MW01138849

Magellan's Navigator

A Historical Novel

Kenneth D. Schultz

Olympicvista Publishing

Kenneth D. Schultz

Cover artwork by Stanislav Pobytov

Map adapted from Wikimedia Commons

ISBN-13: 978-1539972570

ISBN-10: 1539972577

DEDICATION

To all the past, present, and future intrepid explorers of
the Earth and the Universe.

CONTENTS

ACKNOWLEDGMENTS

I have attempted faithfully to represent Francisco Albo's memoirs as I found them, and used Pilot Albo's log and Pigafetta's *Report on the First Voyage Around the World* to supplement his memoirs as appropriate. Unfortunately, the 1755 Lisbon earthquake destroyed all documents seized by the Portuguese on the *Trinidad*. Until the discovery on Elba of Albo's memoirs, his log was the sole navigational source of Magellan's voyage. (Interestingly, Albo's log was missing for over two centuries before being rediscovered in 1788.)

Pigafetta's book gives a much richer description of the voyage and the people and lands visited. Unfortunately, he tends to the hyperbole typical of travel writers of his period. He is also strangely silent about his shipmates. Few are mentioned other than Magellan, a few disparaging comments about Carvalho, and the captains who mutinied at San Julián. Cano is absent from his book.

Tim Joyner's extremely well researched book, Magellan, was used as a resource for factual information when necessary. Mr. Joyner's book is notable, unlike many books about Magellan written in English, for its use of source materials written in Portuguese and Spanish. Mr. Joyner also graciously read and gave feedback on an early version of this book.

I treasure a copy of his book that he gave me inscribed as follows:
"To Ken Schultz
In the hope that he will add some fascinating stories to this narrative history.
Tim Joyner"

I want to thank my editor, Marguerite Wainio, and my beta readers Laura Henson, David Mueller, and Kerry Stevens.

CHRONOLOGY OF THE ARMADA

September 21, 1519 – Sets sail from Sanlúcar, Spain.
September 26 to October 3, 1519 – Canary Islands.
Late October in November, 1519 – Hurricane.
November 29, 1519 – The coast of Brazil is sighted.
December 13 to December 26, 1519 – Rio de Janeiro.
January 11, 1520 – Rio de Solís
March 31, 1520 – Bahia San Julián in Patagonia.
April 2, 1520 – Mutiny.
Late April, 1520 – The *Santiago* is wrecked in a storm.
August 24, 1520 – The fleet departs Bahia San Julián.
August 26 to October 18, 1520 – Santa Cruz, Patagonia.
October 21, 1520 – The Straits of Magellan.
November 8, 1520 – The *San Antonio* defects.
November 28, 1520 – Into the Pacific Ocean.
March 6, 1521 – Landfall is made on Guam.
March 16, 1521 – The Philippines are sighted.
April 7, 1521 – Cebu in the Philippines.
April 27, 1521 – Magellan dies in battle at Mactan.
May 1, 1521 – Most of the fleet's leaders are massacred.
November 8, 1521 – The Spice Islands
December 21, 1521 – The *Victoria* leaves for Spain.
February 8, 1522 – The *Victoria* enters the Indian Ocean.
May 20, 1522 – Landfall near the Cape of Good Hope.
July 9-14, 1522 – The Portuguese Cape Verde Islands.
September 6, 1522 – The *Victoria* returns to Sanlúcar.

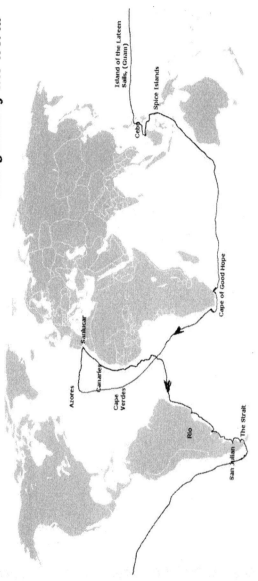

Route of the Armada and Victoria in Their Circumnavigation of the World

INTRODUCTION TO MAGELLAN'S NAVIGATOR

Antiquity's written legacy became ashes with Caesar's inadvertent burning of Alexandria's Library in 48 B.C. Perhaps lesser known is the Lisbon earthquake on All Saints's Day in 1755. This horrendous earthquake, tsunami, and following fire destroyed Ribeira Palace, the Royal Portuguese residence, and with it, all records of the great Portuguese voyages of exploration. Burned with the palace were the journals of Vasco da Gama, the first European to round Africa and sail to India, and the papers seized from Magellan's flagship in 1522. One of Magellan's ships, the *Victoria*, was the first to circumnavigate the globe.

Dissension and tragic misjudgments plagued Magellan's small armada. Unfortunately, the details that remain of these problems are sketchy. An Italian, António Pigafetta, wrote a descriptive travelogue, but his knowledge of navigation was hazy, and he barely mentions the treachery and intrigue aboard Magellan's fleet. The Greek pilot, Francisco Albo, left a logbook, which is essential to understanding the *Victoria's* course around the world, but is silent on the mutiny and other events. Interestingly, this book lay unnoticed in the Spanish Archives for over two hundred and fifty years, until its rediscovery in 1788.

Another important correspondence of this enigmatic Greek navigator has come into my possession due in part to the 2007 financial debacle. My business associate, Wallace Butterfield, successfully navigated the financial meltdown, and when real estate prices cratered, he bought a ruined villa on Elba off the coast of Tuscany in 2009. All that remained of this villa were a few stout walls dating back seven hundred years. Soon after the villa's reconstruction commenced, I received a call from Wallace. His workers had discovered a cache of old journals. Upon examination, I found these belonged to none other than Francisco Albo. The writings span Albo's long life, but what follows in this book is that portion of his memoirs specific to the circumnavigation of the globe on Magellan's ships. They shed light on previously hazy events of that voyage.

Albo wrote in a mixture of Greek and Castilian, which my good friend Gerardus Beekman, a dealer in renaissance books and artifacts, has translated. I then transformed the memoir into modern literary form. Albo's written word is less flowery than most writers of his period, but still much less direct than what today's reader is accustomed to. I hope you enjoy Albo's tale.

Kenneth. D. Schultz
Poulsbo, Washington   November, 2016

ONE – ELBA

The peasants and fishermen here call me the *navigatore Greco antico*. They are literal here. I am indeed an old Greek navigator, so perhaps this name is indeed who I am. I have had many names in my day. They called me Francisco Albo when I enlisted for the Armada de Moluccas, but I was born of the Christian faith as Fragiskos, or Francis, in Thessaloniki.

Thessaloniki. Some of my fondest memories are of sailing on the bay and learning my letters at the local church. Maybe that is why I choose to live out my life here in Elba. The waters here are just as blue, the sunlight just as bright, and the sailboats just as graceful as they glide across the bay. Thessaloniki was then part of the Ottoman Empire under Sultan Bayezid II. It was a vibrant polyglot community of Greek Orthodox, like me, Moslems, and Jews. When I was a small child, Jewish refugees built three new synagogues in Thessaloniki after King Ferdinand and Queen Isabella, in their royal wisdom, issued their 1492 Alhambra Decree, the Edict of Expulsion of Jews from Spain. Recognizing their value as subjects, the Sultan Bayezid sent an Ottoman fleet to evacuate the displaced Jews.

That life ended at age ten when Janissaries appeared at the town square to select the most physically perfect and intelligent Christian boys for the devsirme to be the eventual leaders of the Empire. They picked me. The Janissaries herded other chosen youths and me to Constantinople. They forced us all to convert to Islam. Those lads more perfect of body than mind entered training to become the empire's elite Janissaries, the fiercest soldiers in the eastern Mediterranean.

My wit and intelligence gained me entrance into the elite Enderun College in the Palace. I was destined to become one of the Empire's ruling elite until my dalliance with a fair maiden of the Sultan's harem. I was lucky to escape with my neck still connecting my head and torso. There my luck ended. I fell into the irons of a slaver. The next year as a galley slave was the worst of my life. If God graces me with enough years, I will write of those times.

The great Ottoman Admiral Piri Reis rescued me from the hellhole of the galley bench as a boon to my father. My name as a cartographer assistant to Piri Reis was Naji, but that is another story. Later I joined my father in Rhodes where I was once again Francis. First as a seaman, but then as a mate and master, I sailed olives, wheat, and wine across the Eastern Mediterranean until my father's death.

Around then a new and ambitious man, Selim, ascended to the Ottoman throne. His rule was not as benevolent as that of his father. Selim's fleet was growing, making the waters I knew best a dangerous place, so I plied my trade in the Western Mediterranean, between Genoa, Naples, Marseille, Barcelona, and Cádiz. These peregrinations left me one day in Cádiz and brought about my personal involvement with the most remarkable sailing feat of my age.

There are other stories in my head, which I may write of later. Such as how, after leaving Spain, I was a pilot for Admiral Piri Reis.

My vision is cloudy now. The sails on the boats below are not as crisp and bright as they were in my youth. My mind is still clear. Since it may not always be that way, I will first write of how I was pilot and navigator of the first ship to circumnavigate the world.

TWO – STRAITS OF GIBRALTAR

"Is that one of the Pillars of Gibraltar? The ones inscribed 'nothing further beyond' as a warning to sailors like us?"

Philip, a fellow Greek of Rhodes, pointed at the tall, dark shape off our starboard bow. The moonlight reflected off the whites of his wide eyes as he scratched at the scar etched near his right eye. Its pink flesh contrasted against his tanned face. Despite this, his dark goods looks and carefree attitude made him a favorite everywhere he went.

"It is."

"And was there a reason for the warning?"

"The strait has no patience for unwary sailors, especially those like us seeking a westward passage. If we ventured to the center of the strait, a strong current would push us back into the Mediterranean Sea. If I took us too close to yon pillar, eddy currents would trap us. The prevailing west wind makes passage even more difficult for a sailing ship."

"But the wind is now from the east."

I nodded. "Because I waited until the time that both the wind and tide would work together and take us out the strait into the Atlantic. That's why we're making this passage at midnight. If the wind holds, we'll be in Cádiz before sunset. Go below and get some rest. I want you to help Michael on his watch."

I'd sailed with Philip for three years. He was like a younger brother to me, but right now I wanted solitude. The only others on the deck were the tillerman and the bow lookout. The only sounds were the groaning of the lines and canvas and the soft rush of water along the ship's side.

We were to deliver our ship and its cargo of woven cloth to its Genoan owner's agent in Cádiz, who would sell the cloth in the local market and the ship to the Spanish *Casa de Contratación*, which was paying a premium for ships. Headquartered in Seville, the *Casa de Contratación* controlled and taxed all trade with the Spanish colonies, conducted all exploration, and approved all pilots.

My friend Michael, also of Rhodes, Philip, and I would either sign on with a Spanish expedition, or, failing that, travel on to Lisbon and try to enlist for the annual Portuguese spice fleet sailing for India.

I slept through the heat of the day and returned to the poop deck when a seaman summoned me. Cádiz was a blur of white on its sandspit off the starboard bow. The sun was dipping towards the cloud-shrouded horizon. With the sails filled and taut, we were making a good speed and should make port before nightfall.

"Did you taste the Atlantic's water?" I asked Michael.

"I did. You were right. It is less salty than that of the Mediterranean."

I gestured with my arm. "Can you imagine an ocean so vast?"

"I can't." Michael shook his head.

I knew Michael had reservations about leaving the life he'd known for the past fifteen years, and he was a perpetual worrier. His dark brown eyes with their hooded brows broadcast his concern. I understood his hesitation. He'd sailed his entire life in the Mediterranean without being out of the sight of land for more than a few hours. For safety, most the trade routes there hugged the coast.

Michael continued. "Are you sure we're doing the right thing?"

"Don't you want to be rich?"

"Sure, but I also want to stay alive."

"We could do what we've been doing for a hundred years and never get rich. Meanwhile, every summer the Portuguese fleet returns laden with a priceless cargo of pepper, cinnamon, turmeric, cloves, and nutmeg from India. At the same time, New World gold is filling the coffers of King Carlos of Spain."

"Yes, but you're talking of what makes the Portuguese and Spanish kings and their noblemen rich. Have you heard about any Greek sailors getting rich?"

I hadn't, but I didn't want to admit that.

"Francis, you didn't answer my question."

"Because I don't know the answer to it. However, I do know that to make money, you have to go where the money is. This is where the money is."

Michael shrugged his shoulders. "I hope you're right. It seems more likely that we'll just get ourselves killed."

"If we stayed, a storm or Barbary corsair could also kill us."

Another hour and I made out Cádiz's low whitewashed buildings. Soon afterward, we rounded the tip of the sandspit Cádiz stood on and entered the harbor. A forest of masts awaited us there. I'd never seen so many ships in this fine harbor. Was it a fleet readying to sail for the New World? Could we be so lucky?

I gathered up my possessions: a knife, a few pieces of gold, a set of fine clothes, and, most valuable of all, my *roteiros*, my charts. These were no mere maps. My *roteiros* were detailed instructions that a pilot could use to navigate to anywhere in the Mediterranean and a few other places in the world. I'd bought, copied, and in a few cases stolen them. If necessary, I would kill to protect them.

We turned over our ship to the owner's agent at the dock.

A maze of stacked barrels and boxes filled the pier. Longshoremen were taking advantage of the cooler hours after siesta to ferry the provisions out to the carracks and caravels in the harbor.

Philip bounced along in excitement as we walked along. "Mario back in Syracuse told me 'bout a dice game just off the square." He patted a small bag tied to his waist and gave me a rakish smile. "I need a game."

I hadn't allowed gambling aboard our ship. If I had, either Philip or all the other seamen would have ended up broke, neither of which made for a happy crew. "Those aren't your loaded dice in the bag, are they?"

Philip gave me a fake hurt look. "I got skill. I don't throw rigged bones."

I laughed. "Yeah. Sure. Be careful. They frown on gambling here."

Philip spat to one side. "During the day they may. During the night they'll be blowing on the dice beside me with a wench on their arm with her boobs hanging out."

"If they are there, don't take all their money."

Philip laughed. "Can't help it if Zeus smiles on me."

A brawny man rolling a barrel along the pier approached us.

"Whose ships are those in the harbor?" I asked.

"Captain General Gil González Dávila."

"Where does he sail?"

"To the New World."

We left the pier and started up a cobblestone street towards the main square.

"Looks like we're in luck," said Philip.

"That remains to be seen," groused Michael.

Philip gave Michael a chuck on the back. "You don't know what happens until you throw the dice. Let's get this done with. A game awaits me."

The square was as busy as the docks. Music erupted from a cantina to our right. Two other cantinas were on the far side of the square. To the left was a small church. There were laughing, singing, and shouts of anger, but the voice that caught my ear was someone announcing billets were available for the González expedition. I led my shipmates in the direction of the crier. He stood beside a monument honoring Christopher Columbus, who had launched two of his voyages from Cádiz.

"My two friends and I are as good as seamen as have ever

held a tiller or tended a sail," I announced to the crier in Castilian. I'd learnt my Castilian as well as Turkish and Italian in the Constantinople Palace Enderun. I knew it was good, although I'd never pass as a native of Castile.

A well-dressed man next to the crier eyed me and asked, "Where were you born?"

"Rhodes," I said. To say Greece would ignite a long conversation since the Moslem Ottoman ruled most of my homeland. Saying I was from Christian Rhodes was easier.

"You're Greek?" He said this with a sneer.

"Yes."

"We're hiring only Spaniards for this expedition. We have no use for foreigners."

"But I'm a pilot. I have over ten years of experience across the Mediterranean."

"I don't care how much experience you have. You're not Castilian, Basque, Catalonian, or Andalusian, so I'm not interested."

I gestured to Columbus's monument. "If your King and Queen hadn't hired this Genoan, you wouldn't even know there was a New World."

"Begone, begone."

The hiring agent turned his back on us. This insult incensed me. I reached forward to grab the dolt, but Michael grasped my arm and pointed. "I hear another crier at the far side of the plaza." He pulled me in that direction.

When we reached the crier, he had stopped. I was surprised to see Giovanni Battista di Polcevera arguing there with another man. Polcevera was already old when I first met him in Genoa ten years earlier. That made him now over fifty. His floppy hat hid his baldpate, and the growing darkness obscured the lines on his face.

"But I am authorized by Captain General Ferdinand Magellan to recruit for his armada," said my old friend.

"Who are you?" The man who replied was dressed like a dandy, with shined boots, tights, a flowing blouse, and an immense hat sporting a feather.

"Giovanni Battista di Polcevera, master of the *Trinidad,* Captain General Magellan's flagship. By whose orders are you stopping me?"

"By the order of the *Casa de Contratación.*"

"But Bishop Fonseca, the head of the *Casa de Contratación,* and the King himself have authorized Magellan's armada. I am recruiting on this authority." Polcevera handed the man a paper.

After perusing the papers, the dandy said, "This says nothing about recruiting in Cádiz. I am the *Casa de Contratación's* representative here, and while your armada may have been authorized in Seville, I've received nothing permitting you to recruit here."

"But the King specifically wants more Spanish seamen on the armada."

"Then you should hire them...only do not do it here."

"I have already scoured the other ports, and I still need more men."

"And so does Captain General González whose fleet you see in the harbor. The black death and the demands of the New World have left a shortage of men of the sea."

"Bishop Fonseca will not be pleased when I tell him you haven't been cooperative."

The dandy raised himself to his full height. His lip curled as if he were going to argue further, but then he seemed to think better of it. "You may recruit..."

"Thank you."

A smug smile spread over the dandy's face. "You may recruit, but only foreigners and I ban the use of a crier."

"Those conditions are unreasonable."

"If you find them unacceptable, then go back to Seville. If you accept them, beware. If I hear of one Andalusian signing with you, you will be totally banned from Cádiz."

The dandy turned and left.

"Master Polcevera," I said in Italian. "I know three excellent seamen who might be interested in sailing with you."

Polcevera turned towards me. A huge grin spread over his face. "Albo! How long has it been?"

We embraced.

"Two years ago in Messina if my memory serves me right at that wretched *restaurante* by the harbor."

"Are you seriously looking for a berth?"

"My friends and I are. We tried to enlist in the González fleet, but they wanted only Spaniards."

"And who are your friends?" Polcevera stood back and cast an appraising eye over Michael and Philip."

"This man," I put an arm around Michael, "is almost as accomplished a pilot and master as me. His name is Michael. The good looking younger one," I gestured to Philip, "is an able-bodied seaman. Neither speaks more than a smattering of Italian or Castilian."

"No matter, no matter, as long as they speak the common language of a sailing ship, I can use them. Come along back to my inn. I'd like to talk with you in private."

I explained the situation to my friends, who left to find dinner and a game of dice. Polcevera led me to a narrow, dark street exiting the square. We'd walked half a block when three men burst out of a door. Two men bore swords, knives, and pistols. Each grasped an arm of the third, whose eyes rolled in terror.

"By the Holy Spirit I am innocent of what you say," cried the captive.

A fourth man bearing a tall staff and more finely dressed than the two armed men followed the three out of the door. "Save your breath. You should have spoken up at the Edict of Grace. Now an examiner will decide whether you are brought to trial."

"But what am I accused of?"

"You'll learn soon enough," said the staff holder.

A jeering voice came from overhead yelling, "You're a *Marranos*, Diego. Admit it!"

I stood in confusion. Why was the man called a pig? Then an argument broke out. Polcevera pulled me away and further up the street.

"What happened there?" I asked.

"That was the Inquisition," whispered Polcevera. "Someone accused that poor soul of being a conversos, a Jew who claimed to have converted, but who still secretly practices Judaism. Some Jews decided to convert when King Ferdinand and Isabella expelled all the Jews from Spain. Now the Inquisition is attempting to root out those who falsely converted. There probably are some *conversos*, but more often, the envious falsely accuse the prosperous to rob them of their property…and sometimes their life. Such is the supposed work of God here." He spat to one side.

"But in Greece the Christian, Jew, and Moslem live in relative harmony."

"*Quiet*. Never say that again while you're in Spain. Here the Spaniard and the Portuguese distrust one another, and they both hate the Jews and the Moors. All foreigners are suspect."

I shook my head in disbelief.

"What is even stranger is that young King Carlos is a foreigner. He may be the grandson of Ferdinand and Isabella, but his native tongue is French and he speaks Castilian worse than you and I. He was born and raised in the Low Countries. Most of his advisors are Dutch."

"Enough. Tell me about this Captain General Magellan and his expedition."

We'd arrived at Polcevera's inn. Inside at a dimly lit table, in rapid fire Spanish he ordered wine, a fish stew, and bread for us.

"Why isn't the local *Casa de Contratación* agent helping you?" I asked.

Polcevera quaffed his wine and smiled. "Because Magellan is Portuguese and therefore suspect in the eyes of many Spaniards. Even those supporting Magellan, like Bishop Fonseca, may be doing so to get access to Magellan's *roteiros*. The Portuguese king is also said to be dispensing liberal bribes to thwart this expedition."

"Why?"

"Because of what Magellan knows, or may know. Magellan had a falling out with his king, who by all accounts is a miserly fool. He gave Magellan dispensation to seek employment elsewhere, which he must now rue since the Portuguese spice trade is now at risk. Magellan spent many years in India and even further east in Malacca. He knows the Portuguese trade routes and is intimate with all the secrets of its pilots…Can I trust you with a secret? What I tell you next must not be repeated to anyone."

How many people have you already told this 'secret' to, my loquacious Genoan?

"Your secret is safe with me."

"I have a friend who is privy to what Magellan told King Carlos. Magellan showed the king a letter from a childhood friend of his, a certain Francisco Serrão. Serrão is vizier for rajah of Ternate and runs the kingdom."

"So?"

"The Spice Islands of the Moluccas are the world's sole source of cloves. Nutmeg and mace come from another island nearby. Controlling the spice trade of these islands for just one year would pay for every ship in Cádiz harbor a hundred, a thousand times over. Serrão came to these islands nine years ago with a few other Portuguese and a solitary cannon. He helped the rajah of Ternate defeat his rival, the rajah of Tidore. If a few Portuguese could do that, what could five ships manned by determined soldiers do?" Polcevera's eyes glistened in his excitement.

"But isn't Serrão Portuguese?"

"Serrão is on the outs with his local commanders. He's been commanded to return to India, but he's refused. Furthermore, Serrão in his letter claims Ternate is within the Spanish sphere of influence under the Treaty of Tordesillas. It by rights belongs to Spain."

"Where is Ternate?"

"It is an island in the archipelago of the Moluccas on the opposite side of the world."

"How does Magellan propose to get there? The Portuguese control the African Cape of Good Hope route to India and hence to the Moluccas."

"Magellan says he knows a different route, a western route. He claims there is a strait south of Brazil that gives passage to the Indies."

"Have you seen a *roteiro* for this passage?"

"Magellan is not fool enough to reveal his *roteiro*. If he did, the Spanish would kill him for it."

"Do you believe he even has a *roteiro*?"

Polcevera looked me in the eyes. "I believe he does."

"So, what type of man is this Magellan?"

I'd seen good and bad captains in my time at sea. Men were expendable to the bad ones. A body slipped over the side meant nothing to them. The good ones might be harsh, but they were fair. They also tried to keep their men's bodies as sound as their ships.

"I trust the Captain General. He's meticulously prepared and provisioned our five ships. I've talked with him enough to know he's expert with a chart and an astrolabe. Also, if the stories about him are half true, he is a lion with a sword."

"And how does he treat his men?"

"He is a man of action, not words, but I believe he cares for his men. It is said that when he was shipwrecked off India, he stayed with the common seamen on a small isle until all were rescued. The other nobles left on the first small boat that was available."

"Then, I'd like to enlist as a pilot."

"That's impossible. The *Casa de Contratación* must approve all the pilots and lately all are either Spanish or Portuguese. Most of them are good, either with experience sailing around Africa to India, or to the New World."

"I'm not going to be an able-bodied seaman."

"I wouldn't ask you to be a *marinero*. I'll suggest to Magellan that you be my mate on the *Trinidad*. How good is your friend, Michael?"

"He could be pilot, master, or mate."

"Then I will recommend he be mate on one of the other ships. Come back with me to Seville and meet Magellan. I think he will like you."

"How much is the pay?"

"Two thousand *Maravedis* per month and twelve hundred to your friend Philip as an able-bodied seaman. Plus you'll be allowed to bring two sacks of cloves back, which will be worth a small fortune."

And so, I joined the Armada of the Moluccas. All was as Polcevera had said. Magellan was a captain all seamen should want to serve under, be they Portuguese, Spanish, Italian, or Greek. He was hard, but fair and solicitous of his men's welfare. Polcevera had, though, understated the animosity between Magellan and the Spanish dandies that Bishop Fonseca had foisted upon the Armada.

THREE – SEVILLE

My first experience with the Spanish captains who later would cause so much trouble came a month later. The Portuguese maritime tradition started with Prince Henry the Navigator a hundred years ago and culminated in Dom Vasco da Gama's pioneering of the spice-trading route around Africa's Cape of Good Hope to India, which had now made Portugal one of the richer kingdoms in Europe. The Spanish had no such maritime heritage, and relied upon foreigners like Columbus and Magellan to direct their voyages of exploration.

The hardy Basques of Northern Spain were the exception to this. They had a long tradition as fishermen and whalers. There were many Basques in Magellan's fleet. I respected most as sailors. One, El Cano, I would come to detest. Yet, against my will, our fates became entwined.

One day in Seville, Captain General Magellan sent me to inform the captain of one of his ships, the *Concepción*, of a meeting the next day. It was a brutally hot day. By the time I reached his ship, rivulets of sweat were forming tracks down my forehead and stinging my eyes. When I took my hat off and mopped my brow with my sleeve, a puff of breeze gave me momentary relief. The wind also carried the familiar odor of the *retsina* wine of my homeland. I've never been one to refuse a bottle, but that day the tarry stench, the blistering heat, and humidity by the wharf's edge on the Guadalquivir River had my stomach on edge.

The odor emanated from a vat of pitch beside the *Concepción*. An Irish *grumete*, apprentice seaman, William Irés, tended the fire heating the tar. We were due to sail in a matter of weeks but the *Concepción* was far from ready for the long voyage ahead. Its rigging was still incomplete and her decks a shambles. In a haphazard jumble, ropes and casks littered the ship's deck and the wharf beside it.

Two days earlier, our longboats towed the *Concepción* from the careening wharfs south of Seville after replacement of all its soft planks and the tarring of her bottom. Now a disorganized work party of *grumetes* was tarring the ship's sides above the water. That was fine. The problem was there wasn't a ship's officer in sight.

Then I noticed the kegs stacked beside Irés's fire.

"Mother of God. Do you realize what's in those kegs?"

"No, Mate." Irés's blank blue eyes advertised his ignorance.

"Read the labels, man. What do they say?"

He shrugged. "I don't know. I can read a little Gaelic and English, but not Spanish."

"There's gunpowder in the kegs! Gunpowder! You're lucky I'm not picking up small pieces of you off the dock."

"God forgive me. I…I had no idea." His blue eyes lit up in panic.

"Alfonso, get over here," I ordered. "*Rápido.* Help us move these kegs."

The *grumete* Alfonso tossed aside his pitch brush and ran to help us.

Within minutes, the kegs were a safe distance away from the fire, but by Satan's Blood, where was Master Cano? The *grumetes* needed supervision. Most were sprouting their first whiskers. Not one had been out of sight of land or chummed fish with their breakfast after their first Atlantic swells. I took several deep breaths to calm myself and decided to confront Cano once I delivered the Captain General's message. I climbed the ladder to the quarterdeck and knocked at the captain's cabin door in the sterncastle.

His aide opened the door. Rich fabrics adorned the cabin's wood walls. Captain Quesada sat in a velvet chair at the head of a table with fine inlaid woods with Master Cano beside him. Quesada was a stocky man with a handsome face framed by wavy perfumed black hair. I'd seen him before strutting around Seville in his peacock finery. As captain, Quesada had overall command of the *Concepción* and its crew. The actual navigation and sailing were the responsibility of the pilot, master, and mate. Quesada knew nothing about ships, sailing, or the sea. His main qualification for the job was that he had commanded the Bishop Fonseca's personal guard. The Spanish thought of the sea in military land terms. Quesada was the 'general' of the ship and accountable for getting it to its destination and back according to King Carlos's instructions. The mariners could take care of those pesky details of sailing to the other side of the world and back.

Quesada glanced at me, but continued his conversation with Cano. After several minutes, he turned and asked, "Mate Albo. What brings you here?"

"The Captain General wishes me to inform you there will be a council meeting of all Armada officers at high noon tomorrow. The meeting is to settle the final preparations for the trip down the Guadalquivir to Sanlúcar." Sanlúcar was a small port at the mouth of the Guadalquivir River on the Atlantic Ocean.

Quesada glanced at me for a moment but did not respond before returning to his discussion with Cano. I struggled to control my anger at his rudeness. After several minutes, he finished with Cano and turned to me. "Tell the Captain General my officers and I will be there. You are dismissed."

"Thank you, Captain. And Master Cano should know…"

"I said you were dismissed, Mate. Wait outside. You can talk with Master Cano after I am through with him," interrupted Quesada.

Seething inside at his arrogance, I turned and left. I acknowledged Quesada as a superior, but that didn't mean it was appropriate for him to treat me as a galley slave. I decided there and then that Quesada was a turd, and he must perfume himself to mask his turd smell.

I waited beside Quesada's door for Cano. I knew Cano to be a self-promoter. He'd started on the payroll of the Armada as the mate of the *Concepción*, but two months later, after extensive lobbying with the *Casa de Contratación*, he became master despite his previous trouble with the Spanish Crown for illegally selling a ship under Spanish charter. By rights, I, as mate of the larger *Trinidad*, should have gotten the promotion, but the *Casa* favored Spaniards, even if they were Basques, over Greeks.

Some minutes later, the door opened and Cano appeared. He had a long, straight nose with a dark curly beard and hair. His fine doublet was open in the heat showing his shirt. The rich fabric of his tights made me look like a beggar in comparison.

When Cano saw me, he asked, "You wish to speak with me?"

"I'm sure you'll want to know what I discovered when boarding your ship."

"Discovered? On my ship? My ship is no concern of yours."

"No, but by the Devil in person it should be a concern of yours. You're lucky your meeting with the Captain wasn't interrupted by an explosion."

"What do you mean?"

"When I came aboard no one was supervising the *grumetes*. Not you, not your mate, not even a *marinero*."

"Menial tasks don't require supervision." Cano tilted his head and looked down his long nose at me.

"Master Cano, I found the pitch kettle with its open flame next to powder kegs. I think that's proof that someone should be watching these boys."

"You exaggerate, Albo."

"Not in the least."

Blood curdling screams pierced the air. I felt the pain of the screams in my gut. The shrieks were very near and echoed throughout the waterfront. I rushed to the wharf followed by Cano.

The pitch kettle was overturned and its black molten goo covered the *grumete* Alfonso from the waist down. His peeled back lips were stuck in a grimace. His tanned face turned ashen and his cries ceased. An uneasy silence fell over the wharf.

Irés stuttered, "Oh, Lord help me. I'm sorry. I accidentally backed into the kettle. It was an accident."

"Fetch pails of water. *Rápido*," I ordered. "Pour them on Alfonso."

Irés and I grabbed pails, lowered them into the river, and drenched Alfonso. After several pails, I pressed a finger against the pitch that bathed Alfonso. It was cool to the touch. With two fingers, I pulled on some of the pitch, but it wouldn't come free. Alfonso's breath was ragged, but at least he was alive. The *Concepción's* barber and doctor arrived. He would know how best to care for Alfonso.

Cano shrugged, "Accidents happen. God willed it. They were clumsy fools."

And you, Cano, are a pompous fool.

FOUR –WE DEPART SANLÚCAR

Midnight, September 20, Year of our Lord 1519

My eyes followed harbor pilot Pedro Sordo's gnarled hand into the dark night to the white foam of waves breaking against the bar guarding the Guadalquivir River's tricky channel into the Atlantic. The crash of the waves mingled with the grunts of the men working the sweeps on the main deck below and the bare creaking masts overhead. I steadied myself as the bar's confused currents pitched the *Trinidad* to and fro. We'd sailed from Sanlúcar after midnight to catch the ebbing tide.

"This is where I leave you," shouted Pedro. Pedro Sordo, Pedro the Deaf, always shouted. The evening before in a dirty taverna on the waterfront, I'd raised glasses late into the night with him. Little by little as the wine worked on the ancient man, Pedro had talked about storms that made kindling of ships and the smoke and fury of battles with Algerian corsairs and Ottoman galleys. He recounted these tales as if they had happened yesterday. Now the old man was Sanlúcar's harbor pilot.

I walked with Pedro to the gunwale where his man waited below in the harbor launch. With one leg over the ship's side, Pedro turned and said, "You're in good spirits today."

"By the Blessed Virgin, it's good to be at sea again."

The stout oak deck rolling beneath my feet and the smell of salt air invigorated me. The sea was my element.

"By the Holy Mother, take care of yourself. You're a good man and I'd like to see you again," said Pedro.

"I'll be back within a year. One day you'll see the *Trinidad* appear over the horizon sitting low in the water from its load of spices."

"I hope so. Beware. I've guided many proud ships into the ocean. Like yours, they had bright pennants and flags flying high."

My chest swelled with pride. "And ours will be the most successful."

"Maybe. I've piloted far fewer ships back up the Guadalquivir River than down. Most of the proud ships leaving here end up as flotsam." Pedro Sordo cleared his throat and spat. "Few men have returned. Most have left their bodies to molder in graves across the water or feed the crabs in distant seas. More bad memories have returned up this river than gold and silver."

"I'll be careful. I'm one of the best mariners of the fleet."

"I know you are. But your sailing skills may not be enough to save you." He looked around and lowered his voice. "Your fellow officers may prove to be a more treacherous foe than the sea."

"Don't worry, you will see me again."

"Praise be to God, I hope so," replied Pedro.

He climbed with monkeylike agility down the rope ladder to the pilot launch. I watched as the *marinero* on Pedro's boat set a small sail and started to tack back to the port where the fleet had spent the past month. Pedro's boat passed by the four other *naos* of the armada. First came the *San Antonio*, which was slightly larger than the *Trinidad*, and carried a third of our stores. Behind her came Cano's *Concepción* closely followed by the trim *Victoria*, on which Michael was the mate and Philip a *marinero*. The small *Santiago* completed our five ship fleet. I watched as Sordo's launch disappeared against the dark outline of the retreating coast.

The balmy northeast trade winds of fall had arrived a few days earlier on schedule. We were dependent on the winds. If you took a giant barrel and cut it in half to its bottom, and placed one half on its side in the sea, stuck some masts on it from which you festooned yards upon yards of sails, you had a *nao*. Our fat *naos* sailed swiftly when the winds were behind them filling their sails, but they were helpless if the wind blew from the bow. Piloting a lateen-rigged Mediterranean ship, I could tack against the wind, and, in time, reach my destination. The small lateen sail hanging from the mizzenmast above me on the poop deck gave some maneuverability, but we were still helpless against a wind from the bow. The great success of the Portuguese pilots in fashioning their routes around Africa to the rich trove of spices in India was due to their understanding of the yearly cycle of the winds in the Southern Atlantic and Indian Oceans.

Now the wind barely filled our sails, but it would grow stronger once the sun rose. Pilot Major Estéban Gómez ordered me to have the *marineros* and *grumetes* ship the sweeps, the long oars that powered the *Trinidad* out of the channel, and to hoist all sails for the southwest run to the Canaries. The men had fallen over one another just getting the sweeps out. Would they even be able to get the sails hoisted? It would take time to get the *grumetes* trained and the *marineros* working as a team. The six or seven day sail to the Canary Islands would be an excellent time for the *grumetes* to embark on their journey to becoming sailors, and perchance to even manhood.

All hands swarmed over the sails and rigging. First raised was the main yard, and the sail suspended from it. It was once again as wide as the ship's forty-foot beam. With the addition of a bonnet, an additional sail, to the lower part of the mainsail, the sail would be massive. Next came the foresail, followed by the bowsprit and a triangular lateen sail on the stern mizzenmast. The *Trinidad* was a little more than twice as long as its beam with over sixty men crammed aboard. Once the sails were up, the ships built up their speed. We headed south with our passage marked only by the white florescence of our ships' wakes in the moonlight and the lanterns on their sterns.

Once the sails were up—it took the novices three times

longer than it should—I took a short nap before my watch at four o'clock. At sea, the pilot, master, and mate of the ship stood alternating four-hour watches on the poop deck. Standing with us, as required by Spanish law, was one of the thirteen supernumeraries aboard the *Trinidad*. These were a mixed lot. Many had experience at sea. All were adept with a sword or musket. They'd be at the forefront of any fight with natives or Portuguese. The sailors were broken into port and starboard watches, also in alternating four-hour watches. When running before the wind, most the men had little to do other than the lookouts on the forecastle and topmast, and the man on the tiller. The tiller controlled the ship's rudder, and was in a room open to the sky in the midst of the poop deck, some twenty feet below my feet. Both watches were required to add or remove sails, or if we tacked.

Duarte Barosa's muscular arms pulled him up the ladder behind me as I climbed to the poop deck for my watch. Duarte was Magellan's brother-in-law and had spent several years in India under the Portuguese flag. He was the most experienced mariner of the supernumeraries. By virtue of merit and experience, he should have been one of the captains of our fleet instead of Bishop Fonseca's lackeys.

Pilot Major Gómez, a burly man with intense, hard eyes over a bushy beard, had the watch before me. Once I formally assumed the watch from him, I grasped a line and braced my legs against the swell.

"Well, at least the incompetent bastards of the *Casa de Contratación* can't bother us anymore," said Duarte with a smile.

I laughed. Both of us were tired of wrangling with the *Casa's* petty officials. "I think the ships are fit despite the best efforts of the *Casa*."

Rebuilding the ships for the long voyage ahead had cost a sum near their initial purchase price. I'd stood next to Magellan while he inspected each rib of every ship, marked the punky and rotten ones, and oversaw their replacement.

Food enough for two years filled the holds including biscuits, lots of flour and water hardtack biscuits baked three times to preserve them, dried fish, beans, and wine. We could wage a small war with seventy-one cannon, armor and shields for two hundred men, sixty crossbows, and fifty arquebuses. The fleet had to be sufficient while far from Spain, so we carried lumber, canvas, tools, and vinegar to cleanse. Trade goods included fishhooks, twenty thousand small bells, knives, mirrors, woven cloth, and the like, to trade for spices once we arrived in the Moluccas.

"I've few worries about the ships. The men are another matter," said Duarte.

"There's nothing wrong with the *marinero*s and *grumetes* a week or two at sea won't cure."

"It's not the crew I worry about, or for that matter the pilots, mates, or masters. It's these turds the *Casa de Contratación* foisted on us as captains that concern me."

I was eager to hear Duarte's opinions. Capital General Magellan was a taciturn and private man. He rarely spoke to me, or any of the other officers and crew, except to give an order. I would see him speaking at length to Duarte and some of his other Portuguese friends and relatives. Duarte was more loquacious than the Captain General, especially after a bottle of wine was in him, which was often.

I decided to prime his pump, thinking I might discover from Duarte Magellan's thoughts on the Spanish officers. "I've not been impressed with Captain Quesada."

"Cartagena and Mendoza are from the same mold. They remind me of the parasites that surround King Manuel in the Portuguese court. Those courtiers are little men with big egos with no concept of the ways of the world," said Duarte.

"Why did the *Casa* appoint them?"

Duarte launched a stream of spit over the ship's rail. "It's that slippery Bishop Fonseca's doing. Cartagena's prime qualification is that he's Fonseca's bastard son. Before his appointment as captain of the *San Antonio*, he was an officer of King Carlos's guard. He got that job because of Fonseca's influence."

"What about the others?"

"Captain Mendoza of the *Victoria's* position is said to be payment by Fonseca for Mendoza's family supporting him in his bid to become Patriarch of the West Indies. Coca, the Fleet Accountant, is Fonseca's nephew."

"Let's hope they let us do our jobs."

However, I knew it wasn't in the nature of these self-important Spanish officers to listen to anyone who spoke with an accent, despite the fact most of the Armada's experienced mariners were foreigners. Unfortunately, the sea tends not to forgive fools, even if they are Spanish.

FIVE – THE CANARIES

Two days out to sea, a sudden wave of fear swept over me. I'd felt fear before many times, but this was different and I was ashamed of my fear. *I'd never been so far from land before.* In the Mediterranean, most ships stayed within eyesight of the coast. There were few places in that tidy sea where one was further than a day's sail from shore. This ocean, with the sky touching the horizon for three hundred and sixty degrees around me, could swallow the Mediterranean and not even burp. My life depended totally upon the stout wood hull beneath my feet, the canvas sails over my head, and skills and determination of the crew now lounging on the deck around me.

The enormity of what I'd committed to hit me. If Magellan could pilot us to the Moluccas and back, I should be rich. Would Poseidon permit that?

Three days later, I sighted a low-lying cloud clinging to the horizon in the morning. After several hours, I realized it was not a cloud, but a wisp of smoke. The tall cone of *Cañadas del Teide* materialized under it, still smoking from the eruption Christopher Columbus witnessed in 1492. Our destination was the port of Santa Cruz on the east side of Tenerife, the largest island of the Canaries. The huge caldera of *Cañadas del Teide* was south of Santa Cruz. There was nothing like it in my homeland. Sicily's Mount Etna was its only Mediterranean rival. Lava flows had incinerated *del Teide's* sides, leaving them bare and gray. North of the volcano were lush valleys between rugged mountain ridges. Rocky cliffs rimmed the coast. As our ships nosed into Santa

Cruz's spacious harbor, the cliffs gave way to black sand beaches sparkling in the sunlight. A few caravels rocked lazily on their anchors in the harbor.

I'd read of the Canaries in the chart room of my mentor, Piri Reis, in Gallipoli. I treasured the hours I had spent transcribing *roteiros* in the sunny room overlooking the sparkling waters of the Dardanelles and felt privileged that Piri trusted me to assist with the priceless scrolls. There were copies of Greek and Roman *roteiros* from before Christ as well as one of Columbus's *roteiros* captured by Piri's uncle from a Spanish ship. *Roteiros* were charts and more. They gave specific sailing instructions by season, including winds, currents, and all things essential to a successful sailing voyage. I'd heard it speculated that the Canaries were the lost world of Atlantis. Piri Reis dismissed that idea. The Romans knew of the islands and named them *Insularia Canaria* for the large dogs bred by the native islanders. The islands were poor. There were few visits after the Romans for the next fourteen centuries. The Spanish had invaded a hundred years ago. The native Guanche proved as tough as their dogs and the terrain in which they lived. Only recently had the Spanish claimed victory. Even then, the plague was the real victor over the Guanche, not the Spanish. Fields of sugar cane punctuated by an occasional vineyard covered the hills above the harbor as the *Trinidad* coasted to a stop. Santa Cruz reminded me of any one of several idyllic Mediterranean villages with whitewashed houses topped by tile roofs.

Magellan sent agents ashore to purchase fresh provisions. I supervised the transport of these to the *Trinidad* and their proper stowage.

The sun was nearing the tops of the hills behind me when Michael and Philip met me at an open-air cantina. A light breeze blew in off the water bringing the sweet fragrance of the oleander blossoms outside. Palm fronds rustled in the wind.

Philip sucked a shrimp out of its shell and washed it down with a drought of wine. A mound of translucent shells covered his plate. He rubbed his hard stomach. "By Zeus's beard, this island reminds me of Rhodes. It has the same good wine and sun."

"The wine here is good, but nothing compares to the wines of Rhodes. Oh, to be back home sipping Malvasia Bianca with a smooth-skinned girl by my side," said Michael.

"You can have your white wine any time. It's the Malvasia Nera for me," replied Philip. He scratched the scar on his head.

I laughed. "We don't have either wine here, so you'd best enjoy what's in front of us. It's certainly better than the rotgut stuff that the *Casa de Contratación* bought for us. I've bought two cases of wine here. God forbid that I run out of it."

"That won't last you long," said Michael.

"If I stretch it out, it might last a month. How did the sail down from Sanlúcar go on the *Victoria*?"

"The *Victoria* is a sound ship and handles better than most *naos* whether the wind is strong or weak. She's probably the best sailor of the armada. Our pilot is a professional. He's been on many Caribbean voyages and knows the Atlantic well. He's Portuguese, although not one of Magellan's men," answered Michael.

"Oh? What of the others?"

"Our pilot is by far the best of the three main officers."

"What about Captain Mendoza? And the master of your ship, António Salamón, the Sicilian, was a late hire. What about him?"

"I've seen barnacles with more smarts than Captain Mendoza," answered Philip, "He struts about looking like he has a pike up his ass. He knows seagull shit of the sea. Michael explained to him how the tides work…how they ebb and flow twice a day, and why it's important." Philip, his tongue loose from the strong wine, continued, "But it was like Michael was talking to the mast. Our good captain seems to think such details are unworthy for a person of his august station."

I shook my head in disgust. I respected men of ability and action. Not whom someone's dam or sire was.

"Michael isn't Spanish so of course Mendoza wouldn't believe him." Philip struck his fist on the table as an emphasis.

"Or maybe his head has been up his asshole so long, it's made him dumb as shit," added Michael laughing. "We've all sailed with worse before, Albo. Remember that incompetent Venetian captain we sailed with two years ago? That pompous ass nearly got us killed off Sicily. Captain Mendoza can be no worse."

"And Salamón?" I asked.

"I can't place a finger on it, but I don't like the man. He seems to know his business and he leaves the two of us alone, but he bullies the *grumetes*. He's not a pleasant man. I'm fine with tough masters, but Salamón has a sadistic streak," said Michael.

"We've run into his kind before. Sometimes they turn out to be good men in the end."

Michael arched an eyebrow. "What have you found out about the rest of the voyage, Albo?"

"The Captain General has shared little of what's ahead. Maybe he tells his Portuguese relatives more. Once we're finished loading supplies here, we move on to Monte Roja at the south end of the island. There we'll take on a load of pitch to recaulk our ships with during the voyage. From there we sail on to Brazil. I was with the Captain General back at Sanlúcar when he discussed Brazil with Carvalho, the pilot of the *Concepción*. He told the Captain General of an excellent harbor there called Rio de Janeiro. It's supposed to be a protected place with welcoming natives and ample food. Carvalho claims it's a tropical paradise. The Portuguese visit this harbor once a year for the harvest of brazil wood. They should have recently made their annual visit, so it should be a safe haven for us to rest and resupply after transiting the Atlantic."

"Are you sure the natives are friendly?" Philip asked.

"Weren't Solís and his men devoured by cannibals in Brazil? I heard only a single man escaped to tell the tale."

"Rio will be safe. Solís met his end at a place called La Plata. That's south of Brazil. Carvalho assures me the natives at the harbor in Brazil are quite friendly. He lived there many years and even took a native wife."

An ugly sweet smell assaulted my nose; it was Quesada's perfume. I looked up to see Captain Cartagena's chiseled face as he marched through the cantina with Quesada and Mendoza. Coca, the fleet accountant, and Cano were in tow. Quesada dismissed me with a sneer as he made his way through the maze of tables towards a private back room.

Cano sauntered over to us. "What are you doing here? Shouldn't you be working on your ships?" His voice sounded like a rusty hinge.

"Did you ever hire a replacement for Alfonso?"

Alfonso had died a painful death a week after his tar bath.

"I can probably pick one up here, but that's none of your business anyway. One *grumete* more or less really doesn't make a difference," replied Cano.

"A *grumete* today will be a *marinero* tomorrow. We may be in need of more *marinero*s a year from now. Alfonso was a promising young man. I'm sorry to see his life was cut short through your carelessness."

"Go to Hell, Albo, you Greek bastard," replied Cano.

"Don't go and sell any of the King's property," I sneered.

Cano stomped off after the other men.

"What an incompetent fool," I muttered. "Thank the Blessed Virgin he's not on my ship."

"Yes, but he's only a pilot fish feeding on the scraps the sharks have left," said Michael.

The rest of the stay in the Canaries was uneventful, except for one strange occurrence when we were loading pitch at the south end of the island. The Armada's ships swung about at their anchors during the afternoon watch in Monte Roja's harbor. A five hundred foot high red rock mountain stood sentinel on the eastern point of the harbor. It was hotter here at the south end of Tenerife. It was as if the mountain was a great furnace radiating heat. It also blocked the winds that cooled Santa Cruz leaving us to bake in the sun.

The skiffs and longboats went to and from the beach. Bare backs and strong arms glistened with beads of sweat that sparkled in the sunlight as they pulled the oars. The boats brought casks of pitch to the ships like bees taking nectar to their hive. Hoisting the casks aboard and stowing them in the dark holds below was hot, backbreaking work. The men complained while they labored, but no more than I expected. After three days, almost all the casks were aboard.

Pitch was essential to keep our hulls watertight and to protect them from the wood destroying teredo worms. The teredo would honeycomb an unprotected hull. At least once during the long voyage ahead the ships of the armada would likely need careening to replace rotten planks and clean the bottom. Christopher Columbus's fourth voyage to New Spain turned into a disaster when a poor job of pitching his ships' bottoms left them riddled by teredo. Columbus ended up marooned for a year after beaching the leaking hulks in Jamaica. The pitch gave our ships their characteristic black color when viewed from afar.

Early in the afternoon, a swift caravel rounded the point to the northeast. By all reports, ships were infrequent visitors to Monte Roja. The ship made for the *Trinidad*, dropped its sails, and glided to a stop nearby. Soon the rumble of chain and anchor plummeting into the depths echoed across the water. I recognized the caravel as the Santa Teresa from Sanlúcar. It lowered a skiff and two sailors rowed a gentleman alongside the *Trinidad*. He wore a jerkin over a fine linen doublet. His hose and codpiece were a somber brown. A smile dressed his tanned face.

Seeing me the man called, "Good sir, I have an urgent message for Captain General Magellan. Is he aboard?"

"He is. And who might I say is asking?" I said.

"Señor Bartolomé Costa y Alvarez," was the quick reply. "I must speak immediately to the Captain General."

Señor Bartolomé, Duarte, and the Captain General sequestered themselves in the Captain General's cabin until dark. Then Señor Bartolomé reboarded his caravel and sailed north.

What message could be so important that someone hired an entire ship to convey it? Had Bartolomé brought word of a Portuguese fleet lying in ambush for us? I'd heard rumors at the cantina in Santa Cruz to that effect. We were safe in the Canaries from the Portuguese. The peculiar etiquette of the Spanish and Portuguese royal relations made such overt conflict unlikely. Once we were on the high seas, it would be different. The disappearance of a small fleet like ours was not unknown. Or, if need be, the Portuguese king could denounce a few rogue Portuguese captains for our armada's demise.

Our ships could put up a stiff fight. We had some fifty-eight culverins on our decks or in our holds to batter with cast-iron round shot any ship or fort that challenged us. Magellan could send over two hundred men into a fight, although I, for one, had joined this expedition in search of riches and knowledge, and had no yearning for martial glory. Any battle could be fatal to Magellan's, and my, aspirations. The loss or severe damage to either the *San Antonio* or the *Trinidad* with their great holds carrying trading goods and provisions would be enough to abort our expedition.

However, if Magellan believed the Portuguese were a threat to us, why hadn't he ordered our small fleet made battle ready? Most of our cannons were still in the hold. Our protection was minimal with a small falconet at both the stern and bow, and a larger culverin at the ship's waist both port and starboard. In addition, if the Portuguese were the problem, why hadn't Magellan summoned the Spanish captains from the other ships to confer with them? I was stewing on these thoughts when orders came to ready the ship to sail at midnight.

SIX – WE LEAVE THE CANARIES

Midnight, October 3, Year of our Lord 1519

As the last sand fell through the *ampolleta*s, half-hour glasses, marking midnight, the grinding of the capstans pierced the stillness of the night. Raising the anchor, like most aspects of shipboard life, had its rituals.

I chanted, "*O la fede.*"

My men strained against the windlass on my "*O*" and then finished the chantey with "*de cristiano,*"

And so it went,

"*O non credono…que ben sia,*"

"*O que somo…servi soy,*"

"*O non credono…que nen sia,*" and so on until the dripping anchor was secured.

On my order, the men placed the ash sweeps in their places on the gunwale, two men to a sweep, and waited for my command. The sweeps were necessary to move the Armada away from the dead air created by Monte Roja's red mountain. On Pilot Major Gómez's command, a *marinero* raised and lowered the *Farol* lantern on the stern, the signal for the Armada to get underway. An hour later, sweat glazed the men's backs and their strokes were ragged from fatigue. A stiffening breeze finally cooled the sweat on my cheek. The men eagerly stowed the sweeps and hoisted the yards for the topsails. Once the light night wind filled these, the remaining sails, the bowsprit, the main, and foresails, and the triangular lateen sail on the mizzenmast were set.

Our course was southwest towards the Portuguese-held Cape Verde Islands. The standard route to Brazil was to catch the prevailing easterlies south of these islands. The Portuguese treasure armadas to India also took this route. When sailing often the most direct route in distance takes the longest in time. One might think that to sail to India, it would be quickest to sail down the west coast of Africa, round the Cape of Good Hope, and then northeast to India. The sailor, though, marks his course based upon the winds that sweep the globe. The fastest way from the Cape Verde to the Cape of Good Hope was to catch the easterlies to Brazil, then sail south to catch the westerlies to the Cape of Good Hope. The distance traveled was nearly twice that as a route along the west coast of Africa, but the time taken was much less.

Later in the morning, Pilot Major Gómez ordered more sails put on. I had the men lace two bonnets to the mainsail. With the additional sail area of the bonnets, the mainsail billowed in the strengthening wind. The slap of the sails played against the sound of water rushing along the hull as the fleet hurried south. The ocean filled the horizon around us. The sky was almost as blue as the sea with a few stretched cotton puffs of clouds. The four ships following behind the *Trinidad* were a beautiful sight with their black hulls and large, majestic sails.

I was shooting the sun at noon with Gómez with an astrolabe when Magellan's bearded face appeared over the edge of the deck as he climbed the ladder from the quarterdeck. He was a short man, barrel-chested, with stern eyes that matched his bushy dark beard. Once up on the poop deck, he straightened himself, and limped over to the Pilot Major and me. His limp came from a Moor's spear in Morocco.

"Pilot Major, I would like a new course. The Armada's new course is south by west."

"Yes, Captain General, but aren't we going to follow the Portuguese *roteiro* to Brazil? That's the course we agreed upon with the other captains and pilots yesterday."

Our original course from the Canaries was southwest. South by west meant we'd now be going almost due south.

"You are to follow orders, Pilot Major," replied Magellan.

"Wouldn't it have been wise to inform the other captains of this course at the Canaries?" There was an angry edge to Gómez's voice.

"I have my reasons. You are to follow my command. Send up the flag signaling the course change." Magellan limped back to the ladder and disappeared into his cabin.

"Mate, have the helmsman steer south by west," commanded Gómez.

Why hadn't Magellan consulted with Gómez about the change? On most fleets I had sailed with, there would have been a council of the pilot major, and the other pilots and captains, about such an important decision. It did appear Magellan had planned this course change all along, which meant his meeting yesterday with the pilots was a sham. The new course would take us well to the east of the Cape Verde, so perhaps the course change did have something to do with the Portuguese. Did this change have something to do with our mysterious visitor yesterday?

We strung up signal flags and fired the stern falconet to signal the new course.

This incident left me feeling uneasy. I didn't doubt that Magellan had a good reason for the change, but it would add fuel to the Spanish cliques' distrust of Magellan. Magellan's treatment of Gómez was also demeaning.

That evening the other ships of the Armada came abreast, one by one, gave their evening salute to the flagship, and fell back into position. Magellan gave no explanation for the change in course.

A few evenings later, after the *San Antonio's* customary salute, Captain Cartagena called across, "Pray tell, what is our course?"

Cartagena was a handsome man with a chiseled jaw and steely eyes. His looks far exceeded his brains from what I'd seen so far. My impression was that his little mind could muster bravado, but not much else.

Gómez yelled back "South by west."

Cartagena's face visibly reddened even over the distance between the two ships. He yelled back, "Captain General, the course should not have been changed without consultation with the other captains and officers of the Armada. We agreed upon a course in Seville and confirmed it in the Canaries but days ago! Then you changed the course after half a day?" *And it took you two days to realize this? I'd seen Cartagena on the San Antonio's deck at the time of the change. Evidently, the landlubber hadn't realized what was happening.*

Magellan's face remained impassive. "I was entrusted by King Carlos as Captain General. You need only follow my flag by day and *farol* by night."

"Yes, you are the Captain General, but I am *conjunta persona*, the co-commander, and should be consulted in such matters." Cartagena pounded his ship's railing to emphasize this.

A vein on Magellan's forehead began to pulse. "You need to obey my commands, captain."

"But the course you steer will take us dangerously near Capo Blanco on the African coast."

"I am well aware of Capo Blanco. We'll stand well clear of it. Please take your ship to its proper position. Good night!" With that, Magellan retired to his cabin.

Cartagena stared at Magellan's back as he left. While the *San Antonio* fell away to starboard behind us, I heard Cartagena yelling over the sound of the waves. Another officer appeared to try to calm him.

This was not good. All the men aboard both ships had witnessed this spectacle. All work had stopped to observe this open rift between the Captain General and his second-in-command.

I yelled at the nearest seamen, "To work men, this is nothing of your concern. Back to work!"

I lay half-asleep on my small bed. Suddenly my eyes flew open, my body alert to every sound and movement of the

Trinidad. There'd been a change. When I'd fallen asleep, the ship had been running before the wind, plowing through the waves with a push, hesitation, push, hesitation. Now, the ship's motion and the creaks and groans of the ship's timbers were more erratic with a side-to-side motion. The change augured nothing good.

I sat up in bed. Something fell to the floor. Mother of God, it was my beloved Thucydides. I retrieved it, unlocked my chest, and placed my book with my other favorites, Polybius, Xenophon, *the Iliad,* and *the Odyssey,* next to my diary and Mediterranean *roteiros.*

I yanked on my boots after locking the chest and made my way onto the main deck just as Duarte came out of Magellan's cabin.

"The seas have changed. Is there a problem?" shouted Duarte.

"I don't know. The ship feels different. I think a storm is brewing."

"I feel it too."

Duarte and I made our way up to the poop deck where Pilot Major Gómez had the watch.

I wondered what time it was. My intuition told me it should be around an *ampolleta* before the morning watch. If so, the sun should be lightening the eastern sky, but the horizon was still dark. In the gloom, it was difficult to tell. Clouds appeared to cover the eastern and southern horizons.

"We've lost the northwest wind," I observed. "The wind has changed to from the south."

"I see that, Mate," replied Duarte. "I think we're in for a demon storm."

Gómez's eyes flitted from me to the sea to the clouds swirling above. He said, "I'd say good morning, but I'd be lying. I think we'll soon be in the midst of a storm. Duarte, summon the Captain General. The Armada must change its course, or all the ships will be in irons. Mate, roust the men and prepare to reef the mainsail."

A *nao* in irons was facing directly into the wind, and

unable to make headway and vulnerable.

Duarte hurried off.

I grabbed the first two seamen I found, and sent them to join the tillerman. If a storm did hit us, one man alone wouldn't be able to manage the tiller. Then I yelled to muster the crew on the main deck. That produced half my men. I sent two seamen off to check the *Trinidad's* nooks and crannies where a sailor might have wedged himself to sleep. Minutes later, two dozen bleary-eyed *marineros* and *grumetes* stood by the mainmast.

Seeing my men assembled, Gómez yelled, "Mate, strike the topsails and foresail along with their yards. Take the bonnets out of the mainsail. I am taking her to a course of due west to catch the wind on our quarter."

I barked "Starboard watch, lower the yards for the topsails; port watch drop the foresail yard. Move to it. Look alive, men!"

The sailors lowered the yards that held the fore and main topsails leaving the deck awash in canvas. Time was of the essence. We could clean up the mess later.

Once those were down, I had the men secure the mainsail to take tension off it. That allowed them to remove the rope that laced the bonnets to the mainsail, letting the bonnets fall to the deck.

I felt the *Trinidad* begin to turn to starboard, to the west. The tillermen must be pushing the tiller with all their strength to make the turn. Within minutes, the storm engulfed us as the winds grew in ferocity. The wind from the south grew stronger and the seas more angry. A few large drops of rain plopped on the deck. The deck started to heave as the waves grew into whitecaps. As the seas grew even higher, the wind whipped a stinging spray off the angry ocean. The men now worked more deliberately with one hand for the boat and one hand for themselves; falling overboard meant almost certain death.

The sails down, the sailors hauled the heavy canvas they'd dumped on the deck into manageable piles. Then they hurried to find any dry, sheltered refuge from the storm. The forecastle and the main hold were favorites.

I rejoined Gómez. Magellan and Duarte stood beside him.

Gómez turned to me and shouted through the din of the storm, "This is no common storm, Mate, it's a hurricane, the worst the Atlantic can throw at us. Have the men take down the remaining sails. We'll run with bare masts. If we keep the sails up, they'll only be blown away, maybe taking off the masts with them."

Magellan nodded his concurrence and then returned with Duarte to his cabin. Gómez tied himself to the binnacle as I once again mustered my men. The seas grew higher yet. Waves battered the fore and aft castles. Water towered over the main deck and fell crashing upon it, washing the deck with knee-high water. My men had to fight the storm to get the last sails down. Once finished, the sodden *marineros* and *grumetes* scurried back to their chosen hovels to ride out the storm. I returned to the poop deck and tied myself beside Gómez.

The wind gathered itself in great gusts that howled and sang through the rigging. Sheets of rain pelted the ship. Visibility fell to nothing. I got momentary glimpses of the other ships only to have them disappear behind a wall of rain. The waves grew even greater and soon were washing over the quarterdeck. When the *Trinidad* was in the trough of a great wave, all but the mast tops of the other ships disappeared.

The storm punished the ship for hours until, as if on command, the wind and rain abated. Overhead the clouds disappeared and a radiant sun revealed itself. An eerie calm enveloped us as clouds towered from the water into the heavens all around us.

"Mother of God, is it over?"

Gómez gave a grim smile. "Have you ever been in a hurricane before?"

"No."

"It's not over. We are in the center, the eye of the hurricane. We are only half way through God's ordeal, although the worst should be over."

"How long before it starts again?" I asked.

"An hour, maybe more. Take some men and check all the rigging. Have them make sure that everything is still properly secured."

Nature's fury did return two hours later. Our small ship endured Poseidon's renewed wrath. I felt insignificant as the *Trinidad* tossed about like a wood chip. My mind grew numb. I was reduced to watching our heading and yelling occasional orders to the tired men in the tiller room.

SEVEN – IN THE ATLANTIC

Hours later, I still clutched the binnacle. My wet clothes clung to my body. The worst fury of the hurricane winds was over, but gray skies still hid the sun. Beside me, Gómez's haggard face was now visible in the half-light. The rain had stopped and the wind came in light gusts. Then, suddenly, light illuminated the ship as if God had lit a beacon aloft.

First one, then another of the crew came out of their refuges about the ship.

"Blessed be St. Elmo, the patron saint of mariners! He is watching over us!" exclaimed a *marinero*.

My red, tired eyes stared at the tips of the masts. There the bright blue of St. Elmo's fire shined.

"It is a sign from God!"

"We've been delivered from the storm by St. Elmo!"

I cannot say if the lights were a sign of St. Elmo, but their appearance marked the end of the storm. I'd seen similar lights before and after many storms. As a child, I saw them over two masts after a thunderstorm. My father told me they were Castor and Pollux. I thought the truth behind the glows was better found through Aristotelian logic than from either Christian or Greek Gods. However, the crew's belief in God reached the core of their being, and at times logic was irrelevant.

The little *Santiago* sailed close by our port bow while the *San Antonio* was three miles off the port stern quarter. I sent a young seaman up to the masthead, and was relieved when he yelled down that the *Concepción* and *Victoria* were five miles astern. We fired the stern falconet as a signal for them to rejoin the flagship.

I inspected everything, and was relieved there was no major damage to the ship, so I set the men to repairing the rigging and setting the sails.

When all was finished, the exhausted men fell asleep on sails, coils of rope, or wherever they imagined a bed. I returned to my tiny cabin and peeled off my wet clothes. Shivering, I toweled myself down, pulled on dry clothes, and climbed back into bed. Every muscle ached. Even my bones felt tired. Despite this, I lay awake wondering if more storms like this might lie ahead.

Over the next ten days, three more great winds battered the fleet. Thankfully, none had the ferocity of the first hurricane, but I did not know that when the clouds darkened and wind filled the sails. Each time fear gripped my stomach as I ordered my men to ready us for another blow. After the last, my men were red-eyed specters staggering across the deck half-dead from exhaustion, and muttering prayers for deliverance from the gales.

Their prayers were all too successful. All wind left us. First, the men relaxed, ate, slept, and regained their strength. Then each day became the same, the same dead air, the same Sahara-like heat, and the same water-laden air that left a man's body coated with perspiration. Now daily the men prayed for wind. Instead, a soft, warm rain fell each day. Afterward steam rose off the drenched decks. This went on for days while the ships lolled about, barely moving near the equator. Our food spoiled, our water turned fetid, our clothing disintegrated on our backs. The stench of rotting food assaulted my nose on opening the hatch to the hold. At the end of October, Magellan cut the water ration to half a gallon of water per day along with a cup of wine. He also cut our ration of moldy bread in half.

I'd seen windless times in the Mediterranean, but never this long. On the Mediterranean, galleys were more common than *naos*, and their oars could drive a ship when the wind died. For this purpose, our sweeps were useless.

Tensions rose. The men realized this wasn't the normal

route to Brazil, and, in private, they blamed the Captain General for our predicament. What they didn't realize was that most likely a Portuguese fleet would have waylaid us if we took the normal route. Nonetheless, it was impossible to sleep with sweat clinging to me like a second skin. The voyage had become an indefinite sentence in Purgatory. I knew I could endure this, just as I had as a slave on an Ottoman galley. But when would it end? Would it end?

We still observed the daily rituals. The two main ones of these were evening prayers and the nightly salute to Magellan. For the latter, each ship's master would call out to us: "God save you, Captain General Sir, Master, and good company."

On November eleventh as always, Captain General Magellan and Pilot Major Gómez punctually arrived on the poop deck half a glass early to receive the salutes. By seniority, it was Captain Cartagena's privilege to go first. This day the Captain General waited as Cartagena climbed to the *San Antonio's* poop deck. However, Cartagena remained mute while a *marinero* called out "God save you Captain Sir, Master, and good company."

I swore to myself. This was a major breach of etiquette for these edgy Iberians. Cartagena might as well have called the Captain General's wife a whore. Magellan stomped to the railing and stared across at the *San Antonio*, while I looked on speechlessly. Behind me, Master Polcevera muttered under his breath and then called in a gruff voice across the water, "Master Elorriaga, the salute must be done in the proper manner."

Before Master Elorriaga could respond, Cartagena interjected, "My best *marinero* gave the salute, but if Magellan prefers, I will have it rendered by a cabin boy!" With that, he stormed off to his cabin.

For the next three days, no one on the *San Antonio* performed the evening salute. It surprised me that Magellan didn't demand his due honors from Cartagena, but what could he do, short of boarding the *San Antonio*? By the third day, I thought no more of it.

This changed when Duarte came to me. He had his usual dagger in his waistband, but today it kept company with a sword and a pistol. Had Magellan decided to force Cartagena to comply? The hairs on the back of my neck rose and my skin crawled.

"Mate Albo, you're faithful to the Captain General, aren't you?"

Where is he going with this? "As I am to God."

Relief flashed over Duarte's face. "Can I depend on you to support the Captain General?"

"Of course." I pointedly eyed Duarte's weaponry. He unconsciously placed a hand on his sword's hilt. "You're expecting it to come to blows with Cartagena?"

"By the Blessed Virgin, I hope not, but it may…with Cartagena and the other Spanish captains."

"Cartagena has been insubordinate, but do you expect the other Spanish dandies to support him? Do you expect them to assault us?"

"Nothing that overt. But Cartagena wants to replace the Captain General."

"What evidence do you have to suspect this?"

Duarte leaned forward and whispered, "Remember our surprise visitor in the Canaries?"

"Your father's friend? The man who arrived and departed so mysteriously?"

"Yes, he warned the Captain General that the Spanish captains had been instructed by the Bishop Fonseca to find a pretext to depose my brother-in-law, and to kill him if necessary."

I looked up. Skiffs knifed through the still waters towards the *Trinidad*.

"Are you anticipating an attack now? What is happening? Should I alert my men?" My voice rose uncontrollably. I'd never been in a fight before.

"No. The captains and pilots are assembling here for the court martial."

"Court martial? What court martial? Surely the Captain General isn't trying Cartagena."

"No, no. António Salamón, the master of the *Victoria*, is accused of sodomy along with a *grumete*. The Captain General is convening a court martial of the sinners to determine their fate." I relaxed in the thought that a skirmish wasn't imminent.

Sodomy was a common enough occurrence at sea on some ships, but I knew the pious Magellan would have none of it aboard his God-sanctioned ships. It was unthinkable he would tolerate sodomy.

I said, "It would seem the ships have been caught in Dante's Purgatorio these past weeks. We've been far from Heaven, but not quite in Hell. Days like this are fertile ground for the Devil."

"That's true, but Master Salamón succumbed to the Devil. Spanish law is quite clear. For this, he will forfeit his life. The law is less clear for the *grumete*. If coerced, he may escape with his life. Anyway, will you help me? After the verdicts are reached, we may have trouble with Cartagena. I'll need your knife if we do."

"I am with you." I touched my knife, and made sure it was loose in its sheath.

The first of the skiffs was nearing us. In it was the captain of the *Concepción*, Quesada, along with his pilot, Carvalho. The vain Quesada was wearing a finely sewn doublet with a velvet hat covering his wavy hair. A cloud of perfume enveloped him as the peacock boarded and swaggered to Magellan's cabin for the trial.

Waiting for Salamón was the Armada's *Alguacil major*, master-at-arms, Espinosa. Espinosa stood half a head higher than most his Castilian countrymen. I'd seen him raise a man off the deck with one arm. Other men looked like boys when standing beside him. Espinosa had rugged good looks. Beside him was his man-at-arms. Like Duarte, they sported a sword, pistol, and dagger plus they wore cuirasses that armored their torso.

They waited as the *Victoria's* boat came along side. A grim-faced Captain Mendoza sat in the stern. In the boat's bow, in irons, sat Salamón along with the accused *grumete*. Salamón, a hulking man with a pocked face, appeared sullen and morose. His lank hair hid most of his face. The *grumete*, a young lad from Genoa, could easily have been mistaken for a cabin boy. His face was pale with tears making salty tracks down his fuzzy cheeks. His chest heaved with sobs.

Soon Cartagena of the *San Antonio* came alongside. He wasn't armored or armed beyond his dagger and sword. Nor were the other Spanish captains armed. Also, the men with them only carried daggers. *They don't look like they're coming for a fight. May be Duarte's fears are for naught.* Last aboard was Serrano, captain and pilot of the small *Santiago*. He wore his lined face with its close clipped beard like a mask as he proceeded to the meeting. He only wore his dagger.

I followed the men into Magellan's cabin, and stood in a corner behind the immense oaken table that dominated the room. Magellan sat in a large chair at the head of the table. The four captains sat along the opposite side of the table with their backs to the door leading to the quarterdeck. The pilots and other officers took seats on stools about the room. *Alguacil major* Espinosa stood guard inside the door with his large arms folded. Espinosa's man and Duarte had remained outside the door to watch over Salamón and the *grumete*, Baresa, who sat cross-legged and barefooted on the quarterdeck.

"Let us begin the court martial," commanded Magellan. "Are you ready?" Magellan asked the fleet clerk.

"Yes, Captain General," replied the clerk, hunched over his paper, pen, and inkpot.

Magellan ordered Espinosa to bring in the first witness, a seaman named Juan of the *Victoria*. "What did you observe last night?"

The man stood straight and cleared his throat. He began, "Late last night I rose to use the *jardines*. It was a dark, quiet moonless night. As I climbed to the poop deck to relieve myself, I was surprised to hear muffled sounds. I silently retraced my steps and fetched my friend Níccolo. The two of us returned to the poop deck."

"What did you find there?"

The man hesitated. He looked around the room and squinted. "Master Salamón was there with his codpiece open and his hands on the head of a boy kneeling before him. It was clearly sodomy. I sent Níccolo to wake the Captain, who had the two arrested."

"Who was the boy?"

"António Baresa, a *grumete* of the port watch."

Magellan surveyed the table. "Does anyone have questions?...No? You are excused. Please send in *marinero* Níccolo."

Níccolo's dark eyes darted around the cabin. He was older than many of the *marinero*s. I couldn't tell if the man was afraid or excited about being the center of attention. Magellan asked, "Níccolo Napolés, tell me about last night."

"I was on the midnight forecastle watch. Not that there was anything to see mind you. The ship, of course, was going nowhere and it was darker than an elephant's ass."

"We are more interested, Níccolo, in what you saw that night."

"Oh. Juan asked me to come with him to the poop deck. He didn't say why, but when we got there it was obvious."

"And?"

"Master Salamón was pumping a head back and forth on his carajo. He sounded like he was enjoying himself."

"And whose head was it?"

"The *grumete* Baresa's."

"Did Master Salamón say anything when he realized you were watching?"

"He said 'shit.'"

"Shit?"

"Yes, Captain General."

"Thank you, Níccolo. Does anyone else want to question *marinero* Níccolo?...No? *Alguacil major* Espinosa, please bring in António Baresa"

Espinosa brought the small, trembling Baresa into the cabin.

"António Baresa, you are hereby formally accused of sodomy by this court martial. What have you to say for yourself?" demanded Magellan.

The young Italian attempted to talk. I felt sorry for him. His mouth must be dry with fear. He stammered, but no words came out. He swallowed and then said, "I was the *grumete*...on the midnight watch with...Master Salamón." He stopped and burst into tears.

Magellan waited. When Baresa's tears ended he asked, "What happened last night?"

"The Master started talking of things unmentionable. I tried to ignore him. Then he grabbed my shoulders, pushed me to the deck...and then he forced me to..." his voice fell to an inaudible whisper.

"So you did not do this willingly, Baresa?"

"No, oh no, Captain General. It was awful. Master Salamón is a powerful man. I'm weak by comparison. He forced me."

"Are there any more questions for this man?"

The only sound was Baresa's sobs. I felt sorry for the boy, first coerced by Salamón into sex, and now his humiliation exposed to the entire fleet.

"*Alguacil* Espinosa," Magellan ordered, "take this man away. Bring in Master Salamón."

The leg irons of the burly Salamón clanked as he shuffled into the room. The Sicilian stood slouched before the tribunal.

"You stand accused of sodomy during the midnight watch of the night of November thirteenth. This act was committed with António Baresa on the poop deck of the *Victoria*. *Marineros* Juan and Níccolo have testified to observing this act. The *grumete* Baresa admits to participating in this act. What do you say to these charges?" asked Magellan.

Salamón said nothing. He looked from man to man around the table and shook his head. After some minutes he said, "Do with me what you will."

"Are you aware that the penalty for sodomy is death? Furthermore, your soul will be eternally condemned to Hell?"

"Do with me what you will."

"*Alguacil* Espinosa, remove this man. Guard him carefully."

Espinosa hauled Salamón from the cabin. Once the sound of his chains was gone, an uncomfortable silence came over the room.

Magellan finally spoke, "Master Salamón's guilt is clear. We have two witnesses, the confession of the *grumete* who participated, and Salamón's implicit admission. He has committed, in both mind and body, the sin of sodomy. I will not have this behavior on my ships! Spanish law is inflexible in this regard. The punishment is death. Are we in agreement, gentlemen?" Magellan pounded the table.

The mood of the room was somber. Some of the officers nodded in agreement, while others seemed less certain. Magellan was more severe than most captains, although death was the punishment decreed by Spanish law. It was unfortunate the evidence was so damning.

Cartagena spoke, "We must make an example of this man. Otherwise, discipline and morality among the crew will degenerate. The most severe punishment is appropriate. To best deter this behavior in the future, the punishment should be carried out before the assembled men."

"I'm in agreement with you on the severity of the crime, but perhaps we should all think about the appropriate sentence. I propose we reconvene the Court Martial for sentencing once the Armada reaches Brazil. That will allow us all time to pray for the right sentence," said Father Pedro, the priest of the *Trinidad*. He spoke deliberately. Everyone appeared to respect the quiet balding father.

"I agree. These doldrums are already preying upon the

spirits of the crews. Some men are near their breaking point. I think an execution at this time might be too much for them," added Captain Serrano.

Heads nodded. I sensed that most of the officers were relieved there would not be an immediate execution. Serrano's concerns hit a chord; an execution might make the ugly mood of the sailors even worse.

"Let the conviction of António Salamón for sodomy be recorded," said Magellan to the fleet clerk. "Let's now move on to the case of the *grumete* Baresa. It would seem his case is not so clear."

"I believe that is so," said Father Pedro. He focused on his hands spread on the table. "A sin of the flesh was certainly committed." He looked up. His gaze went around the room, stopping briefly at each man. "But it is not clear a sin of the soul was committed."

"I agree," said Mendoza almost too eagerly. "There was certainly coercion involved. I myself witnessed Master Salamón bullying the *grumetes*. I find Baresa's story very believable."

"I also agree with Captain Mendoza," said Serrano. "Perhaps the young boy should be spared from meeting his maker just yet."

"But he did commit a crime," said Magellan.

"Perhaps," said Father Pedro, "We should let the judging wait for Christ when the boy's time comes."

"Is that the general belief?" asked Magellan.

Heads nodded. I thought Cartagena and a few others were disinclined to spare Baresa, but were unwilling to say so against the consensus. "So," continued Magellan, "What punishment should the *grumete* receive? Despite the mitigating circumstances his deed cannot go unpunished."

There was silence.

Captain Mendoza leaned back. He started to speak, stopped, and then said, "I propose he be committed to the stocks of the *Victoria* for a day and receive two dozen lashes."

"That is severe punishment, Captain, but then this was a severe deed," replied Serrano.

"So are we in agreement?" asked Magellan. "Yes? Record the punishment as so. Baresa's punishment will take place at the beginning of the tomorrow's morning watch. Now, there is an additional matter I would like to discuss." Magellan paused as he looked from man to man. "There have been irregularities in rendering the evening salute. That is an insult, not only to me but to King Carlos, as I am his appointed representative."

Cartagena's neck muscles tensed and his face grew hard. He spat out, "And there are things I would like to discuss. Why didn't you consult the captains and pilots before changing course after leaving the Canaries? We agreed upon a course in Seville and confirmed it in the Canaries. Why did you change it?"

Cartagena's objections were reasonable, unless he wanted to usurp leadership of the fleet as Duarte claimed, but before doing that needed to know Magellan's detailed plan for sailing to the Moluccas.

"There were good reasons for the course change, Captain, and those reasons must remain known only to me. I have sworn my allegiance to King Carlos and I will do all in my power to accomplish the goal of this Armada. I have been trusted with the responsibility of this fleet, and I take that responsibility seriously. You have sworn to obey my commands and to perform your assigned duties. One of your responsibilities is to render the proper salute in the evening."

And Magellan's explanation was just as reasonable, and, as the Captain General, every man on the armada should kneel to him. I certainly didn't want the arrogant, land-loving Spanish captains to assume command.

Cartagena countered, "How can we be sure you're going to be true to that allegiance? What did you talk about with the man who arrived in that strange ship at Monte Roja? After that, you unexpectedly and secretively changed the course. This is all very suspicious!"

"There is no one more committed to his King than I," replied Magellan.

"So you say. What proof do we have of that? And to which King?" retorted Cartagena.

Quesada and Mendoza gave slight nods of agreement.

I watched with wide eyes as the tempers rose. Most of the officers seemed disinclined to take sides. Some took a sudden interest in their fingernails; others stared at the far corner of the room. I looked anxiously first at Cartagena then at Magellan. My hand found my sheathed dagger.

"Are you prepared to render the proper salute, Captain Cartagena?" asked Magellan.

"I will to the Captain General, when we finally have such a man of that stature commanding the Armada," replied Cartagena with a sneer.

The fool! This was the time Duarte anticipated. I drew my dagger.

Magellan sprang from his chair and moved around the table with startling speed. He grabbed Cartagena by the front of his doublet and shouted, "You are under arrest."

Espinosa stepped forward. Duarte burst through the door behind Cartagena with his sword drawn. With surprising strength, Magellan lifted Cartagena out of his chair and pushed him toward Espinosa.

Cartagena's eyes darted to Mendoza and Quesada. He shouted, "Now is the time!"

They said nothing and did nothing. No one showed an inclination to interfere with the dispute between Magellan and Cartagena, so I resheathed my knife.

"Place him in the stocks! This man has threatened mutiny!" shouted Magellan.

The brawny *Alguacil major* sheathed his sword, clasped Cartagena's arms behind his back, and led him away. Duarte stayed at guard beside Magellan.

The officers exited onto the quarterdeck to witness the pillorying of Cartagena. I'd rarely seen a grimmer bunch of men. They watched in silence as Espinosa clamped

Cartagena in the stocks like a common *grumete*. Salamón and Baresa sat unnoticed in silence on the deck.

Quesada quietly said, "Captain General, it pains me greatly to see a captain and the man named *conjunta persona* of the Armada by King Carlos to be placed in the stocks like some drunken *grumete*. This is not a good example for the men to see. We all diminish our dignity and power by this, Captain General."

Magellan said nothing. A vein on his forehead throbbed. A minute later, he said, "I consider myself a patient man, but Señor Cartagena was a fool to threaten mutiny. It is he who caused me to lose dignity before the men by his childish refusal to render the proper salute."

"That is true, Captain General, but we all must keep our honor. I implore you to release Cartagena into my custody or that of Captain Mendoza. On my word, Señor Cartagena will cause no more problems."

Magellan said nothing. I wondered if he'd even heard Quesada. Cartagena stood, suddenly submissive and forlorn, in the stocks like a common thief. What would Magellan do? It might be best if he stood his ground and either executed or marooned Cartagena. Other commanders had done the same for similar offenses. Marooning would be best. Unfortunately, we were leagues from any land, and executing Cartagena might be too extreme.

If similar thoughts went through Magellan's head, I don't know. Finally, he shrugged. "Have it your way, Captain. I will release him into custody. Captain Mendoza, you will restrict Señor Cartagena to your ship. You are responsible for him and his actions. Do I have your assurance for his behavior?"

"You have my word, Captain General," replied Captain Mendoza.

"Captain Mendoza, do you agree to keep Señor Cartagena in your control and to produce him any time at my request?"

"I do."

"Then it is settled." Turning to the stocks Magellan said, "*Alguacil* Espinosa, release Señor Cartagena into the custody of Captain Mendoza. Put Salamón in irons in the bilge. Baresa will return with Captain Mendoza to the *Victoria* for his punishment."

Turning to the other officers, Magellan announced, "I am making António Coca captain of the *San Antonio*. May he be a better captain than his predecessor. Duarte, please take a skiff to the *San Antonio* and request Señor Coca's presence on the *Trinidad*. Once he is here, we will sound the trumpets announcing his appointment."

I was relieved to see Cartagena was gotten rid of so easily, but I felt uneasy. Why had Magellan appointed Coca as captain of the *San Antonio*? He was an accountant, not a soldier, mariner, or leader. Furthermore, Coca was Cartagena's cousin, the nephew of the Bishop Fonseca, and a member of the Castilian clique. Did Magellan think he was mollifying the Spanish by Coca's appointment? This was perhaps Magellan's first mistake.

EIGHT – APPROACHING BRAZIL

The first day after Cartagena's removal, I feared he might lead a mutiny, but naught came of it. Cartagena wasn't that bold. The crew's mood was subdued. Fighting captains are not what a sailor wants to see. Nonetheless, all captains rigorously observed the evening salutes after Cartagena's removal. A few days later, the sea beneath us turned a rich green color. It was the consensus this was a current, a river flowing through the great Atlantic. Indeed, since the court martial, our fortune had improved, and the mood lightened. Two days later, while I was shooting the sun with my astrolabe to mark our noonday latitude, a puff of wind cooled the sweat on my cheek. Light ripples marked the ocean's surface. Overhead a gentle southeast breeze filled the topsails. The current must have taken us to the southeast trade winds that move along the equator. We all rejoiced. The men could talk of nothing else than drinking and wenching in Brazil.

The next morning Magellan ordered a southwest course. Two days later I marked the latitude as zero degrees: the sun was directly overhead at noon. The Armada was on the equator.

The next morning I stood watch with Magellan's bastard teenage son Cristóbal Ravelo and Master Gunner Andrew of Bristol. The sails mushroomed out from a strong breeze with the rigging creaking under the strain. The *Trinidad's* decks oscillated from the ocean's swell.

I wondered why Ravelo often chose to stand watch with me. Did Magellan expect his son to learn something from me, or was he there as a spy?

The Englishman Andrew of Bristol had befriended me in Seville. I'd often supped on botilla sausage and cabbage stew with him and his willowy wife Ana Estrada in cantinas overlooking the broad Guadalquivir River. Those nights were among my most enjoyable in Seville. Andrew often joined the watch from a natural curiosity about the ship and the sea.

"How soon will we make Brazil?" asked Andrew. His fair skin was scorched to a bright pink and his blond hair bleached white from the sun.

"I don't know for sure. Probably two or three weeks."

"That's pretty vague."

I laughed. "It's not intentional. I don't know our longitude for sure after all the time we spent in the doldrums. Even if I did, I don't know how strong the winds will be in the days ahead."

I was pleased. I lived for these days. Our ship moved smartly with the wind. The eastern sky was golden with the coming dawn. Only the occasional odor brought on the wind from those using the *jardines* marred the scene. A steady stream of men, from cabin boy to Captain General, made their way up to the *jardines* upon waking.

The *Trinidad's* bow sliced through the ocean swell throwing green froth to each side. The main and foresails billowed in the equatorial trade wind.

"She's a thing of beauty, isn't she?" I said.

Andrew looked up at the maze of ropes, sails, and masts. "Maybe to you. I just see a tangle of lines."

"Ah, but look. Each line, sail, and yard is perfectly set. Every line in the spider web supporting the masts, yards, and sails has its purpose. The mainsail is for power, while the spritsail on the bow gives us maneuverability. The topsails capture a weak wind better. Getting them all correct is like tuning a fine one hundred-string guitar. Having them all right is like listening to fifty perfectly tuned instruments playing together."

"Mother of Christ, you love ships and the sea, don't you?"

I laughed. "The sea is my life. My first boat at the age of nine was a small sailboat. I spent hours in it running errands to the ships anchored in Saloniki Bay near Thessaloniki. I learned how to tack, come about, and to use the wind to my best advantage. It may sound like bragging, but I consider myself a virtuoso at the tuning and playing of the sails."

Ravelo listened intently to my discussion with Andrew. He looked like his burly father, although his beard was sparser, and he carried less weight on his frame. He didn't have the arrogance of most Iberian nobles, probably because while he was sired by a noble, as a bastard he didn't have a title. He had a bit of a chip on his shoulder, which I understood. I also had one. Ravelo worked hard, was a quick learner, and didn't exploit his relationship to his father.

We fell quiet for a while, enjoying the serenity of the scene.

Ravelo spoke, "I thought you were from Rhodes, Mate, but you said the place of your birth is Thessaloniki. You don't look Greek to me with your brown hair and light eyes."

"Greeks can be dark or light-haired. We're all still Greeks. I spent my childhood in Thessaloniki and was educated by the Greek Orthodox priests in the church there."

"I thought Greece is under Moorish rule," said Ravelo.

"It is. The Moors have ruled in Thessaloniki for over a hundred years and Constantinople fell some forty years before my birth."

"It must have been terrible to live under the evil Moors!"

"The Ottoman rulers were incompetent, but they weren't oppressive. They tolerated us and allowed Christians to manage affairs between one another. Islam as practiced by the Ottomans recognizes Jesus as a great prophet. Nonetheless, I was a second class citizen of my own land." *And, at times it seems, a second class Christian in Catholic Spain.*

"In my Portugal we fought the Reconquista for seven centuries to evict the Moors from our lands! Less than thirty years ago, King Ferdinand finally freed Granada from the last Moors. It was a bitter struggle."

"Well, let's pray my homeland will be freed someday, but I know of no great King that will free it. I left Thessaloniki when in my teens for Rhodes, which I've adopted as my homeland."

"Father says Rhodes is the last bastion of Christianity in the eastern Mediterranean."

"He's right. The Knights Hospitaller have defended the island against the Moslems for years. Their castle in Rhodes is strong, but the knights manning it are few in number. Rhodes will soon fall to the Ottomans without help. It seems the great powers of Europe: the Pope, Venice, Genoa, France, Spain, and Portugal are too busy with their own schemes to help their poorer Christian cousins. I doubt I'll ever see my Rhodes as a Christian land again."

Young Ravelo seemed shaken by the prospect. "I pray that does not come to pass, Mate. I will pray for Rhodes."

"Thank you for your prayers. May God hear them."

And, perhaps God would then whisper something into King Carlos's ear, and even better inspire the other Christian Kings and the Pope to aid Rhodes. However, in all things religious I kept my opinions to myself. I knew my being born under the Moslem Ottomans made me suspect to some, and I didn't want to give any fuel to their fears.

NINE – DISASTER AVERTED

November twenty-ninth, the year of our Lord 1519, was a great day for me, but a bad day for the Armada. Magellan formally named me a pilot of the Armada, although I retained my duties as mate. Now I could openly maintain the *roteiro* that I had been clandestinely keeping.

What was the bad part of the day? Magellan named the Pilot Carvalho on the *Concepción* as lead pilot while we sailed down the Brazilian coast. This appointment made some sense. Carvalho had lived at Rio de Janeiro for several years so he should be familiar with the coast. However, the reports I'd heard of him were not good. By most accounts, he was an incompetent braggart.

A related problem was that Pilot Major Gómez was not pleased with his temporary displacement. He argued forcefully that he could manage fine since he had the Portuguese *roteiro*, *Livro da Marinharia*, which covered the coast well past Rio de Janeiro down to Capo Santa Maria. Magellan refused to rescind his decision to have Carvalho lead.

I found Gómez's argument persuasive. I'd prefer to trust a competent pilot with a good *roteiro* to an incompetent pilot who'd be depending upon his memory some years old. However, I sensed Magellan had based his decision upon more than competency. There was always this subtle tension whenever Gómez and Magellan were together. Gómez resented that Magellan had gained the favor of the king to lead this expedition over himself. Now Magellan was demoting him even further. This was Magellan's second mistake. He needed allies beyond his small band of

Portuguese relatives and friends. Gómez was not a natural ally of the Spanish, and could have been an important ally of Magellan if he had catered a little to Gómez's vanity.

Once the fleet made landfall, it headed south with the green shoreline of Brazil never far off the starboard side. The *Concepción*, with Carvalho piloting, led the way.

I took a deep breath. Even at this distance, the air smelled of earth and vegetation, which was a welcome change from the salty air of the high seas.

"The *roteiro* calls the cape we just passed Capo Sao Tome. Ahead of us is Capo Frio. Once we round that capo, we should sight Rio de Janeiro harbor in a matter of hours," said Gómez.

"And none too soon," I said.

"Why do you say that? It's been an easy five-day sail down the coast."

"But it's been ten weeks since we left the Canaries."

Gómez grunted, "Ten weeks is nothing compared to da Gama's route to India."

"Maybe for you. Most of the men aboard think it feels like ten years. The men are eager to get ashore, eat fresh food, and meet the local girls."

"We should be dropping our anchors in Rio before sunset tomorrow. These tubs are making excellent time with this northeast wind behind them."

Magellan joined us as Gómez and I talked.

As the Armada approached Capo Frio, I sensed something was wrong. My intuition whispered to me that we were off course. The point of the cape was not getting any closer. I lined up a rope of the ship's rigging with the tip of the cape and watched for several minutes. I prayed I was wrong, but my prayers weren't met. It was worse than I feared. The rope I'd lined up with the cape was inching to the starboard side of the cape. We weren't going to clear it.

"Pilot Major, Captain General." The two bearded Portuguese navigators turned towards me. "Even though our bow is pointed well west of the Capo Frio, I think our actual course is taking us to the right of the cape. There must be a current sweeping us towards yonder shallows." I started towards the bow.

Magellan and Gómez followed me to the forecastle. Each of us lined a rope or part of the ship with the point of Capo Frio and stood motionless to see how the ship moved relative to the cape.

Magellan struck his fist on the gunwale. "You're right, Mate, the fleet will not clear the cape."

"There must be a strong counter current running from Capo Frio along the coast back to Capo Sao Tome. It's carrying us into the shore," I said. Within hours, the entire armada would be driven to disaster.

Gómez reacted immediately, "Have the men strike the sails, Mate. Then man the sweeps. We'll need to work the ships perpendicular to the current if we're going to escape grounding. Signal the other ships to do the same. Have the men work quickly now. Our lives depend on it."

I vaulted from the forecastle deck. "Starboard watch, get the mainmast sails down. Port watch, take down the foremast sails. After you're done with the foremast, do the same with the spritsail."

The men spilled the air from the sails and lowered the yards to the deck. The sound of the filled canvas was gone for the first time in a month.

The wood on wood grating of the ash sweeps against the gunwales replaced the groaning of the canvas. News of the danger spread across the *Trinidad*. The supernumeraries, gunners, and every able-bodied man joined the *marineros* and *grumetes* until each sweep had three or four men on it rather than the usual two. Master Gunner Andrew worked alongside two *grumetes*. The men worked with a quiet tension. There was none of the usual banter. Their eyes stared straight ahead, except for occasional nervous glances towards Cape Frio, to see if we were escaping the current's murderous embrace. No one wanted to be shipwrecked, especially on a

Brazilian shore in Portuguese territory.

After half an hour, the pulls were getting more ragged as muscles started to protest.

"I can't tell if we're making any progress," I whispered.

"I cannot either," replied Magellan. "But either this works or it is the beach. Keep the men at it."

Another half hour and the ship's angle to Capo Frio began to improve. The ships were making progress against the current. Would the men's muscles give out before the ships were far enough to sea to raise the sails?

"We're almost there. You can do it. Keep at it," I urged while walking beside the rowers. A cabin boy trotted by my side with a ladle and pail of water for the men.

By late in the evening, the *Santiago*, *Concepción*, and *Victoria* were free of the current's grasp and raised their sails. An hour later, the larger *San Antonio* and *Trinidad* pulled clear. The exhausted men raised the sails and the fleet rounded Capo Frio.

"Damn that ass Carvalho," muttered Gómez.

"What are you saying, Pilot Major?" asked Magellan.

"I was saying the Pilot Carvalho, in whom you place such confidence, almost wrecked your fleet." Gómez glared towards Carvalho's ship.

"Thank you, Pilot Major."

"Pilot Carvalho was supposed to be familiar with these waters. So why didn't he know about this current?" persisted Gómez.

"Thank you, Pilot Major," repeated Magellan. The vein in his forehead pulsed.

I agreed with Gómez, but remained silent. How could Carvalho not have known of this current if he had lived in these waters for several years? How could he forget something so important? Or had Carvalho lied about his piloting duties while in Brazil?

The Armada slid by two small islets patrolled by seagulls and into Rio de Janeiro harbor shortly after noon the following day. Natural, sheltered bays stretched from the east to the west. It was the best anchorage I'd ever seen. Carvalho led us to a native village nestled at the foot of some hills on the southern shore. I stood at the forecastle with Duarte and Father Pedro beside me, throwing out lead on a line, and shouting out the depth to Magellan and Gómez. At forty feet, Magellan ordered the anchors let loose.

A striking large domed rock on our port side dwarfed our fleet.

"I've been many places, but I've never seen such a rock as that one," I said.

"Carvalho told me to look for it. He said the local natives call it *Pau-nh-acuqua* or "high hill" in their language," replied Father Pedro. A wide-brimmed hat sheltered his balding head.

"It looks like half a huge loaf of bread placed cut side down."

"It looks like just a rock to me." Duarte glanced at the rock and returned his gaze to the native village.

"Where is your sense of curiosity?" I asked.

"Oh, I'm curious…about what the wenches look like and what the liquor here tastes like."

Duarte combed his hair back with his fingers. He had changed into fresh attire. I still wore my usual salt-encrusted clothes.

"I'm surprised how big the village is," observed Duarte.

"Carvalho says those large huts are called *boii*," said Father Pedro.

"What are they?"

"Apparently communal houses. They sleep over a hundred people."

Father Pedro left us to join Magellan on the quarterdeck.

"Talk about sleeping, I've heard the girls are quite willing here," said Duarte with a smirk. "Although they say to avoid the married ones. Their men tend to be very jealous."

"Won't that cause problems for you?"

"Precious virgin, no. There should be enough unmarried

ones to keep me busy. Carvalho says the girls are willing to share their bed for a small gift. Just as important, they're very enthusiastic. My carajo is looking forward to being very busy between the thighs of the local maidens."

"I can see where your priorities lie."

"Mate, I've slept with women from Spain to India. I've bedded white ones, dark ones, and tan ones. I plan to screw my way across the world. There's nothing I like better than being between the soft thighs of a woman. I'll take the pleasures of life as I can find them. I try to enjoy life day by day. I may not return from this voyage, but I'll savor it while I'm alive."

"I'll join you ashore soon once I know the ship is secure."

The ripples from the descent of the anchors were still searching for the shore when canoes filled with naked, olive-skinned Tamojo men and women surrounded the ships. The men were beardless and had bald, shaved heads. Many had bright, multicolored feathers attached around their waists with the feathers suspended over their buttocks. The natives shouted to the crew to get their attention as they held up fruit and squawking chickens for trade. Men leaned over the gunwales to trade trinkets for food. The Tamojos were happy to get a metal fishhook or knife for half a dozen chickens. In the Canaries, a dozen fishhooks might buy one chicken.

The sight of the naked women was too much for some of the men starved for sex after so long at sea. One was Juan de San Andrés, a *grumete* hired on in the Canary Islands. He was as dark as a Moor and had the physique of a Greek god. San Andrés was as tall as Andrew of Bristol and strong enough to work the anchor capstan by himself. When one canoe filled with three naked women drew near, he reached over the gunwale to hoist one of them aboard. The natives back paddled away and he lost his balance. His arms and legs flailed about to the jeers of his shipmates and the scowl of Magellan. He retrieved his situation by grabbing a line. He hung suspended above the water for a second before with arm muscles bulging he pulled himself back aboard.

TEN – RIO

Magellan demanded complete obedience at sea, but once our ships were safely anchored he announced all could go ashore except for a small guard. The shallop was brought alongside and the dingy lowered. The men lined up to disembark. I laughed when I overheard the conversation of a couple of my fuzzy-faced *grumetes*.

"Are you sure we should be doing this?" asked Antón de Noya. Antón was a smallish young lad whose beard was only a little thicker than when he had sailed from Spain. I was always a little concerned when he was aloft that I'd hear a scream followed by a thud on the deck.

"I *have* to do this. My *carajo* can't wait any longer. It's been lonely every night since we left Tenerife. What have you brought to trade?" asked San Andrés. His long black hair was oiled and he wore his clean set of clothes.

"I've ten fish hooks, and twenty beads."

"That should work. Just don't overpay. You don't want to ruin the market," counseled San Andrés as he looked over his own stash of fifteen nails and some red cloth.

Once the guards were set, I went ashore and roamed the village. The bacchanals were well under way.

In one hut on the edge of the village, I found Philip kneeling on the ground with a circle of natives around him and a naked girl on each side.

"What are you doing?"

"Teaching them dice," said Philip with a crooked smile.

"Why? They have no gold and you can buy anything they have for a few nails."

"The money isn't as important as is winning."

"Don't let the Captain General see you."

Anyone caught gambling aboard Magellan's ships went under the lash, but was it gambling if no money changed hands? Philip was as addicted to the dice as Duarte was to his carajo and booze.

I shook my head and continued my inspection. Inside the huge native houses, I was amazed to see that instead of sleeping on the ground or in a raised bed like any European would do, the Tamojo slept in netting suspended from tall stakes in the ground. I bought a jug of liquor for a nail and went in search of a woman.

Before Rio, I'd only seen a woman naked beside me in bed. Here they walked about as naturally as Eve. They were most comely. For a small knife and a mirror, I purchased the company of a sweet girl. I probably overpaid, but I didn't care. She led me to a dark corner of one of their huge huts, and I relieved myself of what had been building since the Canaries. Then we ate some fresh broiled fish and vegetables that I didn't recognize. Afterwards we returned to our little love nest. She was enthusiastic and talented beyond her young years.

Late that night I returned to the *Trinidad* on the same boat as San Andrés and Antón. They had disheveled hair and smug smiles.

The next morning I organized work parties to refill the water casks and gather firewood. I accompanied the steward ashore to buy provisions to replace the four months of rations already consumed. Fresh fruits, fish, fowl, and game were plentiful and cheap, but we needed preserved food. Fresh food would last but a week or two once the fleet sailed. The concept of drying or salting meat was alien to the natives. They could always pluck a meal from a tree or dig it from the ground. We tried drying some meat, but it molded in the moist air. A large supply of tubers packed in dried palm leaves were the best we could do.

That evening I went back into the village looking for the girl, but first came across Duarte sitting with his back against a log, his right arm cradling a jug of the local liquor, and left arm around a naked sleeping brown-skinned honey. He had a satisfied look on his face, while staring at a palm gently swaying in the breeze.

When Duarte came out of his drunken trance and noticed me, he said, "This could be a nice place to lord it over."

"I don't think the Portuguese would approve."

"No, no. I didn't mean here. I meant someplace like here with balmy weather, food almost free for the taking, plenty of booze, and most of all, lots of willing women."

"The women might be willing, but in a while I think their men will grow tired of us."

Duarte laughed. "That's what our swords and armor are for."

I shrugged my shoulders. "Our charter with King Carlos is go to the Indies and return with our ships full of cloves and nutmeg, not to conquer land there."

"Oh. Is that what the charter says? Have you seen it?"

"No, but I'd wager you have. What does it say?"

"We are to find a route to the Indies and return with riches of spice...but there is more. The first six islands we discover will belong to King Carlos, but if Captain General Magellan finds more, he can take two for himself...and his descendants. Imagine it. Magellan's cousin Serrão is vizier to the rajah of Ternate and lives like a king there. There are islands even more valuable than Ternate in the Indies. Serrão gained control of the Moluccas with one cannon and a few fellow Portuguese."

Duarte's eyes were alight with his excitement. He took a swig from his jug. "Think what we can do with our fleet and a hundred armed men. We can conquer a kingdom with Magellan as prince. Mark you, Mate Albo, that means gold, and drink, and women for all of us. My brother will need good men to help him in ruling his kingdom. There will be a place for me...and you there."

I was about to ask Duarte more when his eyes closed, and he leaned back against his log, while pulling his wench closer to him.

I left him there, bought a chicken and a jug of wine, and went back to the *Trinidad* to have a cabin boy roast the bird for me. There was much to think about. There were now many more possibilities than I had ever imagined. If what Duarte said was true, then maybe what Magellan really sought was to emulate the success of Serrão in Ternate and to carve out an island kingdom for himself. From the tales I'd heard of the Portuguese exploits in India, our five ships and few hundred men could be enough to conquer a small country. If Magellan was successful, that could mean very good things for one Francisco Albo, whom Magellan seemed to think highly of and had just named a pilot of his armada. Might I have my own island to rule as a prince? My excitement grew. Things could work out very well for me.

Several days later Father Pedro and I returned to the *Trinidad* from breakfast ashore. I had promised to help the good father in the bilge. We found the ship's carpenter Luciano building a chair for Salamón. Two *grumetes* assisted as Luciano bored a hole for the garrote rope through the chair's high back. The day after our arrival the court martial was reconvened and Salamón's sentence proclaimed: death by garroting. A sailor saw enough death by accident at sea. Those deaths, in time, I got over. The deaths inflicted on one another, whether by combat or execution, took much longer before they moved to the recesses of my mind.

"Good morning, Father, and good morning to you, Mate," chattered Luciano when he saw us. I looked askance at the execution chair. Pudgy Luciano whistled as he smoothed the sides of the hole so the garrote could move with ease. *How can Luciano be so cheerful? Doesn't he realize a man will soon die sitting in this chair?*

"Good morning, Señor Luciano," replied Father Pedro as he crossed himself.

I went to the main deck hatch, dislodged it, and climbed into the hold below. Father Pedro followed.

"The air is foul down here, Mate."

"It's the rotting food and shit. The heat and the humidity don't help."

In inclement weather, the crew often used the hold as a latrine rather than attempting to use the exposed *jardines* on the high poop deck.

Having come out of the brilliant Rio sun, I saw only dim shapes. I lit two candles, handed one to Father Pedro, and waited for my eyes to adjust. Casks of provisions, boxes of trade goods, stacked lumber, and other supplies filled the hold. Some barrels were marked as wine, others as salt cod, or anchovies. I heard the sound of little feet, lots of little feet, scurrying among the barrels. The glimmer of beady eyes reflected the candle light. I involuntarily flinched as a rat ran over my foot. It squealed and ran away.

With Father Pedro in tow, I worked my way towards the stern until I found the rough wooden lattice door to the space below. I unlatched it, propped it open, and climbed into the bilge below followed by Father Pedro.

"The bilge makes the hold seem like a palace," said Father Pedro as he held a cloth over his nose.

More rats scampered out of the sputtering candlelight. There chained in irons laid the dejected form of Salamón. It seemed the man's soul had already left him, leaving him a pale cipher of his former self.

Salamón awoke and shielded his eyes from the candlelight.

"Why are you here?"

Salamón's voice was raspy. He probably had not spoken in days or even weeks. He'd been in the hellhole for over a month.

"I have come to here to administer the Extreme Unction," said Father Pedro.

"I wish to confess nothing. Go away. If they are going to kill me, tell them to get it over with. I'm tired of lying here in the filth and dark with the rats. Death can be no worse than this."

"Are you sure you do not want to clear your heart with God?"

"God was done with me a long time ago, Father. I think he has no use for me and I certainly have no use for him. Go away."

I held my nose. Even among all the fetid odors around me, I could smell Salamón. His clothes appeared to have rotted from his body in the damp warmth of the hold. I turned my eyes away. Salamón would certainly go to hell, but it seemed like he was already there.

"God has a bottomless capacity for forgiveness, Salamón. Let me help your soul in the hereafter by giving you the Last Rites. You may soon meet with God. You can discuss your sins with him further at that time."

"Ah, Father Pedro, you are persistent. Go ahead. Do your work and then leave me."

Father Pedro opened a small flask of olive oil. He wet his finger and drew a cross on Salamón's forehead.

"Through this holy anointing, may the Lord pardon you whatever sins you have committed."

He sprinkled oil on Salamón's hands.

"May the Lord who frees you from sin save you and raise you up."

The Father backed away, knelt, and prayed for several minutes. Salamón closed his eyes; his lips moved in silence as if he was also praying. Father Pedro crossed himself and rose.

"Thank you, Father," whispered Salamón.

In the half darkness, I thought I saw tears welling in Salamón's eyes. I did not like Salamón. In fact, I detested the coarse bully. However, I could not help feeling sorry for him like anyone meeting his doom.

"God be with you and have mercy on your soul," finished Father Pedro.

I stood with my countrymen, Michael, now acting Master of the *Victoria*, and Philip in the bright sunlight. The air smelled of cool earth after a morning cloudburst. The bright sun was high in the sky. Dark clouds gathered in the distance. These would bring the evening rains. The bay's water sparkled while the armada's five black ships swung on their anchors. Past the ships to the southeast on the other side of the harbor was the odd rock formation the men now called Sugarloaf. *This place may be as close to paradise as I will likely get.* The weather was pleasant, the food and liquor plentiful, and the girls friendly.

Michael's voice broke my reverie, "Eh Philip, isn't that the young wench you slept with last night? Ah, yes, there's her sister too."

"Yes, that's them. Every part of my body is hurting, if you know what I mean."

My friends, the entire crew, and I stood in ranks to witness Salamón's execution. Many Tamojos had gathered. They seemed to be wondering what these strange white men were up to. The crew and Tamojo surrounded an open area where Luciano's stout chair awaited Salamón. It had bindings to hold his legs, arms, and torso. The garrote rope now ran through the neck hole in the high chair back. The rope had a stick attached behind the chair back to rotate it.

In Greek, Philip whispered, "I don't understand these cursed Spaniards. Why all this? If our pious leaders wished Salamón dead, they should have swung him from the yardarm weeks ago. The deed would have then been over and mercifully done with."

"You are forgetting these are the people of the Inquisition," I replied out of the side of my mouth. "Mercy has nothing to do with punishing evil doers or rooting out heresy in the minds of these Spaniards. The Iberians are as expert at torture as the Ottoman Turks."

"And God approves of the torture?"

"They must think so. The Spanish use it to find the Jews among them."

"Their version of the Christian faith is two-faced. One face is that of a prune-faced priest, all strict and constipated.

The other face is that of a leering, lecherous old man. Look at the debaucheries of this past week."

"Of which you've been at the forefront, Philip."

"Which I freely admit. Salamón is certainly a sinner, are his sins a boatload more than those committed this past week? I've seen both Spanish and Portuguese captains lurching about drunk like demasted ships in a storm. When not drunk they're screwing like rabbits." Philip drew his cap down tight over his eyes.

"You've grown philosophical. I've no answer for you."

Trumpets sounded. *Alguacil major* Espinosa led Salamón, dressed in black, to the chair. Father Pedro was close by his side. A black-hooded executioner followed. A gasp swelled through the assembled host. The Tamojos looked perplexed.

They seated Salamón and tightened straps about his legs and arms. On a sign from Magellan, the trumpets sounded again. The executioner tightened the garrote. Within minutes Salamón slumped. The executioner held the rope tight. Salamón's pants darkened with his urine. The smell of his excrement drifted in the gentle breeze. His head pressed tight against the chair back as the black garbed executioner twisted even harder on the stick. The executioner released the stick and Salamón's head lolled to the side.

Tension had built in my gut while Salamón was strapped in and the executioner worked the garrote. Now my body felt empty. The crew was quiet; I heard murmurs from the Tamojo discussing the death scene.

The revels that night were much subdued.

In hindsight, December twenty-third was a critical day for the Armada. Decisions made by Magellan that day eventually led to the mutiny that tested Magellan's leadership and to a defection that would challenge the success of the Armada.

I remember that day Magellan pacing the length of his cabin, his dark eyes growing angrier with each step. Magellan had convened a meeting of the Armada's officers. Master Cano sat, arms crossed, next to Captains Quesada and

Mendoza.

Magellan stopped and said, "I have ignored the immorality of the *marineros* and *grumetes*. I expected no more of them. But I expected more of the officers and gentlemen of the Armada."

I was silent, as were the other officers present. Duarte had been absent for three days. Magellan's brother-in-law was one of his most trusted aides. After the trouble in the doldrums with Bishop Fonseca's Spaniards, Magellan had relied on Duarte even more. Now Duarte had failed him.

"Well, the sooner the fleet is away from this tropical fleshpot the better," said Magellan with a sigh.

"Here the Devil will always win by tempting the weak with the pleasures of the flesh," said Father Pedro.

Magellan sat down at the head of his oaken table and looked around the room. The vein in his forehead pulsed. I expected him to erupt in anger at any moment. And, Magellan didn't even know yet about Cartagena.

"Where is Captain Coca?" shouted Magellan. He looked in turn to each of the captains present: Mendoza, Quesada, and Serrano. Each shook their head 'no.' The pilots were also of no help.

Finally, I volunteered, "I saw Captain Coca and Señor Cartagena in a large native boii when I was looking for Señor Duarte. They looked the other way, but I am sure it was them."

Cano scowled at me.

Magellan pounded his fist on the table, "Cartagena? Cartagena should be under your direct control, Captain Mendoza! How can this be? And Captain Coca is with him? He is aiding and abetting this mutineer. Captain Mendoza, please explain why Cartagena isn't under your custody!"

Mendoza drew himself up to his full height, leaned back, looked down his nose, and answered, "Captain Coca asked for Señor Cartagena's release into his custody. As he is captain of the *San Antonio*, I felt safe honoring his request."

"Your choice was a poor one," answered Magellan as he

glared at Mendoza, who averted his eyes.

"Well, Captains, we must regain control of the Armada. We will start with the officers. I'm afraid I've no choice but to make an example of Señors Duarte, Coca, and Cartagena."

The businesslike Serrano nodded in quiet agreement.

Alguacil major Espinosa arched an eyebrow. "What are your wishes, Captain General?"

"*Alguacil major*, take a strong force of soldiers ashore, and very publicly bring Duarte, Coca, and Cartagena back in irons. Announce to all the crew you see that they must return immediately as the Armada is preparing to sail. Everyone who has not returned by nightfall will meet the same fate as the officers. Captains, organize parties to go ashore and roust your men. Once everyone is aboard we will sail to another part of this large bay to finish preparations for the voyage."

"As you wish, Captain General," said Espinosa.

"Captains, I want you to immediately post sentries on your ships. They are to ensure no more of these women are board. *Alguacil?*"

"Yes, Captain General."

"Once all the men are aboard, I want you to take a detachment of soldiers to search each ship from forecastle to stern. Evict every woman from the ships. I will tolerate no more of them on board! The time for play is over. We have much work ahead of us. Any man caught concealing a woman will find his head in the stocks and his back whipped raw."

"Captain General, perhaps we should take some of the natives as slaves. I could keep several busy on my ship," asked Mendoza.

"I can understand your use for some slaves, but I must deny your request."

"Why?"

"First, the King expressly forbade it in our charter. Second, we do not know the time or distance to the Moluccas, and hence we don't know how long our food stores must last. Slaves would be additional mouths eating up our stores. Also, obtaining food and water in Portuguese territory are one thing, but taking slaves is quite another."

The Pilot Carvalho leaned forward, "May I have your permission for my son to accompany me?"

A woman with a young lad sporting Carvalho's distinctive hooked nose greeted Carvalho soon after the fleet landed. The boy was proof of Carvalho's previous stay in Rio, although apparently he'd spent more time screwing while here than learning the seas around Rio.

Magellan nodded. "You have my permission."

I was with Magellan when *Alguacil major* Espinosa returned with the three officers in irons. Magellan looked the other way as Espinosa herded the shuffling men into the forecastle. The closing of the forecastle cabin door ended the sound of chains dragging on the deck. I shook my head. There was the trouble in the doldrums and now this. How would it end?

The *Alguacil major* reported to Magellan. "Captain General, Señor Duarte is back as you directed. He claims to be repentant. Captain Coca and Señor Cartagena are also in custody. The crews are assembling on the beach for the boats to take them back to their ships."

"Well done, *Alguacil*. Take Señors Coca and Cartagena to my cabin. Chain Señor Duarte in the forecastle. Mate Albo, summon the other fleet officers to meet me here."

The captains, pilots, masters, and mates assembled in Magellan's cabin in the early afternoon where a bedraggled Cartagena and Coca waited for them. Armed with sword and dagger the *Alguacil major* stood behind the prisoners.

Magellan entered and glared at Cartagena and Cocoa. "Well, Señors how do you explain this?" He singled out Coca. "Why did you take Señor Cartagena ashore?"

"I thought, I thought Señor Cartagena would like to see the sights of this land…Señor Cartagena…was in my custody at all times," stammered Coca.

"Well, Captain Coca, you never asked my permission. I must…be able…to trust my captains…at all times,"

Magellan pounded the table three times to punctuate his words.

"I'm an officer of the Armada. I did not realize your permission was necessary," whispered Coca.

"You did not realize?" said Magellan with a rising voice.

"No, I did not realize."

"Señor Coca, you disappoint me. You've betrayed my trust. Your captaincy has ended. You will retain your position as Fleet Accountant."

Coca bit his lower lip and said nothing.

Magellan turned and glared at Cartagena, "And if you like it so much here in Rio de Janeiro, I am of a mind to leave you here. Perhaps you could persuade the Portuguese to return you to Spain when they come next year for their annual shipment of brazil wood."

"Captain General, I think most would find marooning me to be excessive for what most would see as a small offense, if it even is an offense. My appointment was signed by King Carlos himself," said Cartagena with a sneer.

Captain Quesada twirled his mustache several times. His face broke into a crooked smile. He interjected, "That's true Captain General. I think the *Casa de Contratación* would look very skeptically at such treatment of an officer appointed by the king."

Magellan hesitated.

What Quesada says is probably true. Will Magellan relent?

Magellan stared at a corner of his cabin. Finally, he said, "Have it your way, Captain. I will release Señor Cartagena into your custody. Do not take this responsibility as lightly as Captain Mendoza did. The new Captain of the San António will be Señor Mezquita. Pilot Major Gómez, you will transfer to the San António to support Captain Mezquita."

I was shocked at the appointment of Magellan's cousin, inexperienced Mezquita, to captain the fleet's largest ship. Beside his blood ties, there was little to recommend the stolid Mezquita for the job. I'd trust Mezquita's sword beside me in a fight, but to captain a ship seemed beyond the intellectual capabilities of the man. There were a dozen more deserving officers in the fleet. The two most qualified were Pilot Major Gómez and Duarte. They were the two officers with Portuguese Indian experience. Unfortunately, Duarte's love for his carajo and liquor had left him in irons in the forecastle. And Pilot Major Gómez? Even though he and Magellan were both Portuguese, they barely tolerated one another. Nonetheless, I thought it a blunder to demote Gómez by moving him to the *San Antonio* under Mezquita. What was so wrong about what Cartagena and Coca did? It looked like Magellan was just looking for a reason to get his own man in command of the *San Antonio*, or was his pride more important to him than being reasonable? It was probably the latter. These Iberians, be they Spanish or Portuguese, were quick to take offense, and overreact to the smallest slight.

"I think, Captain General, that I can best serve the Armada in my present position," said the Pilot Major. His face had reddened.

"The San António is our largest ship, Pilot Major Gómez, and you are best qualified to ensure her safety."

"True, and if that is what you really want, I can. But I can best do that as the *San Antonio's* captain, not as her pilot."

"Señor Mezquita will be captain, and you pilot," replied Magellan.

"As you wish, Captain General. I will insure the *San Antonio* is safe." Gómez stood up and stomped out.

"Pilot Carvalho will do the piloting on the *Trinidad* with Albo's assistance. I'll have the trumpets sound and the changes announced to the Armada. We have much work to do, Señors. Let us get the crews aboard and the ships ready for the voyage ahead of us."

Most the crew was aboard by nightfall; a few stragglers returned in the morning. Espinosa's men searched and scoured the ships for women and other contraband. They found a girl in the *Santiago's* forecastle, and another two girls hiding in the *San Antonio's* hold. As previously agreed

Carvalho's son, called Joãzito by the crew and some nine years of age, stayed as his page and cabin boy.

With the crews aboard and the native women off the ships, we rigged towlines from the ships to the longboats and the shallop. The sweeps, three to four to a side, were extended. Then, with the boats towing and the sweeps rowing, we moved the ships to a sheltered spot on the harbor's northern side. There, Fathers Pedro and Sanchez led the celebration of the Feast of the Nativity of our Lord Jesus Christ. I suspected all but the most pious men would rather still be celebrating ashore. The Armada sailed south the following day.

ELEVEN – RIO DE SOLÍS AND SOUTH

After a two-week sail from Rio de Janeiro, we came upon the huge bay known as the Rio de Solís. The Spanish *roteiros* for the coast to the Rio de Solís were complete, but there they ended. The Solís expedition had discovered two rivers at the head of the bay, although records were sketchy. There natives killed and ate Solís and some of his men. The survivors hurriedly fled back to Spain. Taking accurate soundings and latitudes were not a priority for them. Nonetheless, based upon Solís's explorations showing the bay ended in two rivers, I expected Magellan to bypass the bay and search for the way to the Indies further south. I knew Piri Reis's charts showed no strait to the Indies here, but instead a solid land mass blocking the way. If there was a strait, it was far to the south, although I couldn't tell Magellan that. I also thought that the Portuguese had previously explored this area, and that Magellan should know of what they'd discovered.

Magellan surprised me by spending a precious month of summer exploring this vast body of water. Some speculated that Magellan knew where the strait to the Indies was. His long exploration of the bay proved that false. Magellan explored these waters in the way he did everything: methodically. That was fine for outfitting the fleet, but not for trying to find our way around South America before winter set in.

The bay was at the same latitude as Africa's Cape of Good Hope, so perhaps he reasoned that this continent should end at the same latitude as Africa. He sent the shallop ahead where it found Solís's great rivers flowing into the bay. Captain Serrano in the *Santiago* explored the rivers while the ships replenished their fresh water.

While watering, the Irish *grumete*, the redheaded William Irés from the *Concepción* drowned after falling overboard. Like many of the men, he could not swim. He was our second fatality after Salamón. On Serrano's return, we finally sailed south, but at the cost of at least three weeks of good weather, which we'd rue later.

The ever-present animosity between the Spanish captains and Magellan still troubled me, but my greatest concern was the weather. Time was not on our side as the season crept closer to fall. I was anxious to find the strait and be on to the Indies.

A few days later, the balmy weather left us. To the east, a huge gray thunderhead covered the Atlantic Ocean from north to south and reached to the heavens.

"The wind is from the east," said Carvalho as he tugged his hat tighter on his head. "It will drive us into the shore."

"I know. We're trapped. There's no escaping the storm," I said. "Our lives will likely depend upon how well our anchors hold."

"Better have the men take down the topsails and the mainsail," ordered Carvalho. "We'll just run with the bow sprit, fore, and lateen sails. Have the men stow anything loose."

I strode to the quarterdeck railing and barked out orders. The *marinero*s and *grumetes* dashed to their stations, and worked with a sense of urgency as the dark clouds drew closer. Great bolts of lightning soon split the heavens, followed by deep rumblings of thunder that I felt in my stomach. An acrid odor permeated the air.

Then the storm was upon us. Its immensity dwarfed our ships. Waves engulfed us and drove us towards the rocky shore like flotsam on a tide. My concern grew as the shore became closer. Heavy rains drenched us.

Carvalho turned to me, "We'll be driven and smashed on the shore unless we do this right. We'll need anchors firmly set to ride out the storm."

"When do you want to do that?"

"From past soundings on this coast I judge that the water will be shallow enough to anchor when we're about three miles off the shore. Get the sails down now; I'll give the command to let go the anchors. God be with you."

I put some of the more experienced *marinero*s to getting the sails down, while Andrew and I made our way across the pitching deck to the forecastle using hand lines rigged earlier. I stood by the starboard anchor, while Andrew was ready by the second with his knife.

On Carvalho's sign, I cut the line to let my anchor plunge to the bottom, while Andrew did the same. Seconds later the bow of the *Trinidad* pulled to port like a hooked fish. *The anchors had caught but sooner than I expected. Carvalho had waited too long. The water was too shallow.* The ship rotated on the anchors until the forecastle was heading into the wind.

The ship struggled on the anchor line like a hooked tuna. The anchors held fast to the bottom, but the forecastle dove and rose with the huge waves. The remainder of the ship bucked and turned like a fish fighting for its life. Suddenly the *Trinidad* shuddered and vibrated from the keel to the masthead.

Andrew shouted, "By Christ's blood, what was that?"

"We're anchored in water too shallow. That was a terrific culadas, ass hit."

"*Culadas?*"

"The ship's keel struck the bottom on the downward stroke of a wave. Let's pray that it was a wave with an unusually low trough."

"Why?" Andrew's face was white in terror.

I grimaced. "Because otherwise our ship will be slowly beaten against the sea bottom until its keel and ribs give way."

Andrew's face paled further and the pupils of his blue

eyes grew large. He held the railing in a death grip as he prepared for the next *culadas*. "I don't know how much more of this I can take."

"We will survive. I don't think it's our fate to die yet."

The thunderstorm continued for another two hours with several more *culadas*. Thankfully, none was as severe as the first. As the rain and wind abated, Saint Elmo showed his blue fire from the mastheads. I felt an eerie tingling about my hair and scalp. I even saw a faint light about Magellan's head as he stood on the high poop deck at the stern. I joined my men as we all fell to our knees in a prayer of thanks to Saint Elmo. It couldn't hurt.

The weather in the morning was fair. My shaken men raised anchors, hoisted sails, and resumed the search to the south. The storm left me wondering what lay ahead. It was late summer. If the storms were this bad now, what would they be like come autumn and winter?

Despite the winter staring at us, for the next two weeks, the fleet moved cautiously down the coast. We anchored each night. Did Magellan think we might sail past the mythical strait in the night? Nearly two months had passed since Rio de Janeiro and our fresh food was long gone when we came upon a small island teeming with black and white flightless birds and huge seals. Magellan ordered the *Trinidad* and *Victoria* to each put ashore a party. Master Polcevera named Ginés de Mafra to head a small party of *marineros* and *grumetes* to get some meat. Ginés was a Castilian with a curly head of brown hair. He was one of our best *marineros*. About half our seamen could read, but Ginés could read well and he was good at numbers. His readings on an astrolabe were accurate and his calculations of latitude were always close to mine.

"I'm looking forward to some fresh meat tonight. I'll come in the evening with the shallop for your catch," I said as Ginés cast off in the *Trinidad's* skiff.

"This should be easy, Mate. We'll see you later," replied a

cheerful Ginés. He had four men with him in the skiff: two other *marineros*, the dark giant San Andrés, and fuzzy-cheeked Antón.

I'd made a brief visit to the island earlier. The seals might be difficult to kill, because of their size. The birds should be easy. They were tame, flightless and could only waddle until they reached the water. The birds were dark on the back with a white belly and with a dark black horizontal stripe across the top of the chest and a wider, but less dark, stripe across the neck. These birds were less than two foot tall and lived in burrows on the island. They were like no bird I'd seen before, and, although flightless, most reminded my shipmates and me of European ducks. As so, we named the bay the Bahia de los Patos, the "Bay of the Ducks."

Father Pedro joined me at the waist of the ship. "It'll be good to have some fresh meat, Albo."

"Agreed. I'm tired of salt fish."

"I'm tired of hardtack."

Father Pedro and I were continuing our discussion about food when the *grumete* on watch in the masthead called down, "Mate Albo, look westward. See how the sky is darkening there. A storm might be brewing."

I looked towards shore. The clouds were still at a distance, but they looked ominous.

"Come, Father, let's find Carvalho."

The sudden onset of storms on this coast amazed me. An hour earlier, the sun blessed us with its glory. Now white caps formed on the dark water.

Icy gusts were already cutting my face when I found Carvalho watching the building weather with wild eyes beneath his curly brows. I said, "Pilot, we should immediately send the shallop to retrieve the sealing party."

"There's no time for that, Mate. By the devil, it's another of these damned storms. Summon the crew to ready the ship and raise the anchor. Prepare for rough weather. We can get the men later."

"I disagree. There is enough time to pick up the men if

we move quickly."

"My command is for you to ready the ship for the gale. Let me hear no more from you."

"Shouldn't we check with the Captain General?"

"He's visiting Captain Mezquita on the *San Antonio*. Now get the anchor up," commanded Carvalho.

I looked towards the island. Ginés's skiff was barely visible on the beach. I wished Magellan were here. Magellan was a hard man, but he cared for his men. I had no use for men like Carvalho and Cano who put no value on a *marineros'* life. Damn Carvalho.

The storm hit us with a cold fury. The wind came in great gusts that heeled the ship far over. It brought frigid temperatures, although not low enough to freeze the wet lines.

Soon I had little time to think of my men left on shore. I had to focus on saving the *Trinidad* while the storm blew us far into the Atlantic. By nightfall, our helpless fleet was miles off the coast.

The next morning the seas were calm. A favorable wind took us back to the sealing party. The temperature, though, had fallen further. The *San Antonio* came alongside. Magellan was angry that Carvalho had abandoned the sealers. He ordered Duarte to lead a party to find our men ashore. I took the *Trinidad's* shallop and a dozen men while Mate Philip of the *Victoria* took its longboat and ten men.

Duarte stood at the shallop's bow as I steered for the island. Philip's longboat knifed the water to starboard. I watched in silence, my stomach tight with worry for my men, as the oar blades cut the still waters, leaving little eddies at the end of each stroke. The day was peaceful and gulls floated above in the blue sky while they searched for their morning dinner. The only sounds were the birds calling and the squeaking of oarlocks. Yesterday's fierce storm was only a bad memory.

I guided the shallop towards Ginés's empty skiff. From

afar, the rocks of the island seemed to move. As we drew nearer, the rocks turned into large, lumbering seals. These erupted into a cacophony of raspy bellows. My stomach became queasy as the odor of a thousand seals defecating and the guano from thousands of the flightless birds hit my nose.

The shallop's bottom grated across the rocks as it came ashore.

"Where are the men?" I asked of no one in particular. "Ginés, San Andrés. Where are you?" I shouted.

I could scarcely hear my voice above the noisy seals. The largest of them, the bulls, were over fifteen feet long and certainly weighed five tons. They sported large elephantine snouts. The smaller females were more numerous. There were many juveniles of all sizes. The animals looked as if they were wearing moth-eaten coats with chunks of dark gray and brown hair everywhere. They stood their ground and ignored us.

Duarte and I started walking inland with several men, picking our way between the seals. A small bull charged when Duarte got too close. Duarte's strong arms drove a spear into its chest and several of our men then clubbed it to death. The seal's death cries awoke its brethren from their lethargy. With eyes wide and full of fear, the nearby seals panicked and began a clumsy slow motion dash towards the ocean. This provoked a general stampede of the entire rookery into the water. Mangy fur flew in the air. Many let loose their bowels in their hasty rush for survival. I dodged several animals in their mad dash to the safety of the surf. Men bludgeoned to death some of the smaller seals before they reached the safety of the blue water.

Finally, the seals were gone and the island was quiet. One small group of seals remained further inland. I made my way towards the seals calling, "Ginés, Antón, San Andrés."

As I neared the seals, an apparition arose, bloody and wraith-like. It croaked, "Mate Albo?"

Four other figures rose from the group of seals. They

staggered on uncertain feet towards me.

"Mother of God, Mate, we thought you would never come."

The men were black from dried blood and smeared with gore.

"Ginés, I didn't recognize you. Pleased be to God that you're alive. What happened?" Congealed blood matted Ginés's curly hair.

"We'd already killed six of these creatures when we realized the weather was changing. We hurried back to the skiff to see the *Trinidad* and the other ships departing. By the devil in person, why did you abandon us?"

"Carvalho wouldn't let me send the shallop to rescue you. We had a bad night in the storm at sea, but returned once we could."

Ginés gray eyes bore into me. Then he shouted, "A bad night at sea. A bad night at sea! It was a terrible, shitty night here! There's no shelter on this god-forsaken island. The wind swept over the rocks like a comb over a bald man's head. Freezing rain drenched us."

"We'd have died a cold, wet, and miserable death on these damn rocks," said San Andrés, "but Ginés said that if blubber keeps seals warm in the icy sea, why can't it keep us warm above it. We gutted the seals and crawled inside. My nose may never be the same from their foul odor and I may never get the blood out of my hair, but I'm alive." San Andrés prized his long hair as much as his muscles and combed it several times a day. Now it was lank and clotted with seal blood.

"It was a hell of a bunk, Mate, but without it we wouldn't have survived the night," added Ginés.

"Well done. Come along. Let's get you back to the ship, clean you up, and get you some dry clothes."

The haggard men followed me back to the shallop past the other men busy butchering the seals, all the while muttering curses upon Carvalho. A few of the flightless seabirds were still on the island, but every seal had vanished into the sea.

Carvalho wouldn't look at me, or my men, in the face as we came aboard. I ordered water heated in the great pot used for trying-out the oil of the slaughtered seals' blubber. Ginés and the others bathed, ate, and washed their clothes.

Magellan checked on the men and seemed relieved that they were healthy. Then he turned to order me, "Mate, take a skiff around to the other ships. Tell them we depart in the morning. All the seals must be butchered, their meat salted, and their blubber rendered into oil by that time."

This was a message I was happy to take around to the other ships. No one in the fleet wanted to stay in the unlucky bay any longer than necessary.

The next morning, just as the anchors were up and the sails set, a cry came from the masthead. "There's another storm coming, Señors. This time look to the east."

I saw the storm and swore to myself. The bay turned out to be a trap, as there was no time to sail to sea to escape the coming storm. The wind hit with such fury that the *Trinidad* heeled far over on its side as twenty-foot high waves struck it. The crew grasped rails and rigging to avoid washing overboard. The command went out to lower the yards and drop an anchor. The anchor line paid out. The yards dropped, dumping the sails onto the deck. The bow dug into the sea as the anchor bit into the ocean bottom. There was a loud snap and the *Trinidad* started drifting further into the bay towards the rocky shore. *Mother of God, the hawser holding the anchor had parted.*

I scrambled over the pitching deck to the bow where I released the second anchor. The line ran out as the winds and waves pushed us closer to the shore. The anchor line finally went slack for a moment as it hit bottom. Then it grew taut as the anchor gripped hold of the bottom. "Hold, you piece of shit!" I said under my breath. I called a few *marinero*s who helped me hoist the third anchor out of the hold and then let it loose. It too held. The storm continued unabated throughout the night.

It ended as dawn broke. There had been too much wind. Now there was too little. We spent the day becalmed and anchored for the night.

Later an ominous shudder woke me. I dressed and made my way on deck. My face stung from an icy rain when I opened the cabin door. I couldn't see anything. I knew there was a full moon overhead, but thick clouds had stolen its light. The ship shook again, taking my feet out from under me. I pulled myself up only to have the deck fall beneath my feet. I fell again and rolled along the deck to the starboard side. I grasped the deck railing and peered over the side. A great wave slugged me. Horrendous waves reached far over my head. There was a snap overhead followed by a crash on the deck behind me. *That must be a yard or topmast.* I could do nothing to save the ship. It all depended on whether the anchors would hold, and, even if they did, would the ship survive the battering of the mast-high waves. I crawled along the side until I came to the quarterdeck bulkhead and wedged myself there. From the bow came a terrible ripping sound. Boards floated around me. *Were they from the forecastle? What happened to the men berthed there?* I prayed to Jesus, Allah, and Zeus for their souls. There were more sounds of destruction overhead. *Are the poop and quarterdecks being torn away?* The darkness made it all worse. There was nothing I could do except brace myself against the deck's gyrations and hug the railing to prevent the cold waves from sweeping me off to Hades. I fell into a stupor, cold, and with muscles sore from gripping the railing of my salvation.

Day came. The storm continued, but in the light, it wasn't as frightening. The topmast of the foremast was on the deck, but a walk around the deck showed all damage was repairable once the storm was over. The other ships were still afloat close by. I ate a little hardtack and took some salt cod to chew on. The rain grew worse and I took refuge in my small cabin after inviting some of my men to join me. Otherwise, they'd have to cower on the deck as I had last night, or find a berth in the hold. It was too dangerous to use the *jardines* on the poop deck. Men just went on the deck. It didn't matter. The waves immediately swept it away.

Night came again. Another day came and then night. The storm went on. *Three days. I never knew a storm could last this long. Am I dead? Is this the mariner's hell? Has God forsaken us?* One *grumete* huddled in my cabin repeating the same prayer for hours on end. At first, it was annoying, but in the depth of the night, I joined him. Finally sleep came.

I awoke to a gently swaying ship. I stretched my sore muscles, and emerged from my cabin to a bright, almost warm sun overhead. Stays and yardarms littered the deck. The forecastle was a shambles. Carvalho appeared before me, with face drawn and dark circles under his eyes. Father Pedro appeared from the direction of the forecastle. Soon there were more men wandering about, blinking at the sun.

The *San Antonio* and *Victoria* were off our starboard side and the *Santiago* and *Concepción* to port. Every ship was missing its forecastle. The sterncastles were also gone on the three smaller ships and badly damaged on the *San Antonio*. *How many men have we lost?*

Carvalho, Father Pedro, and I entered Magellan's cabin through a hole where the door had once been. A six-foot hole in the ceiling lit the room where another wave tore away part of the poop deck. The furniture was scattered about the room as if tossed about by Titans. I blinked to let my eyes adjust to the change in light. My lids felt like sandpaper on my eyes. However, I had to stay awake. There was much work to be done and my own, and the ship's, survival depended upon it.

A haggard Magellan looked up from the one upright chair in the room. Duarte sat on the floor, back against the wall, half asleep. Ravelo and Enrique, Magellan's Asian slave, slept in the rear of the cabin.

"Never before have I seen such a storm," said a wild-eyed Carvalho. "Three days! Waves of such height." His beard was white with dried salt.

"We may thank God that our anchors held through it

all," said Magellan.

"Yes, God answered our prayers on the third day of the storm," said Father Pedro in a soft voice. "I think it was the power of our joint prayers that ended the storm and saved us. That and I know many men pledged pilgrimages should the Lord grant them salvation from the storm."

"I think God is on our side now, Father Pedro. I knew it when I saw the luminescent Holy Bodies of Saints Anselmo, Nicholas, and Clara appear over the masts. Let us hope He stays with us for the remainder of the voyage," said Magellan.

"I'm sure He will."

Did Magellan really believe that God had saved us? If so, why had God sent the storm in the first place? Possibly, or more likely, the storm had simply exhausted itself.

"I hope we can repay the Lord with many conversions before we are done," replied Magellan.

Ah, or was Magellan going to use converting pagans to Christians as a cover for his carving his own princedom in the Indies? I didn't know the depth of Magellan's religious beliefs, and how much they motivated him compared to his lucrative contract with King Carlos. On the other hand, my experience in the Ottoman Empire was that most the pashas were quite flexible in their beliefs. I didn't think the same was true with the Portuguese and Spaniards, who seemed fervently devoted to their God. I, for one, preferred the pragmatic to the religious in my commander, although I preferred to serve a man who had goodness in his heart.

"The ships have not fared well," I reported. "I don't know how many men we've lost."

"I don't think either they or the ships can take many more storms like this last one," added Carvalho.

"I know that," sighed Magellan. "We must either find the strait to the South Sea or find a safe winter anchorage immediately."

"Perhaps we should return to Rio de Janeiro. There would be ample food and water there," suggested Carvalho.

"That sounds good to me," said Duarte while in the midst of a yawn.

"And that is why we will not be returning to Rio, dear brother Duarte," Magellan scowled. "No, we will head south. I still hope to find the pass, but we will also look for a safe place to winter. We will need food, water, and wood. We will use the time until spring to overhaul the ships and rebuild the fore and sterncastles. Mate, go around to the other ships. Tell them they have one day to make the most urgent repairs and then we head south. Let's get to work, men."

I didn't like agreeing with Carvalho, but I also thought the wood and blood of the fleet had done all that it could. Both needed a rest, but we needed to find a good anchorage, preferably Rio de Janeiro, before the full brunt of winter hit us.

After my rounds of the ships were completed, I wondered if perhaps God had looked over us. Besides all five ships being seaworthy, when the ships' companies were mustered, not a single man had been lost.

TWELVE – BAHIA SAN JULIÁN, PATAGONIA

Some three weeks later, we discovered on the rugged coastline the narrow entrance to what appeared to be a safe anchorage. The *Trinidad* followed the *Santiago* through the narrow opening. To starboard, to the west, was a hundred-foot-high cliff. A short distance to our port was the tip of a vast shoal that extended from the eastern shore. Following behind were the remaining ships of the Armada. As the *Trinidad* emerged from the narrow passage, the water opened up into a large bay. The peninsula to the east should protect the ships from the storms that continued to batter the fleet after the horrific three-day ordeal.

The prospect of staying here for six months until spring did not warm my bones. Now a frosty rime often coated the deck in the morning. What would it be like once winter actually came? The only food in the ship's hold was salt cod and hardtack, and even that might not be enough to last the winter. We needed to find food nearby. Our water barrels were almost empty. We needed a river for its fresh water. No river was in sight; grass, shrubs, and stunted trees covered the shore.

I hoped this bay would prove better than the one we had found two weeks earlier. That one was also sheltered, but for six days a storm trapped us there, unable to rescue a foraging party from the shore. Thankfully, the men ashore had started a fire and sustained themselves with mussels until their rescue. There had been seals and more of the flightless birds there to hunt, but no fresh water. Without water, we were forced to sail on.

Beside me stood Magellan, the Pilot Carvalho, and Duarte.

"This looks like an excellent harbor to me," said Magellan. "These hills around us will shelter us from the howling winds off the ocean. The trees are not much to look at, but they should supply ample wood for cooking."

"Yes, but there's no sign of a village," said Duarte.

A village would mean fresh water and food. Maybe even the natives could not scratch out an existence here.

The *Trinidad* anchored in the middle of the Armada with the *Santiago* and *Victoria* anchored to our east closer to the mouth to the Atlantic Ocean. The *Concepción* and *San Antonio* anchored to our west further into the little harbor. I took care to set the tines of the anchors firmly and leave a good scope of line. The tides had ranged ten to fifteen feet in the other bays, and a loose anchor could be disastrous.

"Duarte, take the shallop. Explore this harbor and beyond the narrows," commanded Magellan. There was a narrows at the far end of the bay. The *grumete* in the mainmast said he could see an even larger inner bay there. There might be a river.

"Keep an eye out for fresh water. Check out the fish and game. Mate Albo, take a skiff around to the other ships announcing that there will be a council this evening. Each ship should send representatives."

I made the rounds of the ships. By the time I returned, the *Trinidad* echoed with the sound of hammers as our carpenter, pot-bellied Luciano, directed the reconstruction of the sterncastle. This was our first opportunity to repair completely the storm damage of the past month. Wood from the hold was stacked on the main deck. By evening, the new sterncastle was taking shape. The beat of hammers reverberated across the water from the other ships.

In evening, just as the captains, pilots, and masters arrived for the council, Duarte returned. He reported a river appeared to enter the far end of the bay. Ostrich-like birds and long-legged sheep frequented the hills around the bay, which should provide ample fresh meat along with the seals and flightless ducks that cavorted in the water around the ships. Magellan assembled his officers in his newly refurbished cabin for which Luciano had already constructed a stout oak door.

Magellan started, "Officers of the Armada, Bahia San Julián here is an excellent harbor. It will shelter us from the storms that have bedeviled us. This afternoon's reconnaissance indicates there is fresh water and game here. The harbor gives us an excellent place to over winter. We will have plenty of time to repair the damage from the storm at the Bahia de los Patos and to rummage the ships."

Someone groaned in the back of the cabin. I too groaned inwardly. Magellan looked for the offender. Not finding him, he continued, "I am, though, concerned whether our wine and food will be sufficient. I regret we will have to reduce rations. The stewards on each ship will be so informed."

There were many sighs around the table. I doubted the wisdom of this measure. The colder weather here would require the men to eat more, not less. The rummaging of the ships, emptying, cleansing, then repacking their holds, would require the men to expend even more energy. I was as eager to find the strait to the South Sea as Magellan was, but we needed to find provisions.

Captain Mendoza spoke first, "For what are we sacrificing, Captain General? Does the strait you seek even exist? We have been at sea for over three months since Rio de Janeiro. My pilot tells me we're fifteen degrees south of the Cape of Good Hope and there's still no sign of a passage to Balboa's South Sea. Let's restore the rations and return to Spain. We have suffered enough. Let another expedition build on the experience of this one at some later time."

Magellan painted on a conciliatory face. "Could you face our King Carlos, and tell him we decided to return with all five ships and healthy crews? I know I could not. You surprise me by suggesting that, Captain."

"What does lie ahead for us to the south? Starvation? Death in some cold and evil storm? How many more storms must we endure? We tempt fate every time one hits. We're lucky that we haven't lost one, or all, of the ships in the storms we've survived already," added Quesada.

Magellan shook his head in disagreement. "Common sense says there is a pass around this continent, just as around Africa. If we have enough courage and faith in God, we will find it. I have never thought Castilians lacked courage or faith in God. We will find the strait. There is food and shelter here. Surely we should not return to Spain just because wine rations have to be reduced."

"I don't think we're yet at the point where we need to return, but if food stores fall too low, I, too, would vote to return," ventured one of the other pilots.

"Great deeds are accomplished only by the exercise of great will. For Spain and God, we must discover a western route to the Moluccas. We must take the lesson of Dom da Gama to heart and be steadfast in our vision. We must be ready to make sacrifices in the pursuit of that vision. We still have five sound ships with crews intact. It would be traitorous to return the Armada in this condition without having achieved our goal. It would be traitorous to let a little cold and tight belts cause us to flinch from our goal." Magellan pounded his fist on the table.

Magellan's hard, dark eyes surveyed the officers. Captain Serrano of the *Santiago*, and a few others willingly met his eyes. Quesada, Mendoza, and Cano gave one another knowing glances. *What did that mean?* No one, though, was willing to argue any further with Magellan. I, for one, was in agreement with him. It was too soon to return to Spain. Successfully reaching the Moluccas would bring fame and fortune to me far beyond my two thousand *Maravedis* monthly wages. Many countries would bid for the services of a pilot of Magellan's fleet if it found the westward passage to the Moluccas. I wouldn't have sailed this far south so late in the season, but now it was too late to return to Rio. The fleet wouldn't survive the month of storms it would take to reach a better anchorage to the north.

Magellan continued, "There will be an Easter Mass ashore tomorrow led by the Fathers Pedro and Sanchez. Afterward all captains, pilots, and officers of the Armada are invited here to dinner." It seemed odd, celebrating Easter in the fall here in the southern hemisphere.

I stared at my plate and the empty seats beside me. Something was wrong. Something was very wrong. Magellan's table had place settings for all the officers of the Armada. Not one was here, except for the officers of the *Trinidad* and Magellan's cousin, Captain Mezquita of the *San Antonio*. Not even Captain Serrano of the *Santiago* had come.

"What should I make of this?" Magellan asked no one in particular while looking at the empty seats about the table.

What should you make of it? Mother of God, it could not be more obvious. Quesada and his cohorts acted strangely at council yesterday, and didn't show their faces at the Easter services ashore earlier today. And now this. A Spanish storm was going to hit, but would it be a squall or a hurricane?

"I think we had best be vigilant, brother. Remember the warning my father sent you in the Canaries. Maybe the Castilians have finally chosen to act," said Duarte.

"If they make a move, we must reply forcefully and with no pity. Duarte, choose some loyal men and man an extra watch for the night. We must not let our guard down. Cousin Mezquita, you had best also be alert."

"Certainly, Captain General," replied Duarte.

"I hope our fears prove unwarranted."

Pedro Sordo's warning at Sanlúcar's bar was happening. The Armada's officers were turning on one another. If an insurrection broke out, Magellan had a hand in bringing this upon himself. He was too autocratic at times, and too hesitant other times. If he hadn't been so methodical in his exploration, we might have already found the strait to the South Seas. If that were the case, I doubted Cartagena's clique would act.

Given the lateness of the season, we should have wintered further north. Warmer weather might also have thawed the cold Spaniards. What would they do? I supported Magellan. He named me a pilot. Still, this matter between him and the Spaniards wasn't really my business. However, if this came to arms, it meant possible death to my men and damage to my ship. If that happened, would I ever see the Spice Islands, or even the balmy Mediterranean? I would have to do all I could to thwart the Spaniards.

It was an uneventful night. The next morning Master Polcevera sent a skiff manned by Ginés along with a *grumete* to the *San Antonio*. He was to pick up a few men there and then collect firewood and fill some water casks from ponds on the shore. The fall air was crisp. The faint disk of the sun was visible through the fog hugging the water. *Were Magellan's and my fears for naught?*

The skiff nosed up to the *San Antonio*. The boat lingered there for a minute and then drew away. It started back to the *Trinidad* with hurried, ragged oar strokes. I waited in silence, dreading what news Ginés had.

"Ginés, why back so soon?" I asked once they were close.

"It's mutiny, Mate. Quesada and Cartagena came aboard the *San Antonio* last night." Ginés panted in his excitement and seemed incapable of speaking further.

"And so," I asked, "What more happened?"

Once Ginés had his breath back, he said hurriedly, "Master Elorriaga was stabbed; he may even be dead. Mezquita is in chains along with my uncle and the *San Antonio's* mate. It's mutiny!" His uncle, Juan Rodríguez Mafra, was a pilot of the *San Antonio*.

I swore under my breath. *The damn fools. My worst fears had come to be. How many men would die because of this?*

I said, "Stay there. I'll get the Captain General."

A stoic Magellan heard Ginés's tale and said, "Mate, go with Ginés around to the ships. At each ship ask who is the captain and ask where their loyalty lies."

At the *San Antonio*, I called out for the officer of the deck. To my surprise, Cano's head appeared draped with a scowl over the poop deck railing. Cano should have been aboard the *Concepción*. Cano said nothing, but motioned to someone behind him. Quesada strutted to the gunwale wearing a breastplate. A helmet covered his wavy hair.

"Captain Quesada. I didn't expect to see you on the *San Antonio*. Why aren't you on your own ship?"

"I am the captain of the *San Antonio*," said Quesada in a proud voice.

"Where is Captain Mezquita?"

"I, a captain lawfully appointed by King Carlos, have replaced him."

"Oh. And to whom does your loyalty lie?"

"King Carlos."

"And to the Captain General?"

"I said King Carlos. Be gone, Mate."

My reception at the *Concepción* was similar, with Cartagena claiming to be its captain.

Ginés then pulled hard against the flooding tide in the opposite direction, passed the *Trinidad*, to visit the *Victoria* and the *Santiago* on the ocean side of the *Trinidad*.

At the *Santiago*, Captain Serrano's lined face smiled when he saw me.

"And what brings you here this fine morning, Mate Albo?"

"The Captain General has asked me to visit each ship this morning after the events of last night."

"Events of last night? What do you mean? It was a peaceful night here." Serrano peered across the water at the other ships.

"The Captain General wants to know where your loyalty lies."

Serrano stroked his short beard. "Why, my loyalty is to him, Mate. What has happened?"

"Quesada and Cartagena have taken over the *San Antonio* and *Concepción*. I must visit the *Victoria* now. God be with you

Captain."

"And with you and the Captain General."

At the *Victoria*, Mendoza was also dressed in armor. Mendoza professed his loyalty to King Carlos, but pointedly not Magellan. Standing behind Mendoza, I saw Michael and Philip. Michael shook his head, 'No.' I was sure my friends were loyal to Magellan, but helpless to do anything.

I met Magellan in his cabin upon my return to the *Trinidad*. *Alguacil major* Espinosa, Master Gunner Andrew, and Duarte were with him.

Magellan asked, "What is your report, Mate?"

I confirmed that three ships had mutinied.

Magellan nodded stoically, as he might if I told him the seas were three feet higher. Then he said almost reluctantly, "Bishop Fonseca's men have finally made their move." He looked at Duarte. "I'm disappointed that cousin Mezquita was not more careful after yesterday's warning."

Duarte nodded in agreement. "You told him to be vigilant. Your cousin is a good man, but he trusts people a little too readily."

"Perhaps," Magellan sighed, "But he is family." His voice became authoritative, "*Alguacil major*, I'd like you and Duarte to choose some men whose loyalty we can depend upon. We will need at least fifteen, preferably twenty. Break out the arms and equip each man. Make sure they're well fed, and then keep them hidden in the cabins. Keep the forecastle and my cabin empty in case we need to entertain visitors. Mate Albo, go back to Captain Serrano. Tell him to raise his anchor and then let the flooding tide float his ship until it's abreast of the *Trinidad* and there drop anchor. He should mount his cannon. Our two ships will block the exit for the *Concepción* and the *San Antonio*. Mendoza in the *Victoria* will still be able to leave, but I do not think he has the spine to sail away on his own. Once Captain Serrano is in place, we will wait for the mutineers to make their move. They have the weight of cannon and number of men on their side, but we have the superior position and block them from the

Atlantic." Magellan turned and ordered, "Master Gunner Andrew, hoist the cannon out of the hold. Ready them for battle. Load them with round shot."

"It will be done, Captain General," confirmed the blond Master Gunner. His fair face was all business as he left to ready his cannon for the upcoming battle.

Magellan's quick response eased my mind in throwing in my lot with him and confirmed the stories of his quick wits in battle. Hearing his orders, I didn't doubt our certainty of victory, although I did wonder at the cost. I hoped it wouldn't be too great.

Duarte and the *Alguacil major* followed Andrew, which left me alone with Magellan. "Captain General."

"Yes, Mate."

"I can't say anything about the other two ships, but I'm quite certain the loyalty of my countrymen on the *Victoria* lies with you."

"Thank you. Am I correct in thinking that there are comparatively few Castilians on the *Victoria*?"

I hesitated while I counted in my head. "Less than half the crew is Castilian. All the more senior crewmembers hail from elsewhere."

"Thank you. Now go to Serrano."

I returned from the *Santiago* to the sight of cannons being manhandled into positions along the gunwales and the main deck cabins in the sterncastle. *Was a fight unavoidable? Maybe.* However, Fonseca's men still had not made their move.

Father Pedro joined me on the quarterdeck and said, "So the Spanish captains have mutinied. It looks like there will be a battle."

"I hope not, Father. A battle means men injured or even killed. It means ships damaged. Our little fleet can ill afford either."

"I will pray that doesn't happen."

"It's our fate in life to have death surround us, but I'm tired of it."

"Death may be God's will. Are you ready to fight, Mate?"

"I'm not a fighter, Father. This isn't my fight."

"Not your fight? Your countrymen are aboard Mendoza's ship. You must fight after all the Captain General has done for you," said Father Pedro. His deep-set eyes bore into me.

"By the blood of Christ, I am the Captain General's man, but I hope a battle can be avoided."

"I wish you wouldn't take Jesus's name in vain."

"You want me to kill someone, but you take offense at my swearing?" I replied.

"Those are two different things. Do you wish to confess before the fight?"

I couldn't avoid a slight smile. "Thank you, but no." *You would be surprised, Father, were I to give you a true confession. About how I swore to Piri Reis that I would become a Moslem if he'd free me from the bench of an Ottoman galley. I would have promised anything including my soul to get off the death ship. My life as a slave chained to an oar was certain to be brief and unpleasant: misery at the oar and then death. Also, I could tell you how I broke my oath to Piri Reis after two years as his apprentice and escaped to Rhodes. I've found that a man has to meet life, and God, with some flexibility. I'm as flexible as the wind, while it seems the Spanish are as inflexible as a rock. We Greeks have found flexibility—some may call it subterfuge and trickery—to be the key to victory.*

"So will you fight?" asked Father Pedro.

"If I have to. But there may be a better way."

The sun was overhead and the morning mist gone when a longboat left the *San Antonio*. Its crew rowed hard against the incoming tide as it headed for the *Trinidad*. As it grew near, I saw the birdlike face of Coca in the boat's stern.

We had here a deadly game, much like a game of chess. Each side had advanced a pawn so far. What piece were the mutineers advancing now?

I announced, "Señor Coca approaches from the *San Antonio*."

Magellan hurried to the gunwale and peered at the

longboat, and said, "Señor Coca is obviously coming to parley. I will be in my cabin; bring him to me there."

I waited with Duarte on the main deck for Coca.

"What brings you here on this fine fall day, Señor?" said Duarte with a sarcastic smile as Coca's longboat drew alongside.

"I bear a message for the Captain General."

"And who is it from and what may it be?"

"It is from Captains Quesada, Cartagena, and Mendoza, captains as appointed by the King. The message is for the Captain General's eyes only."

"Captain Cartagena?" Duarte laughed. "I don't think so. But come aboard and I'll take you to the Captain General."

Coca climbed aboard. He cast furtive mouse-like glances left and right as he walked behind Duarte. I followed.

Coca hesitated before entering Magellan's cabin. He first placed his hands on the doorjambs and looked inside to the left and right. *I wanted to kick his ass through the door.* Coca took a step in. I followed and closed the door. Magellan sat at his table, looking at some papers. He motioned Coca to sit in a chair across from him. Coca made the distance in four quick steps and sat perched on the edge of the chair. Magellan looked up and asked Coca in a pleasant voice, "And what brings you here?"

Coca worked his mouth. He tried to speak, but nothing came out. He finally swallowed and blurted, "I have a message from Captains Quesada, Cartagena, and Mendoza."

"A message?" said the smiling Captain General. "Why, please give it here."

Magellan strong fingers took the sheet from Coca's trembling hands.

"Now let me see. Ah, they say 'I have mistreated the officers and crew and have caused undo hardships.' Hardships! Of course, there are hardships. We are sailing in unknown seas and visiting unknown lands."

Coca took his quivering hands off the table and hid them in his lap.

"Then they say 'we have endured many storms and now the prospect of a winter on half rations.' Did they expect a royal picnic? These accusations are baseless. In any event, they should have been brought to me and discussed openly. Your friends should not have mutinied."

"The captains have not mutinied. They just want their voices heard, Captain General."

"Well, I think most would call it mutiny. Let me read on. They say here if I 'promise to have councils on all major decisions of the Armada they will acknowledge my leadership and kiss my feet and hands.' It seems to me, Señor Coca, that if they are so flexible, we should be able to come to a meeting of the minds. Please ask the captains to come here so we may iron out these differences. Please assure them I will do what is right."

Coca stood, made a brief bow, and scurried back to his longboat.

Alguacil Espinosa, Duarte, and I watched as the longboat departed. *The mutineers were playing it safe, but maybe too safe. They had only advanced another pawn.* Their tentativeness did not surprise me, but I doubted it would be a successful strategy. On the other hand, I'd been surprised at Magellan's pleasant demeanor. What was he up to?

Magellan's voice came from behind me. "Señors, I doubt the captains will come here. Anyway, we have used enough of the honey. Soon it will be time for the flyswatter. Duarte, Mate Albo and I were saying earlier that the *Victoria* has the smallest number of Spanish of all the ships among our fleet," said Magellan in a soft voice. "We will use that, the tides, our superior position, and the timidity of our foes to our advantage. Now here is my plan. When the longboat returns, its crew will be very hungry. Albo, instruct the steward to have a good meal prepared for them with ample wine. He will detain them in the forecastle. I will, in turn, occupy Coca in my cabin. Now when I pull my ear, this is what I want you to do," said Magellan as he confided his plan.

The mutineers' longboat crisscrossed the bay between

their three ships all afternoon. I took that as a measure of their indecisiveness.

The steward, Ginés, and I were ready to greet Coca upon his return.

"Good afternoon, Señor Coca. I hope you bring good news."

"My news is for the Captain General."

"Certainly. Ginés, please take Señor Coca to the Captain General's cabin."

Once Coca disappeared onto the quarterdeck, I turned to the longboat's crew, "You look tired, men."

"That's true, Mate, we've been rowing Señor Coca between ships all day. And they've forgotten to give us our noon day meal," replied a *marinero*.

"Why, then, you must be hungry. The sun is within an hour of setting. Come aboard, a good meal and wine awaits you in the forecastle."

Without hesitation, the longboat crew clambered aboard. They were soon eating and drinking in the warmth of the forecastle cabin. I'd instructed the steward to give them a double ration of wine. I left them there in time to see Duarte leaving Magellan's cabin. Espinosa, Duarte, and I met on the main deck.

Duarte spoke, "It is as the Captain General thought. Cartagena and the others want my brother to meet them on the *San Antonio*. Of course, he won't go, but Coca doesn't know that. The Captain General gave the sign. We're to put the plan in motion."

"So it shall be," replied the *Alguacil major*. "I'll get my men."

Espinosa, his man-at-arms, Ginés, and I rowed to the *Victoria* with the fading rays of the setting sun at our back. Darkness came swiftly once the sun fell behind the hills to the west, while the ebbing tide sped us on our way.

Behind us in the faint light, I could barely see Duarte's trusted men boarding the shallop. No light betrayed the shining armor the men wore and the swords they carried. I doubted force would be necessary on the *Victoria*, but it would be foolish to go unarmed. In the black night, the shallop silently floated on the ebbing tide behind us towards our objective.

The light of the Victoria's stern light pierced the darkness. Minutes later the ship itself materialized in the gloom ahead of us. An eerie silence engulfed the ship. Not even a gull squawked. A man peered over the gunwale when we came alongside.

"I have a message for Captain Mendoza from the Captain General," announced the *Alguacil major*.

A metallic clink preceded Mendoza's appearance at the ship's railing in a full suit of armor.

"You! Hand up the message to me."

"The Captain General instructed me to personally deliver it."

"Hand it up, and you will have personally delivered it."

"But the Captain General wishes me to hear your response. I don't think either of us wants the whole ship's crew to hear us." Espinosa stood up and held his arms out to each side. "As you see, I'm unarmored and unarmed. I'm no threat to you."

Mendoza glared at Espinoza, but then he relented, "Come aboard if you must, but your men must stay in the skiff."

Espinosa climbed aboard. The three of us followed him onto the *Victoria*. Mendoza was already entering his cabin with Espinosa when I reached the deck. No one stepped forward to stop us so we entered the cabin where Espinosa was handing the message to Mendoza.

Mendoza read it, looked down his nose at Espinosa, sneered, and started laughing. He said, 'You may have the message back. Tell Magellan it does not need a reply.'

"Ah, but there is a second part to the message." Espinosa reached forward with his left hand as if to take the message back, but instead he grabbed Mendoza's beard, pulling him forward. He drew a hidden dagger with his right hand and plunged it into Mendoza's throat. The *Alguacil*'s man then leapt forward with a dagger, thrusting it upward through Mendoza's neck into his skull. Mendoza fell to the floor like a sail hurriedly lowered to the deck before a storm. He twitched twice and died.

I felt no pity or remorse that the arrogant Spaniard had breathed his last. Now Cartagena and Quesada remained to be dealt with, and the sooner the better. Once they were dead or captured, we could resume our fight against the season and the cold, instead of a senseless battle against one another.

I stepped outside where the crew stood with anxious eyes. Michael and Philip were in front.

"Mendoza is dead. Are you for the Captain General?"

"We are!" came the ragged shout.

"Then raise Captain General Magellan's flag to the main top."

"What happened?" asked Michael.

I motioned him to follow me and led him into the captain's cabin. Mendoza's body lay there in a widening pool of blood.

I shrugged. "He was overconfident. I hope we can retake the other two ships as easily."

"They'll be extra cautious once they see three ships arrayed against them. We should expect a battle. I'll get the cannon on deck."

"Mother of God, I hate this," I said.

"I don't like it either, but what other option do we have?" said Michael.

"I have an idea. I'll talk to the Captain General."

It was early in the game and the mutineers had already lost a bishop.

Once he arrived in the shallop with the unneeded reinforcements, Duarte stayed on the *Victoria* as captain. *Alguacil major* Espinosa and I returned in the shallop to the *Trinidad* along with rest of the *Trinidad's* men. The night was ominously quiet.

Alguacil major Espinosa rapped at Magellan's cabin.

"Enter," commanded Magellan.

I followed Espinosa into the cabin. A white-faced and trembling Coca turned towards us.

"The *Victoria* is ours, Captain General. Mendoza has met his maker," announced Espinosa.

"Excellent work, *Alguacil*. Now take Coca and place him in irons in a cabin. Lock the men from the *San Antonio* in the forecastle. Then help ready the ship for battle."

"But Captain General, I'm but the messenger. I'm not a mutineer! Please don't confuse my actions with those of the mutineers," protested Coca.

"A properly convened court will determine your innocence or guilt. Meanwhile, just be happy you did not meet Mendoza's fate. Take him away, *Alguacil*."

Once the tide became slack, the *Victoria* moved abreast of the *Trinidad* and *Santiago*. Magellan's three ships now blocked the exit from the harbor.

Master Gunner Andrew had his cannon in place with shot and powder beside them. The decks were clear except for strategically placed barrels of water for fighting fires. Espinosa was arming and instructing his men: assigning some men with crossbows to the tops, others to work the grappling hooks, and the rest were to be in the boarding party. The preparations sent a shiver down my spine. I had to tell Magellan my idea. Otherwise, a battle would soon rage, the acrid smell of gunpowder would fill the air, and men now breathing and laughing would become broken corpses.

"What now, Captain General?" I asked.

"The odds are much better now with the *Victoria* under our control. I expect the mutineers to sail and attempt to break our line using the ebbing tide at first light. There will be a battle, but we will prevail."

"It would be good to avoid a battle."

"Of course," Magellan stared at me with his smoldering

dark eyes, "but how?"

"We can improve the odds even more, Captain General. I heard the *San Antonio* and *Concepción* pulling up anchor lines. They must be leaving only one anchor down so they can make a fast getaway in the morning." I looked at the men around us and whispered to Magellan, "I have a plan. Can we talk in private, Captain General?"

I exited Magellan's cabin minutes later and called the giant San Andrés and his pal young Antón to me. "Pull on some warm clothes. We're going to have a long night. We'll want something to eat and drink. Get a jug of water and some salt duck for us. I'll get the skiff ready."

I put rags around the oarlocks. I wanted them silent. Then I pulled my knife from my belt and tested its blade. It was razor sharp. I was anxious to get going; from the pull of the *Trinidad* against its anchor, I saw the flooding tide was losing its strength.

The crew was absorbed in readying the *Trinidad* for battle. No one noticed as we boarded the skiff. We passed the dark shape of the *Victoria* and headed for the southern shore of the bay.

"So where are we going, Mate?" asked San Andrés.

"Whisper. You know how sound carries over the water. We're just going for a little row. I thought you needed a little exercise."

"Very funny."

I smiled. "It's true and then you'll get the chance to have a little nap."

"Mother of God, enough of your jokes, Mate, tell me what is going on."

"Take us south over next to the shore and then parallel the shore to the west."

"But am I going to miss the battle?" said Antón with obvious concern.

"You are going to have a most important part in the battle."

"How so?"

"We're going to wait until the tide changes. Once the tide is going out strongly, that should be around dawn, we're going to pay a visit to the *San Antonio*."

"Go to the *San Antonio*? A visit? This is no time for social calls."

"No social call. We're going to cut its anchor line."

"Are you crazy? They'll see us. They'll blow us out of the water. You're going to get us killed."

"I'm not crazy, I'm Greek. The blood of Odysseus flows in my veins. Our skiff should be impossible to see right now in the dark against the shore by those on the *San Antonio*. Later, as we approach the *San Antonio*, there'll be a risk we'll be seen in the moonlight, but all their eyes will be in the direction of the *Trinidad*. They probably won't be keeping a keen outlook in the opposite direction. Our skiff should be invisible until we're almost to the *San Antonio*. We'll catch them with their pants down and their butts on the *jardines*."

"You're crazy," Antón shouted.

"Mother of God, quiet Antón," I whispered. "You'll get us killed by your shouting. We can do it. If they see us, we'll just row away. If we're successful, the *San Antonio* will float on the tide down to the Captain General. The *Trinidad*, *Santiago*, and *Victoria* should easily overwhelm the *San Antonio*."

"One blast of their cannon and we'll be chum for the local fish," said San Andrés, shaking his head.

"I don't intend to get anyone killed. You're safer with me than fighting aboard the *Trinidad*. Consider that I'm doing you a favor by taking you on this little excursion."

"But I want to be in the fight. I was part of the boarding party," said Antón. "It was my chance for glory."

"Or your chance to be dead. Your blood would flow just as easily as the great Hector's did when Achilles slew him."

"You've denied me my dream," pouted Antón.

"No, I've given us a chance for victory."

"How is that?"

"You've heard of Troy."

"Of course…the Trojan Horse."

"Yes, the Trojan Horse succeeded where all the direct assaults upon Troy failed at a huge loss of life, including Achilles."

"What is your point, Mate?"

"My point is the great captains avoid direct assaults, but strive to defeat the enemy through surprise and subterfuge, like Hannibal against the Romans. And that is how we are going to help the Captain General defeat the mutineers. Now shut your traps and row."

"But…"

"Quiet."

I'd already been more patient with the *grumetes* than most mates would have been. I didn't want to debate my strategy for hours with them any further and hear more of Antón's idiotic desire for glory. He might have gotten glory, but what was that worth? And if it brought him death, who other than his mother would remember him a year hence?

An hour later, I thought us far enough into the bay and I tied the skiff to the shore. There we chewed some of the salt duck. Soon after, the *grumetes* fell asleep. I piled a blanket over myself to ward off the bitter cold. I planned to stay awake, but the gentle lapping of water on the boat's side lulled me into dreams.

I awoke with a start. Clouds partially obscured the moon's dim disk. Good. That would make the job that much easier. The moon was halfway through its descent to the western horizon. *It should be time.* I dropped a bit of twine in the water, which bore it towards the bay's mouth. The tide was ebbing. I looked towards where the Armada was, but it had vanished. Only then did I realize a dense fog had settled on the bay. The shoreline beside us vanished into the mist some twenty foot away.

Would I be able to find the *San Antonio*? I should have taken a bearing on it when we anchored. I thought I knew its direction, but if I directly headed towards it, the tide would sweep us east of it.

I gently shook the *grumetes* awake and untied us from shore.

I had them row us on a heading well to the west of where I thought our target was. A few oar strokes and the fog enveloped us leaving no sign of the shore behind us. It was essential for us to head in a straight line so the brawny San Andrés had to ease up on his oar strokes to match Antón's oar. Otherwise, we'd spend the night circling the bay. Once I thought we'd gone far enough, I ordered the oars shipped. Then we waited. If my course was right and we'd rowed true to it, and if I'd judged the tide correctly, time and the tide would take us to the *San Antonio.*

We waited. *Shouldn't we have come upon the San Antonio by now? Have I missed it?*

A panic came over me. My heart raced. I inhaled and exhaled to calm myself.

We waited longer.

Then, voices over the water, but from which direction? I thought they were from our port side. I tapped the grumetes on their knees, and pointed towards the voices. They slipped the oars into the water. A few strokes and dim lights showed through the fog. They must be the *Farols*, lights, of one of the Armada's ships, but which ship? We grew closer. From its great bulk, I could discern that it had to be either the *San Antonio* or the *Trinidad.* A minute later and I was sure we'd found our target. I motioned for the men to stop rowing, and held my breath as we silently drew closer to the *San Antonio.* The moon stayed hidden behind a cloud.

Then, when we were only a few oars length from the *San Antonio*, the fog dissipated, unveiling the moon, and illuminating the skiff. It was if someone were focusing a giant lantern on us, leaving me feeling naked and defenseless under the moon's bright orb. My initial reaction was to order the *grumetes* to row away to the west, but I controlled that impulse. The *San Antonio's* bow watchman lounged against the railing, whistling a tune as he stared towards the stern, beyond which the *Trinidad's* faint outline was visible.

112

Otherwise, all was quiet on the *San Antonio*. Blessed Virgin, we hadn't been sighted.

My heart pounded as the skiff grew closer to the *San Antonio*. Two oar strokes were enough to guide us to the rough cords of the anchor line. I paused and listened. There was no alarm, just the watchman's tune coming from above us. Then I heard Cano's raspy voice rousting the crew in preparation for a morning escape.

I unsheathed my knife and sawed at the anchor hawser. The sound of the knife against the line seemed to broadcast our presence across the harbor. I stopped. There was no indication they had heard us. I resumed cutting. When I was down to the last few bundles of fibers, the line parted with a pop, and the *San Antonio* started to drift out on the tide. Still there was no call of alarm.

I motioned for San Andrés and Antón to row in the opposite direction. Once the skiff was at the edge of the fog, I ordered them to stop. Minutes that seemed like hours went by in silence. Then I heard Cano's panicked voice. Minutes later the thunder of a broadside reverberated from one side of the harbor to the other. I heard shouting. *What was happening?*

THIRTEEN – MUTINY

I later pieced together the mutiny's final events from friends aboard the *San Antonio* and the *Trinidad*. Initially in the fog, no one aboard the *San Antonio* realized it was free of its anchor and floating on the ebbing tide into the maws of the *Trinidad*.

After discovery of their predicament, pandemonium ruled on the *San Antonio*. A bewildered Quesada questioned why they were moving before the agreed upon time. Cano, the acting master, initially thought their anchor was dragging. He made ready to drop another anchor, only to realize it was too late and once the anchor line was paid out, they would be beside the *Trinidad*.

Cano then ordered the sails up, while Quesada ordered the cannon made ready. My fellow Greek Simon de Axio was one of the *San Antonio's* gunners. He told me that Jacques, the French master gunner, had no intention of firing upon Magellan, and loaded a weak charge of powder with no cannon ball in his guns.

There was no time to contact Cartagena aboard the *Concepción* for help. Cano realized that not only were they one ship against three, but they were missing all the men Magellan had detained from their longboat. Cano was no fool, and he convinced Quesada to unshackle Mezquita to beg his cousin Magellan for mercy. Cano later told me that Mezquita, to his credit, coldly eyed Cano and said, "It is a little late to avoid bloodshed. You weren't so eager to avoid a fight when it was Elloriaga's blood being spilled instead of your own last night. You're going to have to make your own peace with the Captain General."

Cano was still with Mezquita when he heard the cannons roar and felt the *San Antonio* shudder. The sound of timbers breaking came from an adjoining cabin where the Ginés uncle, the pilot de Mafra, was shackled to a chair. Expecting the worse, Cano and Mezquita threw open the door to the cabin to find Mafra and the chair lying on their side. The faint light of dawn showed through the ship's side where a cannon ball came through, blasting away the legs of Mafra's chair, while miraculously missing him. Mafra later attributed his luck to Archangel Michael looking over him, which I didn't dispute.

Meanwhile, on the *Trinidad*, Andrew busily supervised the reloading of the cannon. Crossbowmen were in the mast tops to pick off Quesada and the other rebel leaders on the *San Antonio*. Grapplers stood ready to fling their hooks and make their two ships fast. Finally, Magellan in resplendent armor headed up the boarding party armed with spear and sword.

Andrew said that Quesada, in gleaming armor with lance and shield, strutted about on the *San Antonio's* quarterdeck like a peacock shouting orders, although only his aide, Molino, paid him any attention.

As the ships drew near, Magellan ordered the men in the tops to hold their fire.

Grapples snaked over the few feet of water between the two ships. Strong arms pulled, and the two ships were quickly bound together. Magellan was the first to climb onto the *San Antonio*. He stood erect on the *San Antonio's* side, one hand holding a sword and the other supporting himself on a stay. Oh, to have seen that glorious sight. Magellan's eyes met those of the *San Antonio's* crew. When they showed no indication of offering a defense, Magellan shouted, "For whom do you stand?" The response from two dozen throats was immediate, "For King Carlos and Magellan," as they threw down their weapons.

Turning to Quesada, Magellan asked, "Will you surrender now, or should I order the men to fire?" while gesturing to the crossbowmen in the tops.

Quesada looked about him. Visibly crushed he said, "I will submit." His lance fell from his trembling hand to the deck.

They shackled all suspected mutineers in the *Trinidad's* hold. Duarte took a longboat to Cartagena aboard the *Concepción*. The Spaniard surrendered without resistance.

The mutiny was over. Magellan unmasked his queen and captured the mutineers' queen. Checkmate quickly ensued, all without a man injured other than Mendoza. Unknown to all but Magellan and my two *grumetes*, my stratagem played a vital role in quelling the mutiny.

A few days later, I pulled the blanket tighter against the morning chill as I conned the shallop towards shore. A few birds hung from the gray clouds overhead and circled looking for their morning meal. Master Gunner Andrew sat in the bow while a contingent of *marinero*s and *grumetes* manned the oars. Andrew turned and stared ahead as the shore grew closer. The raucous quarreling of seagulls pierced the quiet morning. In the dim light, I saw the birds swirled around two misshapen poles onshore. A few more strokes of the oars and the decapitated and quartered bodies of Quesada and Mendoza materialized spitted on the posts. Empty eye sockets gaped where gulls had plucked out the eyes. Vain Quesada's once wavy hair now hung limp from his head, matted with blood and sand. The gruesome sight sent a shiver through my spine.

"Blessed Virgin. Gets the point across, doesn't it?" said Andrew.

"That it does," replied Ginés.

"The court martial was swift, as was the sentencing and execution. Nothing like Salamón's wait before his garroting, eh, António," said a *marinero* from the *Victoria*.

António Baresa, Salamón's victim, stared straight ahead, ignoring the question, while he clung to his oar. According to Michael, everyday poor Baresa endured taunts since his and

116

Salamón's trial in the doldrums.

"Is it true they propped up Mendoza's body along with the other defendants at the trial?" asked Antón.

"It's true; I saw it with my own eyes. Captain Mezquita was the judge. It didn't take him long to condemn to death all forty of the mutineers, including the dead Mendoza. I guess Mezquita wanted to be sure about Mendoza," I said with a laugh.

"Yes, but then we wouldn't have enough men for all five ships," replied Andrew.

"I'm sure that's why the Captain General commuted all the sentences except those of Mendoza, Quesada, and the aide Molino. Then, Magellan commuted Molino's sentence on the condition that he execute his captain, Quesada. Molino didn't think twice when given that choice." I shook my head in disgust. "I guess Molino's loyalty went only so far."

"And so they ended up food for the gulls on this God-forsaken beach," said Andrew. He shook his blond head.

"I think the Captain General has made his point. He was more lenient than many captains I've sailed with; the others should be happy they still have their heads."

"The mutineers certainly made our lives easier!" chuckled Antón with a silly grin on his face. "It warms my heart to see Cano, Cartagena, Molino, and the others scrubbing out the bilges of the careened *Santiago* and *San Antonio*. That's the filthy, dirty work I'd normally be doing."

"I wouldn't want to be in their shoes. They're no more than slaves," said Andrew.

"Why did he let Cartagena live? He was one of the ringleaders," asked Antón.

"Probably because he's Bishop Fonseca's son. Also, he was personally appointed by King Carlos."

On the beach, work parties were rummaging the careened *Santiago* and *San Antonio*. Once they were finished, the remaining three ships would follow. The huge difference between high and low tide at this latitude made the careening easy. We'd floated the ships up on a high tide, which left them high and dry for most of the day. Today my men were to replace damaged bottom planks and recaulk the seams. Once the bottoms were sound, we'd tar them with the Canary Island pitch.

A line of mutineers lugged food, trade goods, and other supplies from the holds of the ships to wooden sheds erected earlier along the shore. There was no need to shackle them. Escape into the countryside would mean death. Cano glared at me as he trudged by with a bolt of fabric. Once the holds were unloaded, they would place the bilge's stone ballast near the water's edge, so the waves and tide could cleanse it. The next task was to shovel out the rat feces, decayed food, and human excrement from sailors unwilling to use the *jardines* in foul weather, and scrub the holds clean and sprinkle them with vinegar.

The men's spirits plummeted over the coming days. The work was hard, the weather cold and dreary, and we all suffered on half rations. I realized our food supplies were limited, but our Mediterranean men needed more food, not less, as they toiled in the cold.

Our hunters had limited success. The ostrich birds were cautious and fleet of foot. Our gunners found it impossible to draw a bead on them. Our crossbow men found their bolts were not powerful enough to fell them, at least not before the injured bird disappeared over the nearest hill. They had a little more success with the long legged sheep and seals in the harbor. There was some shellfish, but not enough to feed more than a fraction of the men. Even the water was more limited than first thought. The river at the bay's west end proved to be illusionary. There was only a network of tidal flats. Men had to transport water from inland lakes.

A month after our arrival the *Santiago's* overhaul was complete and Magellan sent it out under Captain Serrano to find a better anchorage. A few days before the *Santiago* sailed, a past evil once again took its toll. Young António Baresa threw himself into the outgoing tide. A month later, his swollen body turned the stomachs of the foraging party that found it on a beach. He had finally achieved peace.

After a month there was still no sign of the *Santiago*, and with each passing day I thought it more likely they had met an ill fate. Finally, after eight weeks, two haggard and ragged men appeared after trekking eleven days over a desolate landscape. They told us Serrano had found an excellent anchorage teeming with fish but a two-day sail to the south. When leaving it, a storm had driven the *Santiago* against the shore and destroyed it. Miraculously, only one life was lost, but the remaining men required rescuing.

Like everything in San Julián, the rescue of Serrano's men took longer, five weeks, than anyone expected. Only the *San Antonio* had finished her overhaul when news of the *Santiago* arrived, so Duarte led a food-laden party over the bitterly cold and frozen pampas to the *Santiago's* starving survivors and then led them back to San Julián.

The nearly five months at San Julián were among the more unpleasant of my life. We lost three men to accidents, brave Elorriaga to his stab wound, and another to a native arrow plus Baresa and the two mutineer captains. Hunger constantly gnawed at my stomach. My body never felt warm. And, while the mutiny had failed, the mutineers were a constant reminder of how close the expedition had been to disaster and the divisions that still marked the crew.

Amazingly, the insolent Cartagena attempted to foment a second mutiny with only Father Sanchez. The crewmembers he approached were not as foolish as he, and his machinations were squashed.

FOURTEEN – LEAVING SAN JULIÁN

Finally the day came. The shrillness of metal grating against metal pierced the quiet Patagonian morning as we hoisted the anchors nearly five months after our arrival. I hadn't heard as sweet of sound in months. I was eager to leave behind the bone-chilling cold, the nagging hunger, and the death of San Julián.

Soon the grunts of the *marineros* and *grumetes* working the sweeps replaced that of the anchor capstan. The *Trinidad* led the parade of four ships out to sea. I watched with stony eyes as we drew near the small islet where Magellan marooned Cartagena and Father Sanchez in retribution for their second attempt at mutiny. They pleaded and begged us not to leave them. Even a few hardened *marineros* shed tears for the two men. Magellan shut himself in his cabin once the anchors were up.

Master Gunner Andrew joined me as the *Trinidad* drew abreast of Cartagena and Father Sanchez's small kingdom.

"It grieves me to see men left thus, exposed to the elements and the natives," said Andrew.

"They brought it upon themselves."

"I know, but a quick execution like Quesada's would have been more merciful."

"The Captain General was much more forgiving of Cartagena than any other captain I've served under."

"I can imagine. Cartagena would have tested the patience of Job himself," said Andrew.

"He's an idiot. Did he and Father Sanchez really think

their guards would join them in a second mutiny? He gave us enough trouble. They have plenty of wine, biscuit, and weapons. I won't miss them. Perhaps now this voyage will go better."

"Why wasn't Cartagena condemned to death at the second court martial, like Quesada was at the first?" asked Andrew.

"For the same reason he escaped execution at the first— because he's Bishop Fonseca's bastard son. I think Cartagena might even have escaped being marooned until Master Elorriaga's death last month."

Elorriaga's wound from Quesada's dagger seemed to heal at first, but then the flesh around it grew red, he grew feverish, and four months after the mutiny he died. He'd been a good shipmate, a fine sailor, and an honest man. Everyone mourned his painful death, a death brought on by the mutineers.

"I wonder whether the cold or the natives will get them first," said Andrew.

"The worst of the winter is over now, but they'll be easy pickings for the natives."

"I don't understand why the Captain General kidnapped the two young Patagonians. The natives had been friendly until then," said Andrew.

"I agree." There was no reason to trick the tall Patagonians into coming aboard the *Trinidad*. They were two more mouths to feed. How could the natives possibly help the Armada? Blessed Virgin, let the men go. Father Pedro told me the kidnapping went against King Carlos's admonishment to treat the natives fairly. One native was transferred on the *San Antonio* and one kept on the *Trinidad*.

Their capture had led to a fracas between the robust Patagonians and a small scouting party led by Carvalho. The Spanish crossbows and small cannon were no match for the giant natives armed only with their bows and stone-tipped arrows. The Patagonians were expert archers. They fired and disappeared before our men could bring their clumsy weapons to bear. Carvalho's men did not hit a single Patagonian and lost a man to a native arrow.

"I wonder if we'll see the natives again," said Andrew.

The natives had revealed themselves two months after our arrival. The Patagonians towered in height over most our crew with only Espinosa and San Andrés seeing eye-to-eye with them. They were good-natured and imaginative. With their faces painted red, a yellow streak under the eyes, white-shaped hearts on each cheek, and tall sheepskin hats, they had captivated many of the crew.

"There may be more of them at Santa Cruz, but I've had enough of this land and natives, be they interesting or not. I just want to get on with the search for the strait to the South Sea."

"So do I. Hans Bergen talks of icebergs in his home of Norway becoming a solid sheet of ice as you go further north. Do you expect to see them here?"

"We're at fifty degrees south latitude. If the southern hemisphere is like the northern hemisphere, then we're still far from where the ocean freezes. There was a council of the officers last night. Many of the officers, led by Pilot Major Gómez, argued to abandon this route and go east to the Moluccas via the Cape of Good Hope. We're already fifteen degrees south of that cape. The Captain General would have none of it. He agreed to take the traditional route via the Cape only if no pass is found by seventy-five degrees south."

"The sooner we find the strait the better. We can't exist forever on reduced rations," said Andrew.

"The coast has continually receded to the southwest. I think this continent will end soon and we'll find the strait," I explained.

FIFTEEN – OFF THE COAST OF PATAGONIA

Cartagena's marooning didn't change our luck. Fierce headwinds forced us to tack the entire short sail to Bahia Santa Cruz, the bay Serrano had discovered before losing his ship. There we refilled the water barrels with the clean, pure water from the icy river flowing into the bay. We spent the two months until spring salting and smoking fish and seal meat for the voyage ahead. Meat was now ample, although I had only my stash of quince preserves to remind me of the fresh fruits and vegetables of home.

My spirits rose as the days grew longer and I started to regain the weight lost at San Julián. Before sailing, Magellan pardoned the mutineers and reinstated all to their previous positions, including Cano as master of the *Concepción*. Serrano, the captain of the lost *Santiago,* became captain of the *Concepción* while Duarte retained command of the *Victoria.*

I stood on the forecastle deck, my feet braced against the roll of the ship in the following sea. The winds were from the north and our *naos* were making good time now after fighting strong headwinds for two days. My dead reckoning had us less than a hundred miles from Santa Cruz. The coast had ceased retreating to the southwest and for the past day we paralleled the coast going to the south-southwest. That was unlike Piri Reis's map, which showed the coast on almost an east/west axis. However, Piri Reis admitted his information came from the reports of a few Portuguese ships blown off course, who really did not know where they were.

"Mate, I think I see a large bay," shouted San Andrés from the masthead. I'd put the *grumete* San Andrés up there because of his excellent eyesight. The young lad was already a better sailor than many of my *marineros*. He looked like a dark-skinned Apollo with his hair flowing in the wind as he pointed a muscular arm at the bay.

I peered toward the coast. Perhaps there was a bay or inlet, but at this distance, I wasn't sure. San Andrés in the masthead fifty feet overhead had a much better view. I grabbed the rope ladder and soon perched beside the *grumete*.

"See, Mate, there. It looks like a great bay. It goes inland as far as I can see. Is it the Strait?"

My heart and spirits soared.

"It might be. We haven't seen anything as promising as this," I shouted over my shoulder as I hurried down the rope ladder to inform Magellan.

Soon there were hundred foot clay-sided cliffs close by on the starboard side. After we'd passed the cliffs, a large hill of white sand was visible in the distance. The southern side of the inlet was some ten to fifteen miles away.

Magellan's eyes glistened in his excitement. He stepped from side to side like an excited child. "This may be the strait we have prayed for. Pilot Carvalho, go ashore, and climb that high hill to the north. Tell me if there is an opening in the far shore."

The fleet lay to under the afternoon sun's rays while Carvalho trekked to the top of the white sand hill. The sun was disappearing behind the hills to the west when he returned to report, "He could see no opening on the west side of the bay."

Magellan listened to Carvalho in silence. Perhaps he'd begun to doubt Carvalho's competence because he said, "I'm still not convinced. This is the most promising prospect for the strait since the Rio de Solís."

"True, but the far end of this bay looks closed to me," said Carvalho.

"Perhaps, but I'm going to send Captains Serrano and Mezquita to explore the bay."

"How long will they have?"

"Five days."

I watched with satisfaction as the sails of the *Concepción* and *San Antonio* disappeared in the distance along the northern shore. I felt confident they would find something. Surely we were near the bottom of this great continent. My mariner's intuition whispered to me that if there were a strait to the Southern Sea, it would be here. The *Trinidad* and *Victoria* anchored in the shelter of a small bay. I expected five quiet days until the scout ships returned.

The wild Patagonian wind had other plans for us. It arose during the night watch as a breeze from the northeast, and then grew stronger until it became a full gale. The shore protected us from the full fury of the storm's wrath. Or so I thought. Then I noticed the shore was moving. By Satan's Blood, the *Trinidad* was dragging its anchor under nature's onslaught. I rousted the crew. The starboard watch hoisted the anchor, while the port watch struggled to raise the sails.

It took hour after relentless hour of tacking for the *Trinidad*, followed by the *Victoria*, to reach the safety of the open sea. Only then could the *marineros* and *grumetes*, exhausted by the endless adjustments of ropes and sails in the wind and rain, rest for a while. I was tired of these Patagonian storms, but I had no choice but to lash myself to the binnacle while I directed the battle for my ship, my men, and my life.

Once we were in the relative safety of the open sea, my thoughts went to the *Concepción* and *San Antonio*. I considered myself an optimistic man and Captain Serrano of the *Concepción* and Pilot Major Gómez of the *San Antonio* were two of the best sailors in the Armada, but how could they escape the northeaster beating them into the southern shore? I wouldn't have then given five *Maravedis* for their chances of survival. *By the Mother Mary, wouldn't it be ironic to have finally found the Strait only to lose half our fleet?*

The storm lasted until late morning the following day when we returned to the bay. We found better moorage in a bay a little further west along the northern shore. Then we waited.

The day went by slowly with no sign of the missing ships. The mainmast lookout spied smoke far to the west on the morning of the second day. Were survivors of the *Concepción* or *San Antonio* signaling us? I asked Magellan if I could investigate in the shallop, but he refused. Occasional smoke still showed on the third day. My concern grew. The scout ships weren't overdue, but were they broken somewhere on the far shore?

On the fourth day a cannon shot reverberated across the bay. From the west, the *San Antonio* and *Concepción* returned propelled by billowing sails. Thank you, Mother Mary. The Armada was still as one. Serrano and Gómez reported that the storm had swept them through a narrows at the far end of the bay, where they found another bay, then another narrows. Beyond the second narrows was a large body of water that they called the Broad Reach whose water was still salty and tidal despite being miles from the Atlantic Ocean. They thought it could be the Strait. *Could success finally have come to us after so much strife, toil, and suffering?* Magellan visibly wept when he heard their report and Father Pedro conducted a special Mass in celebration of the discovery.

The Straits of Magellan

Two days later, the entire Armada swayed at anchor at the north end of the Broad Reach and I was surer than ever that success was at hand. The water was deep. In many places, my lead couldn't find the bottom before my line was exhausted. The water was salty. Most important in my mind, the tides varied many feet each day. These strong tidal flows meant there was a connection between the Broad Reach with the ocean or oceans. Of course, the narrows we'd sailed through connected to the Atlantic Ocean, but I didn't think that a constricted passage could produce tidal flows of this magnitude. There must be another link. It might just be another way to the Atlantic, but my instinct said it was the long sought Strait from the Atlantic Ocean to the South Sea. We were twenty degrees latitude further south than Africa's Cape of Good Hope. If there was a strait around the Americas, this must be it.

This thought was a great relief. Finding the strait had always seemed the hardest part of the expedition. Now it should be a short sail over the South Sea to the Moluccas of Magellan's friend Serrão, and rich spices. It pained me, although I mentioned it to no one, that if this was the Strait, it meant that we'd spent the long, bitter winter but a few days north of it. If Magellan had spent a few weeks less exploring Rio de Solís, we'd have found the Strait months earlier. Maybe then, the mutiny would have never happened. Maybe then, we'd already have filled our holds full of cloves, mace, and nutmeg, and be headed back to Spain. When the mutiny loomed, Magellan had been quick to take action and make decisions. If only he'd been as quick to move on at the Rio de Solís.

I was anxious to explore the Strait in earnest, to see the fabled South Sea, and then sail to the Moluccas. The Strait's end might be but a half-day's sail away.

Magellan called a council to decide the fleet's next action. He was holding councils more often now that Fonseca's men were gone. Of course, the captains of the Armada were now two relatives of Magellan, Duarte, and Mezquita, and the experienced mariner Serrano. The pilots were mostly Portuguese. The masters and mates were a mixed group of Basque, Genoan, and Greek professional sailors. At council, Magellan gave a forceful speech ending when he swore that 'even though we may be forced to eat the leather chafing gear on the yards, we must go forward and discover what has been promised to the King Carlos…God will help us and bring us good fortune.'

All but Gómez were in favor of going forward. The season was the same as April in the northern hemisphere. The coming months were the best possible time to push forward. Gómez, on the other hand, argued that while he believed this was the pass, there would still be the South Sea and the Great Gulf of China to cross. He voiced his concern that 'should we be delayed by storms or calms our supplies would run out.' I couldn't understand this thinking. After provisioning with the fish and seals at Bahia Santa Cruz, there was plenty of food in the *Trinidad* and *San Antonio's* holds for all four ships. Did Gómez just want to return so he could head a second expedition to the Spice Islands? Perhaps then, he'd be remembered in history like Vasco da Gama was for finding the route to India, while Magellan would be forgotten like Bartolomeu Diaz, who first found the Cape of Good Hope. All except Gómez voted to go forward.

Gómez had raised one good point. Assuming this was the Strait, we didn't know how far it was to the Moluccas because we didn't know with certainty the circumference of the world. My fellow Greek Eratosthenes had calculated the Earth's circumference as 25,000 miles some seventeen hundred years ago. On the other hand, Columbus had calculated the circumference at 19,000 miles based upon the work of the great Arab astronomer Alfraganus. That meant with good wind the Moluccas might be a week's sail away if Columbus was right, or they could be a several month sail if Eratosthenes was right. What seas, islands, and land were between the Moluccas and us? We did not know. What was the wind system of the seas? We did not know. But we would find out.

We sailed southward the next day. Until this time, the way had been obvious, but now we encountered a maze of channels reminding me of the Minotaur's Labyrinth in Crete, and they were likely just as dangerous. The waters were confining. Should a sudden storm hit, there would be little room to maneuver, either to run before a storm, or to find sheltered water to anchor before our frail hulls were broken against the rocks that lined the water. Initially, the land surrounding the strait was flat barren grassland. That changed as we penetrated further westward where trees covered the mountainsides all the way to the shore. These were of medium height and sculptured by the wind into flat forms. The blue-green waters of the strait reflected the snowcapped mountains visible to both the north and south. Several places a river of ice swept down the mountains to end at the water. At times, the way ahead seemed blocked by mountains, but, once we drew close, an opening always appeared. The Mediterranean had nothing to rival what I saw. Nonetheless, the ever present danger of a storm marred the scenic grandeur of the strait.

In his meticulous way, Magellan thoroughly explored the waterways. He sent Mezquita and Gómez with the *San Antonio* to explore to the east. Magellan took the remaining three ships west. *This was a mistake.* The *San Antonio* didn't come to the rendezvous as planned three days later. Magellan sent the *Concepción* and *Victoria* to search for her. Duarte even took the *Victoria* all the way back through the Narrows to the Atlantic in his hunt. The *San Antonio* had vanished. There was no flotsam, no wreckage, and no signal fires. This was disastrous. The *San Antonio* carried almost half our provisions. Each day the food stores in the holds of the remaining ships dwindled a little more.

Magellan finally asked the fleet astrologer to cast a horoscope for the *San Antonio* and the men on her. I don't believe in horoscopes any more than I believe in oracles reading the entrails of sacrificed sheep or fowl, but our astrologer was no fool. Magellan was astute in many things, but other times he could be blind to the obvious. Gómez had been unhappy enough that Magellan's proposal for a westward expedition to the Moluccas won out over his own. Gómez became more resentful and even less communicative after Magellan effectively demoted him and replaced him with Carvalho once the Armada reached Brazil. Then Gómez's appointment to assist the inexperienced Mezquita must have galled him. The astrologer's horoscope was no surprise to me: "Mezquita is a prisoner in shackles and the *San Antonio* is in the Atlantic returning to Spain."

While we waited for the *Victoria* to return, the shallop

explored to the west. It sighted the South Sea but two days sail away. Our search of over a year was over. To a man, we joked and celebrated and we soon forgot our disappointment at the *San Antonio's* loss. We might be only weeks from the tropical paradise of Spice Islands. The fleet might be home by next summer's end or at least by next year's end. I looked forward to a nice bounty from Magellan. Moreover, I'd have my priceless *roteiro*. Or would Magellan carve out a kingdom in the Indies with a nice appointment in it for me? Or if we returned to Spain, what should I do? Would the *Casa* accept my credentials as pilot? Or should I return to Rhodes if it were still free? Then again, maybe I should see if the Turk Piri Reis would be interested in my *roteiro*. There were many unknowns, but the great unknown of passage around the New World landmass was no more.

There was a formal council on November twenty-first. The Captain General sent a written summons to each ship the night before and asked for recommendations in writing from each captain, pilot, master, and mate. It read:

> I, *Fernando Magellan, knight of the Order of Santiago and Captain General of this fleet that His Majesty sent to discover the spiceries…Know thou…that I understand that all of you consider it a grave matter that I am determined to go forward, for it appears to you that there is little time for completing the voyage on which we have embarked. As I am a man who never scorns the opinion and counsel of anyone, all my decisions are put into practice and communicated generally to everyone so that no one need feel affronted; and because of what happened in Bahia San Julián concerning the deaths of Luis Mendoza and Gaspar Quesada and the marooning of Juan Cartagena and the priest, Father Sanchez Reina, you need not be afraid, for all that happened was done in the service of His Majesty and for the security of his fleet; and*

if you do not give me your advice and counsel, you will be default of your obligation to the King-Emperor, and to the oath of loyalty you swore to me; therefore, I command you, in his name and mine, and I pray and charge that whatever you may feel with respect to our voyage, whether to go forward or to return, each of you will give me your opinion, with your reasons, in writing, letting nothing prevent you from being entirely truthful. When I have your opinions and reasons, I will give you mine, and my decision as to what we must do.

At the council, the officers voted unanimously to go forward. The excitement of sailing into the South Sea was palpable.

Five days later, we weighed anchors and set out with banners and pennants hoisted and artillery salutes. We bade goodbye to rainbows dancing off waterfalls cascading off high cliffs and the sun sparkling off snow-shrouded mountains. Then, as the Strait widened, the land became more rocky and stark. Once again, I felt the rise and fall of the ocean beneath my feet.

We never did see the natives whose campfires we first saw at the eastern entrance to the strait. While we negotiated the strait, smoke often rose around us, and we even found the cold remains of their fires, but of the natives, nothing.

Upon entering the South Sea, Magellan named me a full pilot, and Ginés de Mafra assumed my duties as mate.

SIXTEEN – THE PACIFIC OCEAN

We believed we were in Balboa's South Sea. Vasco Núñez de Balboa had crossed the treacherous Isthmus of Panama to find on its south side water stretching to the horizon, which he named the South Sea. Magellan renamed it the Pacific Ocean, because it was so placid when we first sailed on it. If he had waited a few months to name it, he might have called it the Endless Ocean, or the Sea of Misery.

We sailed up the west coast of South America until we caught trade winds blowing west just south of the equator. Then, we sailed, and sailed. Today the memory of the next three months is hazy. Thank the Blessed Virgin, we had good winds the entire way, because otherwise we would have all died of starvation and scurvy. It was now we missed the *San Antonio's* supplies the most as we sailed west into an empty sea.

The scurvy first started on the *Victoria*. Five sailors quickly succumbed there. Then it took hold of the *Trinidad*. Master Gunner Andrew, my blond giant friend from Bristol, England, was one of its first victims. He lay fitfully in his bed with his skin turning black. His teeth fell out one by one, while his gums grew and rotted in his mouth. He cried throughout the night and spoke endlessly of unknown things in English. Little Gutierrez, a cabin boy, and many others showed similar symptoms.

I'd never seen scurvy before, but the veterans of the Portuguese convoys to India knew it. They said it occurred whenever a ship was away from land for longer than a month. No one knew its cause. They said the only cure was to make landfall and to get the men ashore.

Once we came across a small island where we hoped to find succor, but it was uninhabited and surrounded by a jagged ship-eating reef. We sailed on. I stared at the receding island. I felt as if a lover had jilted me. A lover who had asked for a rendezvous, only to tell me our affair was over. I felt helpless. That was the feeling I felt most during our voyage across the Pacific Ocean. Our three ships sailed into an empty horizon. Blessed Virgin, when would the ocean end? The food left was maggot-infested hardtack and whatever rats a person could catch or buy. San Andrés was proficient with a slingshot and turned the ship's rats into gold in his pocket. The maggots were an acquired taste. The sensation of them squirming between my teeth and the little pop when I bit down took some getting used to. My health was miraculously good, although my face and waist were thinner. Many of my shipmates were not so lucky. I heard some of them, especially those suffering the worst from the scurvy, quietly sobbing wherever they'd found refuge from the unrelenting sun. Other men whispered in groups.

On February the thirteen, the year of our Lord 1520, we crossed the equator and Magellan called a conference of all captains and pilots. Captain Duarte of the *Victoria* and Captain Serrano of the *Concepción* arrived aboard the *Trinidad*. Ginés's uncle, who had transferred to be pilot of the *Concepción*, was too far gone with scurvy to attend.

I surveyed the officers in Magellan's cabin. They were in better health than most, but their faces were gaunt.

"How bad is the scurvy on the *Victoria*, Duarte?" asked Magellan. His deeply set brown eyes fixed intently on his brother-in-law.

"Bad, very bad, Captain General. I've lost six men so far: two *marinero*s, two *grumetes*, my blacksmith, and my master-at-arms. Pilot Gallego is gravely ill, and Coca is almost as bad. I've had rats specially roasted for the pilot and Coca, but Gallego is too ill to eat them and Coca refuses."

"Ha, I always thought Coca something of a weasel. I'm surprised he does not relish rat either raw or roasted!"

I thought the joke by Magellan was ill-timed. It got no reaction from the officers, even from Duarte, who could make the toughest *marinero* blush with his language.

Magellan grimaced and continued, "Duarte, it is sad to hear of your men. I also have several men gravely ill."

"My pilot, Mafra, has also caught the scurvy very bad," added Captain Serrano.

"We must find land," continued Magellan, "I've asked you here to discuss our course going forward. We are now on the equator, which is the same latitude as the Moluccas. I'd set a course for south of the Moluccas up to this point hoping to make landfall in the Indies, where we could buy food before making our way up to the Spice Islands. My friend Francisco Serrão wrote that food in the Moluccas was limited to fish and rice, but there was ample food to the south in Timor, Bali, and Java. I do not see how we could have missed those islands. This ocean is many times larger than I thought possible. My concern now is that the Portuguese come upon us in our weakened condition. Our crew of scarecrows would fall easy prey to a Portuguese ship of any size."

"We must avoid that at all costs," urged Serrano. "I'm concerned should we encounter hostile natives. Few of our men could offer much of a fight. We must reach a safe place for our men to regain their health in peace."

"I agree. I propose a course to the north of the equator. The Portuguese don't sail north of the Moluccas, so that is the safest route for us. Serrão has written of many undiscovered islands there. Perhaps there are even lands we can claim there for King Carlos. We'll have to risk the friendliness of the natives when we meet them. That is something we cannot avoid," replied Magellan.

"Should we strike even further north?" asked Duarte, "Reports just before we left Spain indicated Raphael Perestrello found the Chinese very friendly during a visit five years ago. Okinawa should also not be far away and we know those there to be fair and keen traders. Opening up trade routes with these people could be just as profitable as the spice trade."

"I dream of such things, but for now we must focus on gaining a safe harbor. In addition, our commission from King Carlos is to forge a route to the Moluccas. I propose we continue to sail to the northwest from here at the equator. Once we reach fifteen degrees north latitude, I suggest we change course to due west. We should then strike land some thousand miles north of the Moluccas, which should be a safe distance from the Portuguese."

I agreed with the other officers to Magellan's plan, although I wondered if his reason for heading so far north of the Moluccas was more to discover islands to claim for King Carlos and himself, rather than simply to find a safe place to recover our strength. However, it wouldn't matter if we didn't find land soon.

Our three ships continued across the trackless sea, with our crews becoming ever weaker and with some on our sister ships consigned to the briny depths on a regular basis.

March 6, Year of our Lord 1520
Early Morning Aboard the Trinidad

"I hope I screw one more wench before I die," blurted San Andrés.

"Leave it to you to think of women, when the rest of us are praying for our next meal. Why are you thinking of screwing now?" I asked with a smile.

"What else can a man do? When will we escape this God forsaken sea?"

It had been three months and ten days since leaving the strait with precious little food and water for the past month. Many men on our ship were sick with the scurvy, although so far only the kidnapped Patagonian native had succumbed to it.

Beside me, the Genoan Master Polcevera said, "It's a wonder everyone hasn't gone crazy and not just those with the scurvy. Each day has the same blue sky overhead, the same blue seas reaching from horizon to horizon, and the same wind filling the sails."

"We couldn't ask for better weather for sailing."

"Yes, but the sameness will kill us if we don't find land soon. Please, God, give us a rainstorm. Anything to change our fortunes. How much longer can we go without food and a few cups of yellow water each day? I wish I could have a few bites of that maggot-ridden hardtack again."

"Didn't the leather shrouds from the rigging help?"

"It filled the belly, but it couldn't match the muscle that was once under the leather."

Desperate for food, we'd taken the leather covers that prevented lines from chafing against one another and towed them behind the ship for several days to soften them before it was roasted, and so Magellan's vow in the Straits came true.

San Andrés began to complain again when a cannon's bark punctuated his ranting. A cloud of smoke drifted off the *Victoria's* starboard side. The *Victoria* was perhaps a mile ahead of us. It had fired a signal shot. What was she signaling?

"Can you see anything?" I shouted to the *grumete* on watch in the mainmast's round top.

"Nothing yet," was his quick reply.

The *Trinidad's* taller mainmast made her horizon a little further than that of the smaller ships, so our *grumete* should soon be able to sight whatever my friends on the *Victoria* could see.

Within minutes, a call came down from the round-top, "Land three points off the starboard bow."

A dark splotch on the horizon transformed into a mountaintop as we grew closer. This was no barren atoll.

Less than a half hour later and another call came down, "There's another peak two points off the port bow."

I stood beside Magellan on the poop deck. Seventy land-starved men lined the ship's rails watching their salvation inch over the horizon. Each turn of the half-hour glass brought the fleet another few miles closer to deliverance.

Soon even on the deck we saw the second peak to the south. It grew into an island. It appeared larger than the isle to the north so Magellan signaled a turn to port. As we neared the island's northern tip, we saw that lush dense vegetation covered its lowlands. Brown tipped hills and small mountains sprung up in its interior. We were eager to land, but hundred-foot or even higher cliffs barred us from salvation.

Every *marinero* and *grumete* who could summon the energy worked to unlace the bonnets from the larger sails for the first time since crossing the equator. The ships slowed as we searched for an anchorage. Next, the topsails were hauled down. The cliffs disappeared, but now a reef kept us from the food and water we expected to find ashore.

"Smell the land, Pilot, smell the land," said Ginés as he raised his nose to breathe in the damp breeze off the island.

I replied, "The smelling is fine, but I won't be happy until my two feet are rooted in its dirt."

"Is that smoke there in the highlands?"

A wisp of gray rose above the island in the afternoon sky.

I squinted in the direction of Ginés's arm.

"I can't tell, but I pray you are right."

Our small fleet continued down the island's west coast. A peninsula projected westward with a small village visible at its base. There was no apparent way through the reef to the habitation. We sailed on in search of a less dangerous anchorage. South of the peninsula we passed by a still larger village also guarded by reefs.

We rounded a small point and a village on a protected cove came into view. Inland from the village was the mountain first seen when the fleet approached from the east. It was early afternoon when Magellan ordered the fleet to reduce sail. Ginés cast his lead to test the water's depth. When he announced 'one hundred feet,' Magellan ordered the last sails struck and anchors dropped.

I sighed. Perhaps I would live to see the Mediterranean once again. One hundred days had passed since we raised anchors in the strait. Few men had escaped any signs of the scurvy and all were weak with hunger. We'd found land. I didn't care if it were part of the Spice Islands. It was enough that it looked like a fertile land with people, fresh food, and clean water.

SEVENTEEN – ISLAND OF THE LATEEN SAILS

Lateen-sailed outrigger canoes sped towards us from the village even before our ships began to swing at their anchors. Men rushed about our ship for the first time in weeks. Every man able to move was on deck to see the approaching islanders.

I watched from the poop deck with António Pigafetta. Pigafetta was a slightly built affable man impossible to dislike. Like me, he'd escaped the worse ravages of the scurvy, perhaps because his catholic taste in foods. Unlike me, he'd been born into wealth in a Lombard family in the north of Italy. He had been a member of a papal delegation to King Carlos's court. There he had met Magellan and became captivated by our Captain General and his quest.

Below us, Magellan stood at the center of the main deck where he shouted orders for meeting the islanders, "*Alguacil major* Espinosa, pick the ten fittest men and arm them well. We don't know these people." He gestured to the approaching lateen-rigged craft. "Let's hope they are friendly and honest people like those of Rio de Janeiro, but we must be prepared if they are kindred spirits of the cannibals that were Solís's fate. Stay back, *Alguacil*, when the natives arrive, but be ready for my orders."

Then Magellan commanded, "Get some of the trade goods up here from the hold for display. Let's have a nice assortment so we can find what these people covet most. I want to trade for as much fresh food as possible for the men stricken with the scurvy."

Turning to his slightly built Asian slave Enrique he said, "Stay close, I'll need your help in finding what food is available here and where else supplies might be found. We also want to find out what these people know of the Spice Islands: are they near or far?"

These preparations didn't involve me. I waited as the swift canoes approached.

"These boats are like dolphins in the way they leap in the water from wave to wave. Look at the way they change directions. In one moment the stern becomes the bow and the boat is at once moving in the opposite direction," said Pigafetta.

My eyes were transfixed on the approaching flotilla.

"They fly through the air, barely touching the water. I have never seen such boats or sailors."

As they drew closer, the different colors of the boats became clear: some were white, some white and black, and some were red. Their sails were made of fiber woven mats. The boats were fifteen to twenty feet long, and as wide as a man was. An outrigger on one side balanced the little boats. Three to six well-built brown-skinned men expertly piloted each of the small canoes converging on the fleet. The boats drew up next to our ships. Without fear, the islanders climbed aboard.

The first man over the *Trinidad's* side was a muscled giant. A small cap sat atop his head. Otherwise, he was dressed in the skin of his birth. Standing barefoot on the deck, he towered over Magellan. His broad smile proudly showed teeth colored black and red. He looked about the ship as if it were his own. Dark hair flowed to his waist. Oil anointing his body accentuated his muscles.

Another twenty men, a little smaller in size, but of similar looks and spirit, joined the first man on the main deck of the *Trinidad*. Other islanders climbed aboard the *Victoria* and *Concepción*.

Enrique addressed the first islander, indicating in sign language the willingness to exchange the trade goods for food. The chief nodded and shouted to his companions who had already spread about the ship. Three islanders were on the quarterdeck. One started up the ladder to the poop deck. I planted myself firmly at the top of the ladder barring the way. For a moment, my eyes met his dark eyes. I shook my head 'no' and the native decided to go elsewhere for easier pickings.

Like locusts, the brown-skinned men picked up anything not fixed to the deck and threw it into their boats. Knives, ladles, and ropes disappeared in moments. The chief's men attacked the small pile of trade goods, jostling Magellan and Enrique aside. Mirrors, knives, cloth, and beads vanished in a moment as the natives appropriated them.

"*Alguacil*! Clear these thieves from our ship!" Magellan's voice rose in anger.

Swords drawn, Espinosa and his men emerged from the cabins under the quarterdeck. Most of the islanders, concentrating on finding new spoils, were oblivious to the glint of steel in the sunlight. The chief barked a warning to his men. He looked offended as Espinosa's men approached, made an obscene gesture, and dove overboard. Naked men filled the air diving off the *Trinidad* into the water alongside their boats. They cast off with their loot and raised their sails for shore. The chief shouted and two boats joined his. They made for the shallop tethered to the *Trinidad's* stern. They cut the shallop's line and towed it back to their village.

It was over in a matter of minutes. I stared at the departing boats in a state of bewildered shock. Not only was there no prospect of food, but the thieves had stripped the deck bare and taken the shallop as a dessert.

Magellan and the other officers joined Pigafetta and me on the poop deck to get a better view of the retreating islanders.

Magellan said, "I'll have food and water from these people and I will have my shallop back. If necessary, these people will feel cold Spanish steel and the hot shot of our cannons. I'll have none of this thievery."

"Do you want me to organize a punitive party?" asked a stone-faced Espinosa.

"Yes, start choosing able men and have them prepare their weapons and armor. Be sure you leave enough men to defend our ship. Do not sally just yet. Let's first see if these people will reconsider their ill-made decisions and return to compensate us. I'll send the skiff to Duarte and Serrano to tell them to prepare what forces they can."

By now, the islanders' boats had returned to the village. There was commotion ashore. Ten canoes, all much larger than the smaller ones that first visited us, pulled away from the shore.

"*Alguacil*," shouted Magellan. "Load the cannon with powder." Turning to Ginés he ordered, "Raise the anchor and make ready to get underway. Signal the other ships to do the same."

Ginés ran off shouting orders and gathering his men as he made his way to the anchor capstan.

"Captain General, shall I load solid or grape shot?" asked Espinosa.

"Neither should be necessary, *Alguacil*. Just load them with powder for the first round. I am willing to wager just the sound and smoke will repel these heathens. Have some grape on hand if they are so foolish as to ignore our warning barrage. Ready now, quickly."

The war canoes continued their steady approach, while the clamor of anchor chains reverberated over the water.

"They are majestic," Pigafetta whispered as if in a trance. "The graceful lines. Their vibrant decoration. The perfect synchronization of the rowers. Their paddles are cutting the water at the same time and same angle with each stroke."

I smiled, "That's all true, but look. The chief stands with a spear in the foremost canoe. He isn't coming to kiss you. He's mad as hell and coming to kill you."

Ginés's men had the anchor up and mainsail, the bowsprit, and the lateen on the mizzenmast up by the time the chief's men drew close.

"Good work, men," shouted Magellan in encouragement. "Pilot, take the *Trinidad* parallel to the shore so we might give these canoes a broadside. Be careful not to mask the guns of the *Victoria* and *Concepción*."

Our ships gained momentum in the breeze as the native boats arrived. The chief slowed his fleet, as if deciding the best way to attack. The gaudily painted war canoes started to approach after the rowers had rested for a few minutes.

"Espinosa, be ready to fire on my command. Albo, be ready to lower the signal flag," Magellan watched the canoes near. "All right, *fire!*"

The *Trinidad*'s cannons roared.

The chief was urging his men forward when the thunder of the *Trinidad*'s cannon filled the air. I could imagine that the islanders had only heard such a loud roar before in the middle of a terrible hurricane. A minute later, our two other black ships also erupted in fire. The black smoke that belched from the ships created an acrid cloud that hung above the water.

The chief's men back-paddled. The evening breeze caught the sails of our ships, which accelerated us away from the war canoes. The islanders did not pursue, but turned their war canoes and paddled back to the village.

I watched with a cold rage as the villagers receded. I thought of Andrew lying in his bed, dying. The thieving islanders stood between us and the fresh food and water he desperately needed.

Once well offshore, Magellan ordered sails lowered and summoned the officers to the *Trinidad*.

The last time I'd seen those from the other ships was during the conference at the equator. All were now haggard and tired beyond their years. Others from our meeting on the equator were either dead or dying.

More than ever, Captain Serrano's face looked etched like a ship's rigging. He was the first to speak, "My men sorely need food. It's a pity these islanders are so belligerent, but the lives of my men depend upon getting them food fast."

"I think the only way we'll get food from them is to teach these heathens to fear our wrath. Then they will be more cooperative," said Duarte.

"I agree," said Magellan. "We will return to the village tomorrow at first light and we'll send ashore a well-armed party to demonstrate our martial superiority. Either we will get some cooperation from these people, or, if it is their will, we'll take what food we need. Plus I want my shallop."

"I concur. May I lead the party?" asked Duarte. He appeared eager for action after months of inactivity crossing the Pacific.

Magellan nodded. "You'll lead twenty men in the *Victoria's* longboat. Espinosa will be your second in command and lead another twenty in the *Concepción's* longboat. Captains Serrano and Duarte, once our fleet is off the village's beach tomorrow morning, I want you to each send your longboats to the *Trinidad* with ten men apiece. You should each send two arquebusers and two crossbowmen along with four men armed with sword and lance, and two *marineros* to guard the longboats. Draw your men first from the men-at-arms, gunners, and supernumeraries on your ships. Men from the *Trinidad* will fill out the company so you will have eight arquebusers, ten crossbowmen, eighteen swordsmen total. Fully armor everyone with cuirasses, cuisses, greaves, and helmets. Gather what food and water you can find, torch the village, and then return with my shallop. Are there any questions?"

"What if they resist?" asked Duarte.

"I do not want you to needlessly slaughter these heathens, but if they fight do not spare the use of force. A volley from the arquebuses should put these people to flight. Firm and overwhelming might should win the day and keep our casualties to a minimum. Are there other questions? Very well, I'll see you come the morning. Keep a close watch on the *Trinidad's* signals tonight. We will start sailing back to the village in the early hours of the new day. *Alguacil*, prepare the

Trinidad's men for this raid."

Espinosa turned to me. "I need everyone who can walk and swing a sword. You are one of our healthiest men. Will you come with me?"

"Certainly, *Alguacil*," I replied without hesitation. I would have preferred that it not come to this. I didn't want to fight or kill anyone, but there was no choice but to seize what we needed.

The *Alguacil* and I went to the supernumeraries' cabin. Only five of them could walk steadily: a Frenchman, two Portuguese, a Castilian, and the Italian, António Pigafetta. Together we went to the armory. There, my stomach tight with anticipation, I armed myself with an arquebus and then rummaged amongst the armor for a breastplate, helmet, and greaves.

On the way back to my cabin, I stopped at the hospital cabin. Master Gunner Andrew appeared near death. Occasionally he woke in a delirium. I felt helpless. I doubted any food I might find would help Andrew, but I had to try. Two Castilians were also far along with the scurvy. They begged me to bring back the entrails of any natives killed, in the belief that eating these would reverse their scurvy. I feigned deafness. My stomach, already tight, turned at the thought of their request. Instead of returning to my own cabin, I found a cooler and quieter place on the deck to rest. Nonetheless, I had trouble sleeping.

The next morning, with Pigafetta by my side, I waited to climb into the longboat while cradling an arquebus. The full moon reflected off our small squad's armor.

"God forgive me, but I'd give anything to come along wearing armor and shouldering an arquebus," blurted San Andrés.

"What?" I exclaimed. "Why is that?"

"The excitement of it. Don't you understand?" said the fuzzy-cheeked Antón, whose eyes danced in excitement.

"I do and I don't," I replied.

"There you go, straight and grim-faced, all in shining armor to battle with the heathens."

"You're a romantic, and only see knights in armor. I'm going to either kill or be killed over a damn shallop and some food."

"Where's your sense of adventure?"

"If I weren't adventurous, I wouldn't be standing here. But I have no wish to fight."

"One day, Pilot, I too will be sailing into battle."

The sun's rays exploded over the hills behind the village as the bows of our two longboats headed towards the shore. The smell and smoke of the arquebusers' matchlocks' smoldering wicks hung like a small cloud about us. In the half-light, I saw the village women and children fleeing into the hills. Numerous warriors stood on a hill just behind the village's palm thatched huts, where they shouted taunts and shook spears.

The boat shuddered as its bow ground into the beach. Vomit rose in my throat. I took a few deep breaths, which calmed my stomach. When I stood, the weight of my armor made me top-heavy. I steadied myself, threw an armored leg over the side, climbed out of the longboat, and lumbered to where Duarte and Espinosa were on the beach. Immediately, a hail of sling bullets peppered us.

"Form up, men. Let's show these heathens what Spanish arms can do," ordered Duarte.

Duarte and Espinosa aligned us and ordered our little armored phalanx to advance. I staggered as a stone battered my cuirass. The stone's impact left a small sting, but no other damage. The plunks of stone sling bullets hitting those around me grew louder.

"Enough of this, men. Arquebusers, give them some lead to eat!" shouted a red-faced Duarte.

I pushed my flash pan lid aside, took aim at a slinger, and pulled the trigger. The fuse met the gunpowder in the pan, and then, with a delay, the pan's fire set off the powder charge in the gun. The deafening roar of my gun joined that of the seven other gunners. The sound reached up into the hills and echoed back. I saw three brown warriors fall from the volley before smoke obscured my target.

"Forward. Arquebusers, reload," commanded Duarte.

I emerged from the cloud to find most of the enemy had fled. A few of the braver warriors remained. These rushed forward to fling spears, which we easily avoided. Espinosa and the other crossbowmen took aim at the remaining warriors. This went on for some minutes.

I finished reloading, but few targets remained. One tall warrior rushed forward to throw his spear. A moment after its release, a crossbow bolt entered his shoulder. The warrior looked aghast at the leather-fletched bolt sticking from his chest. He reached around his back. I saw the warrior's hand recoil; he must have felt the bolt's point, which had gone through his chest. The man must have had no idea what had happened to him. The warrior grasped the fletched end and pulled. The bolt came free. Great spouts of blood pumped out of his chest. He collapsed onto the sand.

I looked around and relaxed a little. The battle was over. Seven warriors lay dead or dying. The only damage to our force was aching shoulders from the recoil of the arquebuses. Our steel armor was invincible against the islanders' stone sling bullets and fishbone tipped spears. Looking back to the ships, I saw the *Trinidad's* skiff, commanded by Ginés, coming in with *marineros* and *grumetes* to assist in gathering provisions. The skiffs of the other two ships followed him.

"Arquebusers stand guard for any counter attack. The rest of you search the huts for food and load it in the longboats. Launch the *Trinidad's* shallop." The men hurried about following Duarte's orders.

The battle had gone well, but we were all eager to be away. We filled our boats with coconuts, tubers, and a slender yellow green fig-like fruit that was new to me. Later I found out this fruit was a banana. The *grumetes* caught a pig and several chickens. *Marineros* filled several casks with fresh water from the village stream. Once the food was aboard,

Duarte ordered the native huts and boats torched. We left a few huts and boats on fire, but we were more interested in getting the food back to the ships than destroying the village.

The sun had already grown high in a blue sky when we returned to the fleet. Smoke streamed overhead from the burning huts we'd left behind. As the heat of the day built, I sweltered in my armor. The two longboats, reclaimed shallop, and skiffs were low in the water with men, food, and water. I realized my hands were trembling as the shallop approached the *Trinidad*. The sight of the doomed warrior pulling out the crossbow bolt and dying reran in my mind like a bad dream, but I also realized the battle had been the most exciting time of my life.

Two days later, Father Pedro and I watched as the Island of Thieves, which was our new name for the Island of the Lateen Sails, faded to the east. The islanders followed us to hurl insults after we'd sailed west from the islands. Now, silhouetted against the green island were the multi-colored sails of the islander canoes as they returned to their village. I was happy to see the last of the thieving natives. I still thought of the fight ashore. It had only lasted a few troubling and exhilarating minutes, but there were few things I had experienced as fully. Escaping from the Sultan's harem, riding out the hurricane south of the Canaries, and cutting the *San Antonio's* anchor cable during the mutiny came to mind. I was lucky to have survived them all. For all my fear and excitement, it had been an unequal fight. The islanders fought with stones and bone blades. We fought with steel and gunpowder, which must have been a horrific surprise to the simple natives.

I'd been surprised when the natives ventured out to trade on the afternoon of the battle. I'd expected them to flee for the hills after our guns slaughtered their warriors. Instead, men and women brought fruit, tubers, and some fish to trade. The men were naked as before. The women covered their pubic area with a thin bark material. The women were well built, similar to the men. Their very long dark hair framed their well-formed breasts and rounded hips. Both sexes were shrewd traders who bargained at length over every piece of food.

The second day a flotilla of canoes surrounded us. The natives had discovered the magical properties of iron and wanted it in any shape or form. They brought more food to sell, but supplies appeared limited on this island. Enrique signed with the natives; they knew nothing of mace, cloves, or nutmeg, but they indicated more and larger islands lay to the west. We sailed the next day to the jeers of the natives.

What food we'd gotten was a godsend. I took some to Master Gunner Andrew, but he was too far gone in his illness to eat. The two Castilians were disappointed I'd brought back no human entrails. Their scurvy ridden mouths made it difficult to eat even the soft roasted tubers, but they managed to swallow a few spoonfuls.

I sat down to feast with Father Pedro. My tale of the battle saddened him.

He shook his head, "I wish I'd had time to tell them of God's Word."

"Would they have listened?"

The Father turned to me and fixed his sad dark eyes on me, "In time, Jesus Christ would have bade them to listen."

Jorge, Magellan's brown-skinned, barefoot cabin boy from India, padded to Father Pedro's side.

"Father, Father, you should come. Master Gunner Andrew is fading. He worsens with each passing minute. Please come." The black-eyed boy anxiously shifted his weight side to side.

Father Pedro and I rushed to the hospital cabin. There San Andrés was at Andrew's side; the dark giant gently mopped Andrew's brow. When San Andrés moved aside for Father Pedro, I finally saw my friend. His skin had a grayish cast. His mouth lolled open revealing toothless and rotting gums. His breath was ragged and exuded a foul odor. I closed my eyes and remembered the smiling jovial Andrew of six months ago. Damn the scurvy. Father Pedro began to administer the last rites and I opened my eyes. The rites once over, I sat and watched with San Andrés. Father Pedro grasped Andrew's hand.

We sat in silence beside my dying friend. There was nothing to say. There was nothing we could do. Gradually, Andrew's breath became more labored. Then he did not breathe for several seconds. He gasped, breathed in again, exhaled, and then relaxed when his noble spirit left his wretched body.

I stared at Andrew's still gaunt body and then closed my eyes. I pictured Andrew's blond hair, blue eyes, and sunburnt face. I remembered Andrew's curiosity about the mysteries of the ship's rigging and sails. The Englishman had been a true friend; I would have placed my life in his hands if need be. I opened my eyes. Only this foul-smelling, scurvy-wracked body remained of the man I knew as Master Gunner Andrew of Bristol. I would miss him.

I turned to the cabin boy, "Put Andrew's gear in my cabin. I'll give it to his wife."

I remembered the dinners in Seville with Andrew and his wife Ana Estrada. While I looked forward to seeing Ana's tawny, willowy beauty once again, I wasn't looking forward to telling her of Andrew's death.

"It's been six days now since we left the Island of Thieves and we've been here before, Pilot," Pigafetta noted with a disgusted look on his face. "There's a strong wind behind us, only blue water from horizon to horizon, and the last of our food and water will soon be gone. This all seems perversely normal."

Pigafetta and San Andrés were with me as I stood watch.

"I hear you. Let's hope the thieves weren't also liars. What if they sent us west into an empty ocean when land was actually to the south or north?" My stomach grew tight at the thought. "They might think sending us to our death is a proper return for the warriors we killed."

My remark brought San Andrés out of a daydream. "My God, would the natives do that to us? Do you really think that's true?"

"It might be. I'm not confident how much they knew about the islands and lands about them. They didn't appear to have true seagoing vessels. They couldn't have ventured more than a few days' sail from their island in their canoes. They simply couldn't have carried enough food and water. Their war canoes could have carried more, but they didn't look as seaworthy. So maybe their knowledge of the world about them comes from visiting ships like ours. What will they say about the land we came from? Maybe that it is seven days east of their island?"

"Are we doomed to sail this cursed ocean for days and weeks again?" asked Pigafetta.

I shook my head in disagreement. "I don't think so. The people at the Island of Thieves looked more like Enrique than us. Also, look at those birds off to starboard. They are never far from shore. The birds we saw in the open ocean are now gone. I think we'll find land within days, not weeks."

"God, I hope so," San Andrés peered intently at the birds on the starboard bow. "One bird looks like another to me. Will the natives be friendly at the next landfall?"

"I suppose it will all depend upon their past experiences with strangers. Unless they've had unfortunate experiences, I expect them to be wary, but friendly. I think the natives of the Island of Thieves were unusual because they'd had little contact with people outside their few islands. It seems they thought they were acting from the more powerful position before our guns corrected that misconception. They believed in their martial superiority despite having only weapons of stone and wood. That means they've had little, if any, experience with those from beyond their own islands."

"I overheard the Captain General say we will have to deal with many local rajahs, some powerful and some weak, some Moor, and some pagan," said Pigafetta.

"Then you know more about rajahs than me. Of Moors

and pagans, I know something since the Moslem Ottoman rules my homeland. I'm a little surprised that Islam has spread so far across the world, but a Moslem rajah shouldn't necessarily be a problem for us. Many of the great traders of the eastern Mediterranean are Moslems. They dominated the spice trade with Asia for centuries before da Gama found the water route around Africa."

"That sounds like blasphemy. I don't see how you can speak so kindly of the Moors. Are you saying Catholicism isn't the one true religion?" retorted Pigafetta.

"Of course not, but that doesn't mean I think I must kill all Jews and Moors. I consider tolerance a virtue, as I think Christ would. In Axios, my hometown in Greece, Christians, Jews, and Moslems lived in relative harmony together."

"I can't agree with you," said Pigafetta. "There is only one true God, a Catholic God. I pray we have many converts of the natives and they increase the Pope's flock."

"I, too, hope many are converted to Christianity, but while we are adding to the Pope's flock here, Hans, the German gunner on the *Victoria*, tells me the Pope is in danger of losing many of his flock in the German states to the black sheep, Luther…"

"Jews, Moors, and Luther. Your talk confuses me," interrupted Pigafetta.

"There's no need for confusion. I believe in Christ as much as you, but enough of this talk. Let's hope we find the Spice Islands and are soon sailing home with our hold filled with cloves and nutmeg."

EIGHTEEN – LANDFALL

I was putting away my astrolabe after the noonday sun shoot when the *grumete* lookout in the mainmast shouted that land was on the western horizon. A cheer went up from the crew, which had gathered for their meager noonday meal. From the forecastle I saw what I thought were mountain peaks. Mountain peaks! Magellan had spoken of the volcanic peaks of the Indies. Had we finally crossed the Pacific Ocean? The heights inched higher as the day went on. By afternoon, an island took form under the mountains. Magellan named it San Lazarus. Reefs and cliffs rimmed the island's shore and dashed my hopes for food and water. The need for sustenance was urgent. The forecastle was full of men nearing the time to pass over the Styx. Gutiérrez, a likeable quick-witted Castilian cabin boy we all would miss, took Charon's boat while the Armada turned south and searched the coast for villages or a place to land.

The sun was nearing the horizon when we reached the southern edge of San Lazarus. Since it was dangerous to sail at night in these unknown waters, we anchored by a small island there. Large islands were visible in the fading light to the south and west and there was a small island southwest of our anchorage.

We made for this island in the morning and, within two hours, we made landfall. En route, we sighted several canoes. Villages or even cities must be nearby. The canoes turned and sailed west when they saw us.

For once, reefs did not ring the island. A shallow bay on the island's northeast shore was the best anchorage I'd seen since the Straits five months earlier. The island was uninhabited, with a few coconuts trees swaying in the breeze and several dense stands of banana plants, but otherwise nothing else to eat. There were two streams of sweet water. I bathed in one to flush the salt and oil out my hair for the first time in nearly four months.

We erected tents ashore for the two dozen sickest men in the hopes that being on land would counteract their scurvy. The sickest, including Ginés's uncle the Pilot Mafra and Coca, could only drink coconut milk. Magellan ordered the slaughter of a pig from the Island of Thieves for those able to eat.

Ginés led a work party from the *Trinidad* ashore to clean and refill our water casks. He returned early, screaming he'd found gold. He presented Magellan some sand with yellowish flakes that glittered in the sun. Gold! We'd found the Strait, crossed the vast Pacific Ocean, and now we'd found gold. For the past two months, I'd second-guessed my joining the Armada. Now it was looking like I'd made a good decision after all.

The night was warm, but I slept well. The ordeal of the Pacific Ocean was finally over. I felt confident we could find food somewhere in these islands. The uncertainty of when, and even if, the fleet would ever find Asia was over.

The new day was balmy. Magellan, Duarte, and I watched as some of the crew swam in the crystal blue waters. Others caught colorful fish for their dinner.

"Most of the men are recovering quickly. A little food and change of scenery does wonders," observed Magellan.

"Yes, but there's little food here and that from the Island of Thieves will soon be gone," I replied.

"I know. My first priority is obtaining more of it. Only then can we think of finding the Moluccas."

"What about the gold that was found yesterday?" asked Duarte.

"It might be worth mining if we had some slaves," said Magellan.

"Or maybe we can trade for it from the natives," said Duarte.

"We'll know more once we meet the locals."

"But are we in Portuguese territory?" I asked. My question was actually a trick one. The Treaty of Tordesillas brokered by the Pope set a longitude meridian that divided the New World between Spain and Portugal. The treaty was somewhat vague as to how it applied here on the far side of the world. I was curious as to Magellan's approach to this potential problem for his ambitions.

"I don't know," Magellan's face broke into a crafty smile. "No one can be certain of the longitude here on the far side of the world. In any event, if we find heathen lands that are undiscovered by the Portuguese, I'll claim them for our King."

"Our alliances with the natives, trading posts, and forts will be more important than some arbitrary longitude," said Duarte.

"Duarte, stay for dinner. Please join us, Pilot. Enrique has caught a fine snapper for our meal."

I was pleased to get the invitation, although I'd like to hear more talk of getting to the Moluccas and less talk of trading with the natives here hundreds of miles from the Spice Islands.

The exercise, heat, and food had the men nodding off. A call from the topmast interrupted their siesta.

"Hello! There's a canoe approaching from the south."

I joined the general scramble across the deck to the gunwale where I saw a large boat approaching.

"Make way men, make way," said Magellan as he went to the main deck rail nearest the boat. "Stand back, men, Enrique and I will do all the talking. *Alguacil* be ready with your men, but keep any arms well hidden. I don't expect any trouble with these people."

The boat swiftly came up to the *Trinidad*, lowered its woven fiber sail, and glided to a stop feet from us. It held nine men whose grins displayed nine sets of white ivory-colored teeth. The men were similar in build and features to Enrique, and less so to the robust Island of Thieves warriors. Four wore loincloths made of a coarse fiber. The other five wore cotton loincloths and colored bandanas. The oldest man wore an embroidered loincloth. Tattooed geometric designs adorned his shoulders and upper arms.

Magellan signaled for the men to come aboard. The five wearing the cotton loincloths climbed onto the deck. The chief barked out some orders to the four remaining in the boat, and they departed. The remaining five, Magellan, and Enrique sat in the middle of the main deck. I stood close behind Magellan while the crew gathered around us. Some hung from the rigging while others sat on the edges of the quarterdeck and forecastle.

The natives signed that they were from a nearby island. Magellan ordered some of the trade goods brought out. Unlike at the Island of Thieves, these natives appeared familiar with iron and European goods. Nonetheless, the cloth, combs, mirrors, and knives piqued the interest of the natives. Enrique indicated the goods were to trade for fresh food. While Enrique and the chief signed to one another, the lookout yelled that the original boat had returned with a second boat. Once both boats were alongside, the chief aboard the *Trinidad* shouted orders. In the boats were fresh fish, a jug, large and small bananas, and two coconuts. All were brought aboard and given to Magellan, who, in turn, gave some of the trade goods to each of the natives. They smiled and signed to Enrique. Enrique announced that in four days they would be back with more and a greater variety of food. Once the boats left, Magellan tasted the liquid in the jug. He announced it was a clear, alcoholic drink. Magellan shared it with all the men, from officer to cabin boy. The Spanish wine was long gone. My swallow was like honey on the tongue.

Four days later a small fleet of canoes appeared. Accompanying the chief from the prior visit was a man with finer clothing than all the others. He sported tattoos on his arms, legs, and breast. Two heavy gold rings dangled from his ears and thick golden bands encompassed each arm. Gold jewelry adorned many of the others. There was no doubt that there was gold here. Of more immediate importance, the boats carried jugs of a fruit wine, oranges, coconuts, and chickens. The food was too late for a *grumete* on Michael's *Victoria* who had succumbed to scurvy the day before.

The following day we brought the sick back aboard and readied our ships to sail. We made for the large island to the west. Upon reaching it, our ships paralleled its shore heading south. An island appeared on the port side and formed a strait. As the westward island ended and the fleet came to a westerly course, a strong easterly gale with heavy rains battered the fleet. Fortunately, we found shelter in a bay on the lee of the western island. I was surprised the storm lasted three days. Had we caught the edge of a Pacific Ocean hurricane? Nonetheless, the storm was a summer picnic compared to those that savaged the fleet a year ago off the eastern coast of South America. The delay was fatal for some. Coca and Ginés's uncle died the day we set sail again.

A small island appeared to the southwest a few hours after we left our refuge from the storm. We came upon a beach with large boats pulled up on it. Huts were visible among the palm trees just inland of the boats. Magellan ordered the anchors dropped. The three circular waves from the anchors were still spreading out when natives ran to a canoe and launched it. The men aboard it were more cautious than the last we'd met. They stopped a safe distance off and hailed the *Trinidad*.

I was surprised when Enrique began conversing with them in a strange tongue.

"So you know their language, Enrique?" asked Magellan, who had been watching the exchange. "What are they saying?"

"Their language is my birth tongue, Master. They say their master is the Rajah Colambu."

"Ask them to come aboard and I will reward them with many gifts."

Enrique spoke with the Asians, who replied but stayed in their boats.

"They are afraid to come aboard, Master. They are going to return to tell their rajah of our arrival."

"Tell them to wait. We have some gifts for them and their rajah."

Magellan ordered a mirror and red cap placed on a wooden plank in the water. A gentle push floated it over to the natives' canoe. The men took the gifts and paddled back to their village.

Before long, there was activity ashore. Two ships cast off from the beach. These were small galleys and by far the largest native vessels we'd seen. The larger had twenty rowers per side and the smaller fifteen. Both had outriggers on each side and a mast with a furled sail. The aft of the larger one had a platform sheltered from the sun by a roof of mats. Once they grew near, I could see a beefy man, his dark hair flecked with gray, seated on the platform. Large gold loops dangled from his ears. Elaborate tattoos covered his broad chest and strong arms. The rajah barked an order and the rowers shipped their oars. His ship coasted to a stop a stone's throw away from the *Trinidad*.

The rajah's eyes scanned our ship and locked onto Enrique. He cleared his throat and spoke in Enrique's language. I grew more and more anxious as the two talked on for some minutes. I realized then how reliant we were upon Enrique's honesty and faithfulness to his master.

After a while, Enrique turned to Magellan.

"The chief says he is the Rajah Colambu. This small island is but a part of his realm. He comes here for hunting and fishing. His capitol is to the south on a much greater island. He asked what we wished to trade for. I said fresh food, and possibly spices. I said we have many goods to trade in exchange. He then asked if we are the Portuguese he'd heard of. I told him no. I said our King Carlos rules the

Spanish Kingdom, which is much more powerful than the Portuguese Kingdom."

Magellan whispered to Enrique to welcome the rajah aboard.

Enrique conveyed his master's invitation. Evidently, the rajah was unwilling to come, although he sent three warriors aboard. Magellan gave them a large basket containing cloth, five mirrors, and three combs. They returned to their ship and gave it to the rajah. He put it aside without looking. Then he gave his warriors a basket, which they delivered to Enrique.

The basket held fresh ginger and a small bar of gold. Magellan took the ginger, but returned the basket to the warriors with the gold. The rajah then departed back to his village.

After watching the ships depart, Father Pedro and I followed Magellan to his cabin.

"Captain General, why did you refuse the gold?" I asked in confusion.

"We don't want the rajah to learn how much we value gold or how much we value spices for that matter. Things considered of little worth here might be worth a fortune in Spain. We must play the canny trader with these people."

I smiled. Magellan must be part Greek. "I'll be most careful. What is your next step?"

"I will send Enrique ashore in the morning. I hope that he can gain the confidence of the rajah. Then we can get the food we need and information about the surrounding area."

"We're fortunate that Enrique can speak their language."

"Yes. You know what that means?"

Father Pedro gave Magellan a blank look. I knew. *Enrique was home.*

"It means that Enrique is the first man to circumnavigate the earth. I acquired Enrique as a young boy twelve years ago in Malacca, on the west coast of the Malaya Peninsula. The slavers must have bought or captured him from somewhere near here and now he has returned once again to them, moving to the west the entire way. Let us pray we will be able to say the same someday," said Magellan.

The next morning Ginés took Enrique ashore in the shallop to parley with the Rajah Colambu. From the *Trinidad*, I saw Enrique enter a large hut where he remained for over an hour. He then came out, appeared to talk to Ginés, and disappeared back into the hut.

Ginés returned and announced that the rajah would soon come to the *Trinidad* with Enrique in his *barangay*, the galley of the day before.

Within the hour, the rajah's *barangay* pulled aside the *Trinidad*. The Rajah Colambu, back straight, came aboard, followed by Enrique, and eight warriors bearing two fine blunt-headed dorado close to five feet long, and three large rice-filled porcelain jars. Magellan thanked the rajah for his gifts and gave him a finely made red hat and a red and yellow robe of fine Turkish cloth. He then gave each warrior a knife and mirror.

The other officers and I followed Magellan and Columbu into Magellan's cabin. There Magellan poured the rajah the last of his personal Porto wine. They toasted. Enrique refilled their cups. After several glasses, the rajah said something to Enrique.

"Master, the rajah would be pleased if you and he would become blood brothers by *casi casi*," said Enrique.

"Rajah, we are not familiar with *casi casi*," said Magellan.

"We must drink one another's blood. We make the blood with the cut of a sharp knife on the arm," interpreted Enrique.

Magellan did not hesitate. "Tell him I would be honored."

They drew sharp knives, drew them across their forearms, and entwined their arms. Each licked the other's blood from the open cut, shook hands, and had another toast of Porto.

Magellan unrolled a large chart onto his table and placed a compass beside it. Magellan traced with his finger the route of his fleet across the world. The rajah nodded knowingly. I doubted he understood anything of what Magellan was saying.

Magellan motioned for the rajah and his men to follow him. Arrayed on the main deck atop blankets was an assortment of trade goods, including cloths of many colors for his inspection. The rajah seemed pleased with them.

"Enrique, ask the rajah if he would like to see our cannon fired?" Magellan pointed at the two starboard cannon.

Enrique asked the rajah, who agreed. Magellan gave a sign to the gunners. A match to the guns produced a thunderous explosion and a cloud of smoke. The rajah didn't flinch although his warriors visibly recoiled in fear. They calmed after Enrique chattered to them in their language.

Next *Alguacil major* Espinosa stepped forward in a fine set of plate armor. San Andrés and two other *grumetes* assailed him with knives and swords. Of course, he was invulnerable to their attack. Magellan then escorted the rajah to the *Trinidad's* armory stocked with swords, bucklers, and armor.

"Tell the rajah a single armored warrior is worth a hundred native warriors. Tell him also that our ships hold two hundred such soldiers."

Enrique passed on Magellan's boasts to the rajah.

Enrique told Magellan the rajah's reply, "Then it is truly good that we are blood brothers. Let us talk of peace, not war."

Magellan nodded in agreement.

Enrique continued, "The rajah also invites some of your men to come ashore for entertainment and to see his favorite hunting island."

Magellan looked surprised. His eyes landed first on Pigafetta and then me. He commanded, "Señor Pigafetta and Pilot Albo. Please accompany the rajah back to his island. Enjoy his hospitality and keenly observe all about you."

Why us? I laughed inwardly. We were probably chosen because we're trustworthy, observant, but also, if the rajah was duplicitous, expendable. I believed I was an excellent pilot, but even after the losses to scurvy and the defection of the *San Antonio*, there were other good pilots aboard the armada. Thinking about it more, I realized that to Magellan virtually every man on the armada was expendable if we kept him from fulfilling his dreams, excepting his close family including Duarte and his son Ravelo.

I watched and listened as the *barangay* glided back to the village. The warriors' muscles bulged as they pulled their paddles in perfect unison. Memories I'd long suppressed surfaced. Memories of another galley, in another sea, in another time. It was the eastern Mediterranean. It was an Ottoman galley. I was one of many galley slaves. A slave because I was at the wrong place and the wrong time. That was then. Let me rejoice in today, I thought. I am a free man. I am free because I was in the right place at the right time when my father's friend, Piri Reis, chanced to see me. Now I am free. I am a pilot of the Armada of the Moluccas. I am an emissary of King Carlos to an Asian rajah. Let me enjoy this moment.

Raindrops dotted the calm water around the *barangay* as a brief shower cooled the afternoon's heat. The rain stopped as the *barangay* nudged into a dock. The warriors stood aside for the Rajah Colambu who stepped ashore and raised his hands to the sky. He turned and signed to Pigafetta and me to do the same. The rajah took Pigafetta by the hand and a muscular warrior gently took mine. They led us along a path paralleling the shore with six warriors leading and four behind. Lush tropical foliage framed the well-trodden trail.

We came upon a reed-edged inlet where a large, decorated *barangay* floated quietly. It was the most beautiful ship I'd ever seen. Ornately carved and colored wood formed its bow and sides. The designs mimicked the rajah's tattoos, only their colors were a vibrant red. I estimated the ship's length at over seventy-five feet, as long, or even longer, than the *Trinidad*. The rajah led us to an aft deck where he indicated Pigafetta and I should sit beside him on a reed mat.

A woven palm canopy sheltered us from the hot afternoon sun, while a soft breeze off the ocean cooled us. The warriors arrayed themselves around us, arms at the ready, which was a little disquieting. Nonetheless, I'd taken a liking to the rajah and my impression was that he was trustworthy. Half-naked with his strange tattoos, he was like no man I'd seen before, different from the woolen clad Iberian officers, the well-dressed Venetians, and turbaned Ottomans. He was a natural leader with his firm authoritative commands. His men appeared to respect but not fear him.

A girl appeared with a pottery jug of what I learned later was rice wine, followed by a servant with a plate of skewered pork basted with a savory sauce. The fragrant sauce's aroma filled the air. I relaxed despite the armed guards surrounding me. I motioned thanks to the rajah and smiled at Pigafetta. I knew he had a dilemma. It was Good Friday and meat was on the platter before him. Would Pigafetta offend his host by not eating the dish or his God by eating the pork?

The servant carefully poured the wine into three glasses. The rajah motioned us to wait. With his two hands, he raised his glass to the heavens. Then, taking the glass in his right hand, he thrust his left fist towards Pigafetta. My muscles tightened as I saw Pigafetta's eyes open wide and then involuntarily blink. Pigafetta did not flinch as the rajah's fist stopped short of his face. The mood eased as first Pigafetta and then I imitated the rajah's toast. The rice wine warmed my throat and stomach. The sip of liquid from the jug a week ago had whetted my appetite for alcohol. I took one deep drink and then another, and became a little light-headed as the wine took effect.

Our host gestured to the plate of pork skewers. I flashed a smile at him and looked pointedly at Pigafetta while retrieving one after dipping it in the sauce. My companion gave me a wan smile, realizing I knew his dilemma. He shrugged and reached forward and took a bite of the forbidden meat. He chewed it slowly, while gesturing to the rajah that it was good.

Later Pigafetta took out a pen and paper and started pointing to things about the dinner setting. The rajah would say his word for an object, which Pigafetta wrote down. The rajah appeared captivated by the pleasant Italian.

After a third drink, two manservants arrived, each with a large porcelain platter. The first had a large roasted haunch of pork. The second had heaps of rice. We tore off hunks of pork, this time Pigafetta didn't hesitate, and ate them with balls of rice. It was my best meal since the Canaries. My stomach was full and I was growing lethargic when the rajah rose and signaled us to follow. It was dusk. A few of the brightest stars were visible in the tropical sky. After a short walk, we arrived at a thatched roof house built on tall pillars. I was surprised at the agility of the rajah as he climbed a ladder and disappeared into a room above. I followed and entered a palm-thatched room. The floor had a plush rug. The rajah lounged against one of the many large pillows strewn about. Pigafetta and I had just relaxed against our own pillows when a fourth man, who resembled the rajah, joined us. He was the rajah's eldest son and crown prince of the realm. Lithe bare-breasted girls delivered a large baked dorado flavored by fresh ginger. A half hour later, three girls returned with a roasted fish swimming in a brown tangy sauce and another dish of rice, all with more rice wine. I grew sleepier.

The girls stayed. One olive-skinned girl nestled beside me and turned her face towards me beaming a radiant smile. She was beautiful with dark eyes and hair. Her sweet smell was more intoxicating than the wine. A warm feeling seemed to flow from her body into mine.

The rajah suddenly became more garrulous and his eyes grew a hot red. He rose and shakily departed down the ladder.

I stroked the soft flesh by my side. Her ruby lips were soft and pliant. Our kisses grew more passionate. We fumbled at one another's clothes. Then our bodies molded to each other's in a tight embrace. My hard manhood searched and found its goal. Our breathing rose together like the onset of a hurricane; it reached a crescendo, and then, like the calm after a storm, grew quiet.

I awoke in the morning to Pigafetta's gentle snoring across the room. The crown prince's muted breathing came from my right. The girls were gone. Or had they been the houris of a drunken dream?

The morning was beautiful with a bright sun, but my head throbbed as I returned to the *Trinidad* with Pigafetta.

Some days later, I admired Colambu's *barangay* as it danced about in the wind ahead of our ships. An expert sailor must be at its helm. A quartering wind from off the island of San Lazarus to the east propelled the fleet. The wind direction made it slow going for the Spanish *naos*, while it was child's play for the lateen-sailed *barangay*. Our destination was the city of Cebu, three days to the northwest of Colambu's Limasawa, where the rajah had assured Magellan he could purchase ample food.

The past days had been relaxing, yet some of the events troubled me.

Easter Sunday was two days after my dinner with Colambu. Magellan decided to have Mass ashore. The Rajah Colambu glowed like a schoolboy when told there would be an important religious ceremony.

The Captain General was intent on a grand display. We wore our best and most luxurious garments. The bows of the shallop and longboats grated on the beach sand precisely at high noon followed by the roar of the fleet's cannons. An effusive Magellan stepped ashore first, embraced the rajah, and anointed him with perfumed water. Our men formed into a three-abreast column fifteen men long. The sun glinted off our meticulously polished swords and armor, making the little formation look like a multi-faceted gem. San Andrés and his friend the *grumete* Antón carried Spain's and Magellan's flags at the van of the little troop. The ceremony mustered all the pomp and pageantry possible on the far side of the world from a proper church. At the end of the Mass, once again the roar of the fleet's guns reverberated about the island.

After communion, a drummer started a beat. A flute joined in. Four of Cano's Basque countrymen did the Basque sword dance, the Ezpata Dantza. The four linked themselves to one another by the hilt and point of their swords. The dance reminded me of those of my native Greece. The dancers ended with a flourish and a round of applause.

We followed the rajah to a large banquet area, where natives carved two roast pigs. I loaded a plate with tropical fruit, steamed rice, roast tubers, and crowned it with a huge chunk of moist pork. With the platter in one hand and a mug of rice wine in my other, I joined my countrymen Michael and Philip under the shade of a palm tree. Full bellies and several glasses of the local wine left Europeans and Asians alike snoozing during the balmy tropical afternoon.

What followed is what troubled me the most. I got up to seek out the girl I had slept with two nights before. There was no sign of her. I happened on Magellan talking softly with Duarte and his son Ravelo about the Rajah Colambu's enthusiastic observance of the Mass. Magellan took this to mean that the animist rajah and his people would be willing converts to the Catholic religion.

Magellan was mistaking the Colambu's captivation with the ceremony with something much deeper: true belief in God and the teaching of Jesus. It would take Father Pedro, or men like him, months and years to teach and explain this to these people. Unfortunately, our Captain General seemed to think it could happen overnight.

Few of the crew seemed to share Magellan's religious fervor. All claimed to be religious, but few were. Most didn't truly care about God unless they were facing death by storm or disease. What they wanted most of all was freely flowing liquor and willing women. A handful, of which I was one, were focused on the ultimate prize and wanted to get on to the Spice Islands. The people here were friendly, but there was no sign of spice here other than ginger. The rajah told many stories of gold, but I'd seen only modest amounts of gold jewelry. So I was relieved when Magellan announced the fleet would search a few weeks more in these islands for spice and gold, but unless we found it, we would sail south to Serrão's Spice Islands.

The Rajah Colambu volunteered to guide us to the largest city of the region, Cebu, after the rice harvest. It seemed likely that fresh food could be obtained anywhere throughout these islands. Nonetheless, we needed storable food for longer voyages. Little islands, like the rajah's Limasawa, could not adequately supply the fleet. After helping with the harvest, we set out for Cebu.

NINETEEN – CEBU

The second day, under full sail with a following wind, our ships out-sailed Colambu's *barangay*. We reduced sails to avoid leaving the rajah behind. On the third day, we sailed southwest through a channel with the island of Mactan on the left and the large island of Cebu on the right. Visible on the starboard side were a large number of huts built on stilts as the channel widened and Mactan fell away to the port. The huts became the city of Cebu. Nervous, excited conversation surrounded me as we drew close. This was by far the largest city I'd seen since Spain.

Magellan's agreement with the King gave him his choice of islands if more than six non-Christian islands were found not previously contacted by the Portuguese or Spanish. Mother of God, there were hundreds of islands around us. Cebu looked large, but not so large it would be difficult to conquer. It looked prosperous. Would Magellan carve out his empire here, or would he sail for the Spice Islands?

Magellan wanted a grand entrance to awe and impress the locals. Flags and pennants flew from the masts. On a signal from the *Trinidad*, the morning quiet was shattered as all three ships discharged their cannon.

I laughed at the natives' reaction. It wasn't what I think Magellan wanted. Screams of terror echoed over the water. The natives crowded the streets as they fled west into the safety of the hills.

The fleet dropped anchor offshore from one of the larger buildings. Magellan ordered Enrique and Ravelo ashore with a small lightly armed guard to find the local rajah. They returned to say that the local Rajah Humabon had proved difficult to deal with. The haughty ruler demanded a tariff of a tenth the value of all items traded, which Ravelo indignantly refused. Magellan was also alarmed that a turbaned man was with the rajah. He was evidently a Moslem trader whose Siamese junk was in the harbor. The Rajah Colambu heard their story and went ashore to tell the Rajah Humabon of his experiences with us.

Enrique and Ravelo went back ashore the next day. Evidently, Colambu made an impression. The Rajah Humabon announced he waived the tariff. He even offered to pay tribute to King Carlos. Ravelo replied that tribute was not necessary and that we desired only to trade. The rajah seemed pleased and proposed *casi casi* with Magellan. He also said it was a Cebu custom to give presents to one another.

A *barangay* filled with natives came out to the *Trinidad*. Enrique announced the rajah's son-in-law, the crown prince, and Humabon's heir apparent, Tupas, as he came aboard the *Trinidad* along with other chiefs. Tupas was a self-assured slender young man who wore a smile like a mask. His dark eyes flashed about, observing everything. The chiefs followed him aboard. Some looked bewildered, while others were as controlled as Tupas.

I followed them to the quarterdeck where Magellan waited before two velvet chairs. After Magellan and Tupas sat in them, the officers, chiefs, and I took seats on cushions around them. Magellan launched into a long sermon, carefully translated by Enrique. I had expected discussions of trade. Instead, Magellan's discourse ranged from the Greatness of God to how God created the heavens, Earth, and all who were on the Earth, and ended with Jesus Christ and his rise from the dead. This went on for an hour. I thought no one could doubt Magellan's passion given the earnestness in his voice and expression, but I wondered what Magellan's motivations were. The charter from King Carlos emphasized trading. Spreading the word of God was secondary; otherwise, there would have been more priests aboard the Armada originally than Father Pedro and the marooned Father Sanchez. Nonetheless, Tupas and the chiefs seemed intrigued and impressed by the power of Magellan's beliefs. They diplomatically asked that two men to be left behind when the fleet left to instruct them in this faith.

I was surprised when Magellan replied he could not spare any men. The fleet's holy man, Father Pedro, could, though, baptize them if they wished to become Christians. Magellan said he would return in the future with an even larger fleet with many priests.

Tupas and the chiefs talked among themselves. They announced that they would have to consult the Rajah Humabon before such an important decision as to become Christians.

Magellan thanked them for listening to the word of the One True God. He told them that they should not become Christians for fear of cannons, or the might of our fleet, or to please us in any way. They should become Christians because of their love of God.

What were Magellan's motivations? Was he thinking of founding a small princedom here? What should I think of his long sermon? I knew Magellan was religious. Most men were. Being religious was one thing, starting a crusade to promote Christianity was another. We had business to attend to.

I was relieved when finally the conversation turned to the secular. Magellan and Tupas swore to peace between Spain and Cebu. Magellan, with tears in his eyes, took the hands of the Rajah Colambu and the crown prince, and uttered a prayer for eternal peace between their two lands and Spain.

Tupas ordered the delivery of the Rajah Humabon's gifts. Hoisted aboard from the *barangay* were three large boxes of rice, one for each of the three ships. Three pigs, two dozen chickens, and a goat followed. In return, Magellan presented Tupas with a bolt of fine linen, a red hat, several glass vases, and a gilt glass cup. Tupas's chiefs received glass mirrors and knives. Shrewd Enrique had not noticed any glass in Cebu and then discovered the people coveted it.

Afterward Pigafetta, Enrique, and I returned with Tupas to present gifts to the Rajah Humabon. The sun was halfway to the horizon when Tupas's and my party arrived at Humabon's palace.

The grunts of a rooting pig and clucking of a flock of chickens were the only sounds as I stepped ashore. Otherwise, the streets were empty. We followed Tupas up a broad street towards what appeared to be the palace. Bordering the street were heathen statues of sitting creatures. These were the height of a man. Their legs were spread out, the soles of their large feet pointed out, and their arms open wide. They had grotesque faces, dominated by angry mouths with four large teeth. Each face had its own strange personality. All were painted fancifully in gaudy colors.

The palace, the largest building in Cebu with a thatched roof and walls of woven grass, was almost empty when we entered. Seated in its middle on a dais covered by palm fronds was a squat, corpulent man, the Rajah Humabon. His loincloth of cotton with silk stitching hid little. A loose turban embroidered in silk sat atop his head. Tattooed geometric patterns covered his body. He sat on a cushion with two large porcelain plates before him filled with eggs. Tupas explained they were turtle eggs. The rajah smacked his lips in delight as he ate the eggs and sipped some palm wine through a reed. Drinking through a reed had never occurred to me. His eyelids drooped. It was my impression he had been drinking for several hours. Minutes passed before he scratched his ample belly and asked something of Tupas, who whispered an answer. The rajah seemed satisfied with Tupas's news. Pigafetta presented the rajah with a robe of yellow and violet Sicilian silk, a very fine red cap, glassware, and two gilt glass cups, all on a silver platter. The rajah beamed and invited us to partake of the eggs and wine. At a clap of his hands, servants appeared with more wine and eggs. With Enrique as an interpreter, Pigafetta quizzed the rajah and Tupas. I listened until the wine began to have effect. It was dark when the rajah took his leave and suggested to Tupas that he entertain Pigafetta and me at his house.

Four finely featured girls were waiting at Tupas's house. Their jet-black hair cascaded down their bare backs to their waists. Small veils topped their heads and palm fiber skirts hung from their hips. They formed a musical quartet, with each playing different strange instruments. One struck a note to set the key and the four began playing. The music was foreign, but pleasant and relaxing. Of course, given how much wine I'd drunk, any music played by four half-naked girls would sound good. Pigafetta stood and announced we must leave when the four girls started dancing seductively before us. I reluctantly followed Pigafetta and Enrique back to the *Trinidad.*

The next day things finally got down to business. The Rajah Humabon granted the use of a building on Cebu's central square for a trading post. The locals eagerly traded gold for the harder metals of iron and bronze. We bought food with the small trade goods, combs, knives, and such. Magellan wanted to keep the value of gold low, and only the official trading post could trade for it. Any crewmember caught doing so would go under the lash.

I had my fun ashore, but I stayed focused on the remainder of our voyage. The ship's clerk and I inventoried the hold's contents. Our inventory was satisfactory compared to the books, although we had incentive to finish it quickly. A putrid smell filled all the below decks areas from the rot and accumulated filth of the past months in the hot and humid tropics. I was anxious for a cleansing swim when Pigafetta approached me.

"Pilot, did you hear Father Pedro baptized another hundred islanders after Mass this afternoon? That makes nearly a thousand." Pigafetta had an idiotic smile on this face.

"Wonderful." I pulled off my threadbare pants. I hadn't worn a shirt in the miasmal hold.

"Do I detect cynicism in your voice? You are such a skeptic," replied Pigafetta.

"It's my nature. I find it difficult to call the Rajah Humabon 'Charles' now. Or Tupas, 'Ferdinand', the Rajah Colambu, 'John', and, most of all, the Moslem trader, Ali, 'Christopher.' Do you really think they've converted, or even know what conversion means? I will wager Ali does understand but still prayed to Allah last night." I walked to the gunwale for my swim.

Pigafetta followed me like a duckling follows its mother. "These conversions are all that Magellan, Father Pedro, and I have prayed for. The rajah has even removed the idols from the streets and his palace."

I was anxious for my swim, but turned to Pigafetta while straddling the railing. "I'd like to believe these conversions are real. Maybe these people even believe they have converted, but I'd bet the trolls will be back up within a month of our leaving. Did you see the look on Humabon's chiefs' faces at their baptism? I don't think they were willing participants."

"But have you seen how the rajah talks for hours about the Lord with Magellan. Have you seen how Magellan's eyes shine then?"

"I've seen that and it worries me. We came here to resupply before sailing to the Moluccas. Our men are strong again. It's time to be off."

"But we can't leave this success," said Pigafetta.

"I don't see the same success. I think we are wearing out our welcome here. How do you reconcile the carnal lust of the nights and the mass baptisms of the day? The nights are like Rio. Discipline among the crew is getting worse each day. Duarte is missing again. We need to leave here."

"Yes, but the Captain General has replaced Duarte."

"But with his own son. Ravelo is a bright man, but he is fifteen to twenty years junior to men more accomplished than he is. I'm loyal to the Captain General, but I don't understand his decisions. Are they in the best interest of

King Carlos and the Armada?" I argued.

"But soon this entire land with be allied with Spain. Just today messengers were sent out to the neighboring rajahs demanding that they submit to the Rajah Humabon and King Carlos as overlords."

"That just sounds like more trouble to me." I turned and dove into the cleansing blue water. I swam to the *Victoria* and back to the *Trinidad*, all the while thinking.

I had second thoughts about helping Magellan establish his princedom here, if that was what he intended. Trade and religion when combined with the natural instincts of the crew resulted in a volatile mix. Magellan appeared to believe all was well here, but it wasn't. He obviously hadn't noticed the scowls of the Cebu men who clearly were not happy having their daughters and even wives screwed by the foreigners. It was best we be on our way, but Magellan showed no sense of urgency to be off while the sham conversions continued en masse. I sensed other of the armada's officers felt as I did, but like me were hesitant to face the strong-willed Magellan when all appeared to be going well.

A week later Pigafetta walked beside me as we entered Humabon's Palace for a meeting.

"God continues to smile on us, Pilot, despite your fears. Almost all the neighboring rajahs have submitted to the Rajah Humabon and King Carlos. Your fears have been unjustified," gloated Pigafetta.

I stopped and stared at him. "I heard that little magic word 'almost.'"

"Two rajahs on the island of Mactan have resisted. The Captain General has dealt with one already. A raiding party torched the offending rajah's village and carried away his livestock. We're meeting to discuss what to do about the other, one called Lapulapu."

"They should have been of no concern to us."

"God is on our side here. Remember the miraculous cure of Humabon's brother."

Humabon's brother, Lamdagan, had been deathly sick and unable to even talk for four days. Magellan told the Rajah that this was God's punishment since the people of Cebu had not destroyed all their idols as promised. Magellan said if the idols were destroyed and his brother was baptized, then God would save the Lamdagan.

Humabon agreed. Magellan destroyed the heathen statues in Lamdagan's house and Father Pedro baptized Lamdagan, his wives, and children. Finally, Magellan had Lamdagan bled and ordered food for him, including some of his quince preserves. The next day Lamdagan could talk and in five days, he walked. He began spending long hours with Father Pedro discussing the Father, Son, and the Holy Spirit. Lamdagan was, after Humabon and Tupas, the most important chief in Cebu. Lamdagan then personally oversaw the destruction of the remaining idols. The news of Lamdagan's miraculous cure spread about Cebu. Those few who were still unbaptized sought out Father Pedro's magic.

I rejoiced for Lamdagan's recovery for his own sake. Unfortunately, things like this just fed the Captain General's appetite to intervene in the politics among the rajahs. He was well along to establishing his control over the neighboring islands, but to what purpose? These people had no spices, and the longer we stayed here, the more likely it was that a spark would ignite the growing animosity of the local men.

Pigafetta and I had arrived at Humabon's so-called palace. As we entered, I whispered to Pigafetta, "God may be on our side, but I think we shouldn't rely upon him too much."

The council had been called to decide what to do about Lapulapu. Humabon and his chiefs were there as was Magellan. Oddly, few other Europeans were there. Magellan announced he had sent an ultimatum to Lapulapu: submit or his village faced destruction. The rajah's answer was defiant: 'He, the Rajah Lapulapu, will be waiting for Magellan.'

Humabon announced he would take a thousand warriors and Lapulapu would be no more, if only Magellan came along with a force of cannon and armored men to support him. *Fine. Do it, and then let's be done with Cebu and get on to the Spice Islands.* However, Magellan's reply alarmed me: "That this Lapulapu is nothing and he would personally rout him with his Spanish forces." Magellan announced to the Cebu chiefs, "Within two days he would take a force to destroy Lapulapu's stronghold. The Rajah Humabon's men would not be needed." I swore under my breath. This was what I had feared.

That night Magellan convened the officers of the Armada aboard the *Trinidad*. Magellan asked for our support in dealing with Lapulapu.

"We must punish this upstart rajah," argued Magellan. "His response was an affront to the Rajah Humabon and King Carlos. I should take a hundred men to his village. He must be dealt with firmly."

"A hundred men! We do not have the men to spare for this, Captain General. We barely have seven score men left. A hundred men would leave less than fifty on the ships," replied *Alguacil major* Espinosa.

I was surprised to hear the heretofore ever-loyal Espinosa argue so vehemently against Magellan's proposal.

"It will only be for a little while, *Alguacil*. The battle will be over and the men back within a day," said Magellan.

"We can't afford to lose any more men. The loss of even twenty men might imperil the success of our entire voyage," continued Espinosa. "Captain General, I have served you faithfully, but why are we interceding in the squabbles of these natives? It is time for us to set sail for the Spice Islands as King Carlos instructed us to. Only then can we sail for Spain. I know you have a wife and child there; my wife, son, and daughter also await me."

"But we must support the Christian Rajah Humabon. We have here the opportunity to establish a great Christian Asiatic kingdom."

"Perhaps," calmly interjected Serrano, "but I too believe we should be sailing on to the Spice Islands. They are the objective King Carlos contracted us to find. Our men are refreshed now. It's time to sail on. Involvement in the wars of petty native chiefs is against the spirit of King Carlos's orders to the Armada."

Many heads nodded in agreement with the respected Captain Serrano. I was pleased to find the other officers felt like I did.

"Please, Captain General, let us sail south. You've spoken many times of wanting to see your cousin Señor Serrão. Let's sail south so you can do so," added Pilot Carvalho with a quavering voice.

"You will not support me in this?" shouted Magellan looking from man to man. The vein in his forehead pulsed. Serrano and Espinosa met his eyes directly and shook their heads 'no.' Carvalho, and most the others, avoided Magellan's intense eyes.

Magellan looked stunned. Never before had Serrano and Espinosa voted against him. Even his brother-in-law, Duarte, was silent. Magellan quietly said, "We must punish the Rajah Lapulapu or all our work with the Rajah Humabon is wasted. Will you support me?"

We all remained silent.

"Then I will mount this operation with volunteers. I'll vanquish this rajah with only sixty men. I do not need your support."

"I beg you to abort this mission, Captain General, but if you won't, put someone else in charge. We can't risk losing you. Send Ravelo or Duarte to lead the attack," argued Serrano.

"That is unnecessary, Captain. There is little risk. The natives will flee before the hard steel of our men. I'll be back before evening tomorrow. You'll be embarrassed to hear how easy the expedition was. Once I return, we'll start planning our departure for the Spice Islands."

TWENTY – MACTAN

The stars shone bright in a moonless night as the shallop pulled away from the *Trinidad*. The dim outlines of the longboats of the *Victoria* and *Concepción* were close behind us. Across the water came the shouts of Humabon's men in many *barangays*, although I couldn't see them.

My breathing was shallow and perspiration dotted my face. In a few hours, for the second time in my life, I was going into battle. This time, I would be fighting side by side with Magellan himself. After a pull on the oar, I looked back to where Magellan stood at the shallop's stern.

I had first declined when Magellan asked for volunteers to punish Lapulapu. Once I'd dreamed of working by Magellan's side founding an Asiatic empire. More somber thoughts had replaced those dreams as Magellan became more and more erratic. I wanted only to leave Cebu and sail for the Moluccas.

I would have stayed aboard the *Trinidad*, while Magellan fought at Mactan, but then António Pigafetta came to me with his silvery tongue. "I've heard you refused to help your Captain General defeat the renegade rajah, Pilot Albo."

"Most of the fleet's officers refused, António. Are you going?"

"I volunteered without a moment's thought. I would do anything Magellan asked. I can't believe you aren't supporting him."

"It wasn't an easy decision," I replied.

"How could you refuse after all the Captain General has done for you?"

"I know. He had the faith in me to make me the mate of

the *Trinidad.* He made me a pilot. I've now worked by
Magellan's side for two years, but I am a sailor, not a warrior.
I signed on for a voyage to the Moluccas and back. I didn't
enlist to fight Asian rajahs."

"But the Captain General says it is essential to bring this
upstart under control." Pigafetta's face showed his anguish at
my failure to support his idol.

"I will defend myself, my ships, and my crewmates if I
must. I fought at the Islands of Thieves…and I enjoyed it.
However, I don't want to enjoy it. I have no stomach for
killing. I've seen too much death in my days. Go if you will,
Pigafetta, but please don't ask me to come. The other
professional mariners feel much the same as I do. The
Mactan battle is not ours and has nothing to do with King
Carlos's commission for the Armada."

Later, I changed my mind when I realized San Andrés
and his friend Antón had volunteered. I felt responsible for
the lads. Reluctantly, I joined Magellan's ragtag company.

Now, rowing towards Mactan in the dark of night, I was
second-guessing my decision. I trusted Magellan beside me in
a fight, but where were Duarte and *Alguacil* Espinosa, who
led the assault at the Island of Thieves? Where were the
other officers? Where were the *Alguacil major*'s men-at-arms?
Those men were the core of the attack force before. They
had stood before the spears and sling bullets with no thought
for their own safety. I looked at the faces about me. Many of
Magellan's volunteers were *grumetes* and some even cabin
boys.

At least there were some supernumeraries like Pigafetta
beside me. Most of these had some military training. Would
they be enough?

San Andrés and Antón worked the oar in front of me. I
sensed the tension and excitement in their voices as they
whispered to each other. We wore cuirasses covering our
chests and helmets, but no greaves or cuisses to protect our
arms and legs because of the heat. Another thirty men were
in the other two longboats, with Ravelo, Magellan's son,

skippering one boat and a *marinero* the other.

I saw Magellan staring ahead at the dim outline of the northwest point of Mactan.

"Are we there?" I asked.

"We are close. The infidel's village is at the center of a large bight beyond this point," said Magellan. "Don't worry, by late morning we will have defeated Lapulapu and be preparing to sail for the Spice Islands."

After our small flotilla rounded the point, outlined against the sky was the eastern side of the bay. The faint light of a few fires marked the rajah's village at the south side of the bight.

"Are we going to attack now?" I asked.

"No. There's at least an hour until the break of day. I will not hazard a night attack over unknown ground. There is always much confusion at night, which can produce panic and fear in those not inured to battle. No, we will wait for the dawn. Bilbao steel will win the battle for us. I'll take this time to give Lapulapu one last chance to submit."

Magellan ordered his little fleet to lie to and called Humabon's *barangay* alongside. Through Enrique, he asked 'Christopher,' the Moslem trader Ali, to approach Lapulapu one last time. Ali was to tell him that 'the King of Spain and Emperor of the Christians wished for the rajah and his people to be his friend. This could be if the rajah and his people agreed to obey him as their lord and to pay him tribute. If they didn't wish to be friends, then they would learn by experience how our lances pierce.'

I watched as Ali's skiff disappeared in the dark towards the shore. I questioned whether Ali would faithfully parley with Lalupalu. I doubted his conversion to Christianity and suspected he was still a Moor at heart. In any event, I thought his purse would hold more gold if Magellan were unsuccessful than otherwise. We waited in the dark for an hour. The sky was brightening with the approaching dawn when the skiff reappeared out of the gloom.

Ali gave Lapulapu's response that. 'His men are ready

with sharpened weapons. The Spaniards should come when they will.'

Magellan ordered our three boats forward as the sun's rays began to break over the eastern shore of the bay. The creaks of the oarlocks and sound of the oars hitting the water broke the silence of the dawn. No one felt like talking. Halfway to shore I heard a sudden crunch and I lurched forward into my oar. The shallop was fast aground still half a mile from the beach. The longboats managed to go a hundred feet closer before their keels gripped the bottom.

"Well, men, let's have at them. Let's show this puppet rajah how Spaniards fight," shouted Magellan as he jumped into the thigh high water.

Butterflies in my stomach, I followed him and started the slow wade to shore. Eleven men remained to guard the boats and man the shallop's falconet, a small cannon.

Pigafetta and I shuffled through the water after Magellan, Ravelo, and Enrique towards the village. The water was cool against my bare legs. San Andrés, Antón, and two supernumeraries followed behind. The rest of the men fanned out to each side.

"Father, it looks like the fight will be out of the range of our cannon. Shouldn't we wait for the high tide to get our boats closer?" asked Ravelo.

"We did not need the cannon at the Island of Thieves to rout the natives there. It should be the same here. A few volleys from our matchlocks and crossbows should put them to flight. Then we'll torch the huts and put an end to the arrogance of this rajah."

The trudge ashore continued. The water depth fell first to my knee and then to my calf. The twilight of dawn was gone when I finally stood on the sandy shore.

Warriors waited for us in fields just beyond the village. Several hundred warriors to my left armed with wooden shields, bows, and lances first caught my eye. Magellan ordered us forward. Once beyond the village huts, I saw another five hundred warriors straight ahead. Then a cheer arose to my right. My gut twisted when I saw another enemy cohort there. Could all these men be from Lapulapu's village? I didn't think so. Had the refugees from Bullaia, the village Magellan razed a few days earlier, joined Lapulapu? The warriors beat their lances against their shields and yelled taunts.

What had Magellan told the Rajah Colambu: that one of our men was worth a hundred native warriors? That was an exaggeration, but how many could we fight and hope to be victorious? Here we're outnumbered thirty-to-one. I looked at the golden beams of the morning sun and thought it might be the last dawn of my earthly life.

We advanced. When I saw the warriors' headdresses, Magellan's deep voice ordered the arquebusers and crossbowmen to open fire. The opening volley was deafening. One warrior fell to my gun. Arrows from native bows began to pelt us. Their aim was not good at this distance, but I was glad I was armored after one glanced off my breastplate. The firing of the arquebusers became more ragged as the inexperienced men struggled to reload and as guns jammed.

After fifteen minutes, a few more warriors had fallen to our bullets and bolts. I heard Magellan order us to hold fire and conserve our ammunition. I stopped, but sporadic firing continued. Most arquebusers were oblivious to the order; their ears must be ringing and deafened from their gunfire. Without thought, the men continued to reload and fire. The report of the guns stopped only as the men ran out of ammunition.

"Let's take them with cold steel, men," shouted Magellan as he trotted forward, lance in hand, towards the central group of warriors.

What was Magellan thinking? Forty men against fifteen hundred? Mother of God this was foolish. Yes, a few Spartans had held off the Persians at Thermopylae, but they were the most disciplined soldiers the world had ever seen and they were in an easily defendable narrow pass. Even then, in the end they had died. Gloriously, perhaps, but they had died. I was not eager to meet death just yet.

Nonetheless, I piled by gun with the others, drew my sword, and followed Magellan, Ravelo, Pigafetta, and Enrique. The other men advanced on each side. A hail of arrows and steel-tipped lances met us. I was eager to get to blows with the natives, but a ditch guarded by sharp, fire-hardened stakes appeared before us. It was useless to attempt to go further; we could not get over the ditch to wield our swords and lances against the Asians. But the ditch was also our savior. If it were not there, Lapulapu's men would have surrounded us like a tsunami washes over a pebble.

Magellan shouted, "Back to the village men. Stay together now!" Then he turned to Ravelo and ordered, "We have to get them out from behind their ditches, so we can fight them man to man. Fire some of the huts. Maybe that will draw them out."

Smoke started to rise from a dozen huts. Soon flames were reaching to the sky.

It had the affect Magellan desired. Fifteen hundred warriors pulled out the protective stakes and let loose a curdling cry. Then they charged. Like a flooding tide, they swept towards us. Instinctively we moved closer together, falling back towards the water. From the corner of my eye, I saw a man from the *Victoria* take a spear in the throat. Blood pulsed from the wound. He lost his footing and vanished under the wave of warriors. It was all I could do to deflect the spear thrusts of three natives before me with my sword. Perspiration poured down my face and fear gripped my stomach. I stayed by Magellan's side, as step-by-step we retreated to the water's edge.

Lapulapu's men aimed their arrows and lances at our bare, unarmored legs. Magellan took an arrow in his leg. Ignoring the wound, he shouted for us to fall back to the shallop's cannon, whose protection he had scorned minutes earlier.

We edged backwards into the water. Five men on the

right threw down their weapons, turned, and ran back to the boats. Another three men joined the flight and then two more. I stood my ground with Magellan's small party five hundred feet offshore while the rest of our amateur soldiers fled to the boats. Our cadre edged backward. The native warriors followed us screaming insults. We had to get back to the covering fire of the boat's cannon. Then we'd be safe.

My arms were leaden. I parried another spear thrust when I heard cannon fire behind me. Thank God, we are saved! The cannon would chase away the warriors before us. Perhaps this was not my day to die after all. Glancing back, I saw three of Humabon's *barangays* coming to our rescue. However, Lapulapu's men weren't the gunners' target. In the confusion, the Spanish gunners were firing at the *barangays*. I heard screams as shot tore into one of Humabon's ships. The *barangays* retreated. I cursed the gunners. I wished Andrew's cool head was directing the cannon, but Andrew was dead. A spear thrust came from my right. I deflected it at the last moment.

A chief—was it Lapulapu?—with oiled skin and covered with bold tattoos, led twenty archers to a short distance away from our forlorn band. The chief shouted an order and the nearest warriors fell back. Another order launched a cloud of arrows towards us. Pigafetta flinched as one zeroed in on his face; he put a hand to his cheek. An arrow pierced Ravelo's throat. He fell into the water. His head bobbed in the gentle waves with a red cloud spreading around him. I heard metal hitting armor and helmets around me. A supernumerary of the *Trinidad* slumped and disappeared in the water. Enrique cried out as an arrow brushed him. The arrows mercifully missed me. Magellan waded to his son, the one person he most loved of all of us.

The warriors rushed forward. Magellan fought like a lion while he defended his son. A dozen or more tattooed bodies floated about us. Undeterred, the warriors became bolder. One rushed Magellan with a bamboo spear. Magellan impaled him, but his lance remained stuck in the dead

184

warrior's body. Magellan reached to draw his sword, but another warrior's lance pierced his sword arm. Three more warriors rushed him. A heavy spear pierced his left leg. Magellan fell forward. The warriors closed in. Magellan disappeared from sight. A supernumerary from the *Concepción* went to his aid, but a sword thrust to his hamstring cut him down.

I'd been fighting near Antón and San Andrés. Awkward Antón stood his ground against two tattooed warriors. I lost sight of Antón for a moment when another warrior rushed me. The next time I glanced Antón's way, his body floated in water dyed red by his blood. Beside him, a warrior clutched Antón's severed head.

"Antón," screamed San Andrés. The dark giant pulled his spear out of a man he had just impaled and rushed the warrior standing over Antón. San Andrés feinted with his spear. The native reacted and San Andrés ran him through. The man's eyes rolled back in his head. As he fell, Antón's head fell from his hand and disappeared from sight. Pigafetta and I each grabbed an arm of San Andrés and pulled him towards the boats. Enrique followed. The four of us were all that remained of Magellan's escort. Our getaway was unnoticed while the natives hacked away at Magellan's body.

Once on the shallop I sat down in shock. My leader of the past two years was gone. We were on the opposite side of the world, surrounded by hostile natives, and without the man who led us here. I looked around. The others sat, eyes glazed, nursing their wounds. Lapulapu's warriors shouted insults, but dared not come within range of the cannon. San Andrés's head hung between his legs as he sobbed, muttering "Antón, Antón, Antón." Beside him, Pigafetta stared ahead. Blood oozed from a deep gash in his cheek and reddened his shirt. Enrique was also bleeding. I was lucky to have escaped unscathed.

Humabon came alongside in his *barangay* and motioned for us to follow him back to Cebu. In a daze, we started the long row back. A squall descended on us. I became drenched, but barely noticed it as I thought about the loss of Magellan and what it meant for our small fleet…and me. Our losses in numbers weren't large, Magellan, his son, Antón and four others. Over twice that number of our men were wounded including our Asian interpreter Enrique and Pigafetta. The natives would mourn far more tonight, but that meant nothing. Lapulapu had driven us from the battlefield in full view of our allies. We were no longer invincible in the eyes of those around us.

TWENTY-ONE – CEBU, THE FEAST

The news of Magellan's death ricocheted amongst the crew like a cannon ball across the deck. The stunned men listened solemnly as Pigafetta and I told of Magellan's last minutes. I feared the men would panic, but all seemed to understand our plight. The remaining officers, *marineros*, and *grumetes* understood our position in Cebu better than Magellan had, but then they didn't have the promise of a princedom distracting them. All were of the same thought as I was: to be gone from this Godforsaken piece of Asia and to leave immediately for the spice islands of the Moluccas. We elected Duarte and Serrano as joint commanders of the fleet. They closed the Cebu town square trading post and reloaded the trade goods. Next, we needed pilots knowledgeable of the way to the Moluccas. Humabon should be able to supply these to us. I followed Duarte as he went to Enrique to have him make our request of Humabon.

Enrique lay in his bunk in the captain's cabin, his face turned to the ship's side. His right arm had a nasty cut from a warrior's lance and his neck a scab where an arrow cut his flesh. Enrique gave out with a weak moan when we entered. The cabin was stifling in the tropic heat. If I were he, I'd rest on the deck, where a breeze blew, but perhaps he did not want to talk to anyone.

Duarte, with his usual lack of tact, jostled Enrique. "Get on your feet. I have work for you." Duarte's rough voice reverberated through the cabin.

Enrique ignored him and feigned sleep.

"Damn it, get up, slave. I need you to go to the Rajah Humabon."

Enrique bolted up to a sitting position when he heard the word 'slave.' "I'm no longer a slave, Captain. My master's *testamento* set me free."

"*Testamentos* be damned. You aren't free yet, Enrique. You do as I order or I'll return you in chains to be Lady Beatriz's slave. I have important work for you."

Enrique glared at Duarte. What was he thinking? Perhaps that he fought beside his master while Duarte lay drunk in a wench's bed in Cebu.

"I won't ask you again, Enrique. I want you to go to the Rajah Humabon. I need pilots to guide us to the Moluccas. On your feet, man, or I'll have you flogged."

Enrique flinched at the word 'flogged,' and stared hatred at Duarte. "But my wounds, Captain. I need to rest until they heal."

"There is a skiff waiting for you. You'll have even more wounds unless you're on it immediately."

"I will do as you wish. There is no need to threaten me," Enrique added a smile to his face. He sauntered to the skiff by the main deck. As the boat pulled towards the shore, he turned to look back at us with an evil smile.

Enrique returned to the *Trinidad* with the joyous news that Humabon wished to present us with exquisite jewels for his brother King Carlos. He invited the captains and officers to a special feast tomorrow to commemorate his friendship with King Carlos. He promised exquisite delicacies and limitless rice wine. Tupas's dancing girls were to entertain. The rajah would bestow the gems at this dinner.

My first impression was this was all too much like a Trojan horse, but Duarte eagerly accepted. Captain Serrano said he would stay behind and ready the fleet to sail the next day, but Duarte taunted him. "Was Serrano afraid of a little wine and dancing girls? Was he afraid of the fat rajah?" Serrano relented and agreed to go. News of the banquet spread through the three ships. Servants and *marineros* begged officers for permission to accompany them.

I watched the next day as two longboats departed for the feast with Captains Duarte and Serrano, Enrique, Father Pedro, Pilot Carvalho, and *Alguacil major* Espinosa. Twenty other officers, clerks, stewards, gunners, coopers, blacksmiths, *marineros*, and *grumetes* jostled in the boats in anticipation of one last bacchanal before leaving for the Moluccas. I saw nothing to celebrate so soon after Mactan. Pigafetta surprised me by not going. He was never one to miss a party, but his face bore ugly scabs from his wounds at Mactan.

Am I the fool for not going? I don't think so. I might miss a feast if my suspicions are misplaced, but if my suspicions are right, I keep my life…and will have the chance for many more dinners in the future.

Once the boats left, I began inspecting the rigging for our sail tomorrow. I was done with the mainsail when movement towards shore caught my eye. A longboat with Espinosa and Pilot Carvalho was returning. I shouted to them, "Leaving the party so soon?"

Cebuan music reverberated over the water from the Palace.

"Things didn't seem right," replied Espinosa. "Like Captain Serrano, I questioned the sincerity of Humabon. I almost didn't go to the dinner. Then, on the walk to the palace, the Pilot Carvalho and I saw the rajah's brother Lamdagan take Father Pedro's hand and lead him away."

"Father Pedro and Lamdagan have become close friends. Maybe Lamdagan wanted to honor him with a private dinner."

"Perhaps. I know Lamdagan credits the Father, and God, for his miraculous recovery. Of all the 'Christians' baptized in Cebu, Lamdagan is one of the few who've taken any effort to learn the Bible. Father Pedro has spent hours reading the Bible to Lamdagan and discussing it with him. I think Lamdagan was saving his spiritual mentor and savior."

So, Lamdagan is probably the one true convert in this entire city.

The longboat pulled alongside. Carvalho stood and looked back to the city. "I hope we haven't been too cautious. It sounds like a good feast."

Music and laughter continued from the palace.

A gong echoed across the water. What in God's name is that? The music stopped. Carvalho, Espinosa, and I huddled on the poop deck of the *Trinidad* and stared towards shore. Shouting and the clank of metal on metal replaced the music. The other longboat lingered at the Cebu wharf, until warriors approached it. The *marineros* on the boat cast off and franticly rowed back to the fleet.

"I think our fears were well founded. I feel helpless here," whispered Espinosa.

"Let us hope our friends at the palace weren't caught unawares. We must do what we can to help. Albo, hoist the anchor and prepare to sail. Signal the *Concepción* and *Victoria* to do the same," ordered Carvalho.

"We don't have enough men to make an assault, but they should still fear our cannon. I'll have them made ready. We'll punish the rajah if our fears are true," added Espinosa.

One gunner was at the feast. Andrew was dead. Espinosa and his man-at-arms assisted the two remaining gunners in lifting gunpowder and shot from the hold to the deck, and loading the guns.

Ginés and I assisted a crew depleted by Mactan and the partygoers in the raising of the anchor and hoisting of the yards. It took an hour before we had the *Trinidad* making way towards the quays with the decks cleared and ready for action. I hadn't heard any sound of fighting for some time. Cano's *Concepción* trailed the *Trinidad*, while the shorthanded *Victoria* was just starting to make way. I watched with apprehension as we neared the docks.

Shouts of exultation in the native tongue filled the air, but I heard no Spanish voices.

Carvalho ordered, "Let them have some round shot, *Alguacil*. Aim near to the Palace, but not at it. Some of our men may still be alive there."

The two starboard cannon spat out shot. The men around me cheered when a building north of the Palace caved in. Enthusiastic hands reloaded and let another volley loose. A throng of natives filled the streets fleeing in panic. While the gunners were loading for the third time, Humabon, along with a group of warriors, left the Palace and headed down to the dock. As they grew closer, I realized they were leading someone, a captive. Carvalho ordered us to lie to a few hundred yards off shore. Only then did I realize Humabon's prisoner was the stalwart Serrano flanked by a native warrior on each side. Next to Humabon were Tupas and Enrique. *Enrique?*

"The rajah demands you cease fire immediately, or Captain Serrano will die," shouted Enrique over the water.

"What has happened, Captain?" shouted Carvalho.

"We were attacked without warning," replied Serrano. "Our men fought valiantly, but we were badly out numbered. Most are now dead. They've taken a handful of us as prisoners."

Carvalho glared at Enrique. "Are you a prisoner or in league with the rajah, Enrique?"

"I am a free man, and I'm home once again after many years."

"Are you an ally of the rajah, Enrique?"

"What happened was fate."

"When you go before God, you'll have to explain the blood on your hands. Tell the rajah to free his prisoners."

There was a quick conversation between Enrique, Humabon, and Tupas.

"The rajah will free the prisoners if he is supplied with two cannon."

Now we talked. We all agreed that two small cannon were a small price for our comrades. We manhandled two falconets into a longboat and I leapt in with four sailors. When we approached the dock, I motioned the rajah's men back. We pushed the cannon ashore, and backed the boat off the beach. I was close enough to Serrano to see blood caked on his close-cropped beard and doublet.

"We've met our promise. You have the two guns. Let

Captain Serrano and the others free," I shouted.

The rajah whispered something to Enrique, who replied, "The rajah says deliver two more cannon and we will let them go free."

"We'll give you what you want, but first let me see all our men in a place of safety. Then we will make the exchange."

Enrique started to speak, but Serrano shouted, "The rajah is stalling and waiting for reinforcements. You must get away now, or you'll all be lost. It is better that I die than that all should perish."

"We can pound this city into submission with our cannon. Enrique, tell the rajah we will begin firing unless our crewmen are freed."

After a short consultation with Humabon and Tupas, Enrique announced, "The rajah demands two more cannon. He will negotiate no further."

"Sail, for God's sake, sail," ordered Captain Serrano. "They are simply playing for time for *barangays* to arrive with more men."

Enrique spoke to his confederates. Tupas punched and gagged Serrano.

I felt helpless. I shouted to Serrano, "God be with you." Then I ordered my men to take us back to the *Trinidad*.

TWENTY-TWO – WE FLEE CEBU

Our three fleeing ships plowed through the waves under full sail. The *Trinidad*, with the only two pilots left, Carvalho and I, led the way for the *Victoria* and *Concepción*. The course was southwest, several miles off the lush eastern coast of Cebu Island. Carvalho's anxious pacing was annoying, so I went forward and joined the forecastle lookout, San Andrés. I played the events of the last few days repeatedly in my head.

I hated myself for leaving Serrano. Could we have saved him with a concerted assault? We'd never know. Even if still alive, Serrano would never see Spain again, and spend his last days as a slave. I'd always respected Serrano's quiet competence. He was a brave man. Would Carvalho have told the fleet to sail away without him? Never. Could I have done it? I'd like to think I would have.

Magellan had his faults, but he was a leader. With him gone, the Armada had lost the one man either respected or feared by all, and the one man able to herd our polyglot crew in the same direction. Who would lead us now? Carvalho? I hoped not, but feared his election. He was the most senior of the surviving officers.

Many good friends were gone: men I'd shared meals with, bantered with, endured storms with, and fought beside in battles. I remembered Antón's youthful naivety. What of the others who went to the rajah's banquet? I assumed Duarte was dead, fighting until his end.

The ships were now shorthanded. I was one of the few original officers left, and of those two were Carvalho and Cano, an incompetent and a braggart. My friend Michael and the stalwart Espinosa I respected, but Espinosa was no sailor. Enrique's betrayal left us without a translator, although the Italian Pigafetta had made great strides learning the local language. However, my chances of smelling the sweet orange blossoms of Valencia had fallen after Magellan's death at Mactan. The odds of my return had plummeted after the slaughter of my shipmates at Cebu.

As the false energy of battle wore off, I realized the logical conclusion of our situation just as clearly as if Aristotle had explained it to me. If I was going to see home again, I'd have to make it happen.

We were sailing into unknown waters without a local native pilot. The sun was halfway to the western horizon. We had to find safe anchorage before dark. It was dangerous enough to sail these seas in daylight and potentially fatal to sail at night.

I'd sailed many seas and only my home waters of the Aegean Sea had as many islands as there were here. However, the Aegean islands were very different. There the islands were stark rocks with villages of whitewashed stone houses surrounded by tidy olive groves and vineyards. Here dense woods covered the islands. Villages were of thatched huts built on stilts, often over the water, to give some respite from the ever-present clouds of mosquitoes. The blue waters were treacherous. Reefs could be anywhere; a lazy lookout or careless pilot could mean a holed and broken ship. A wreck meant being marooned in Asia to rot in the heat and humidity, with little chance of finding our way home.

A shout came down from the top mast. "Boats off the port side."

Carvalho shouted frenzied orders for the crew to prepare for battle. San Andrés hoisted the battle flag to signal the *Victoria* and *Concepción*. The crew stored unnecessary gear, loaded the cannon, and made sure arquebuses, crossbows, and hand weapons were ready.

I joined Ginés at the port gunwale. "What is the problem?"

"Over there. Those boats just appeared over the horizon to the east. They may be coming in our direction."

"They're too far away to tell their angle on the bow. They may not be heading towards us."

"I mentioned that to Carvalho."

"I would think a threat would come from the north, the direction of Cebu, and not the east."

"True, but Carvalho, in his present state of mind, would panic at the sight of a floating coconut," laughed Ginés.

"Even if they wanted to attack us, I don't think they could catch us. We're making good speed in this quartering wind, which is perfect for us. Remember how we outdistanced the Rajah Colambu's *barangay* under similar circumstances on the sail to Cebu. Our only danger would be if their pursuit continues into the night, forcing us to have to sail into unknown waters."

Ginés nodded in agreement, "I know. Tell that to Carvalho."

After a half hour, it became clear that the boats would pass to the stern. They were probably fishing boats returning to a village south of Cebu, or maybe to Cebu itself. Carvalho went to his cabin. And so ended our little alarm, which reflected the horrors of what we'd left at Cebu, and a crew and officers still in shock, more so than any threat from the distant boats. I'd never feared Humabon behind us. What I feared was the unknown ahead of us.

I kept our small fleet a mile off the Cebu coast. Another island had crept over the horizon on the eastern, port side. We'd left Cebu City far behind when the sun started to grow close to the horizon. The island to the east grew closer. There was no sign of a pursuit by Humabon. Even had he followed us, I believe our cannon would have been more than a match for his *barangays* and junks. When Carvalho returned smelling of liquor, he agreed that we should gingerly approach the coast until the water was shallow enough to moor for the night.

There was no sign of Humabon's boats in the dark or in the morn. Once it was light, I threw lead to navigate us through some shallows, and then guided the fleet to the middle of the channel between Cebu and the eastern island. We'd traveled south but an hour when the land to the east started to fall away into a great bay. I made for the shelter of the bay and its quiet water in the lee side of the eastern island.

It pleased me that there were no signs of habitation. A month ago, I'd been desperate to find a village; now I did not want to see even two natives fishing from a canoe. We'd fled Cebu with little preparation and less organization. There were many decisions to make.

Where to go next? Who would lead us now that so many of the officers were dead? We hailed the other ships to announce a council of the remaining officers, *marinero*s, and supernumeraries. Men crowded the *Trinidad's* deck for the meeting.

In five minutes, we made the first decision. King Carlos's charter was to find the Spice Islands of the Moluccas. We would find them. We knew the Moluccas were on the equator roughly south of us. In theory, we could sail south to the equator, and then explore to the east and west until we found the Moluccas. That was in theory, but in reality these waters were dotted with islands and ship-destroying reefs. We had to find a native pilot who knew a safe course to the Spice Islands.

The second decision forced upon us was obvious after the short sail from Cebu. There were not enough men to man all three ships. The *Concepción* required pumping around the clock and was in the worst condition of the three ships. Of the five original ships, she had been the oldest. I also thought Cano was negligent in her upkeep. So we stripped the *Concepción* of everything useful and apportioned its crew between the *Trinidad* and *Victoria*. Then we burnt her to deny her use to any Asian.

After that we held elections. To my great disappointment,

the crew elected Carvalho captain of the *Trinidad* and Captain General of the two ships. He'd also remain pilot of the *Trinidad*. I was the obvious choice to pilot the *Victoria* and was so elected, which made me happy. I had my own ship and was away from the hapless Carvalho and his vacillation between bravado and cowardice. Carvalho reminded me of a dog with a lot of bark, but that was quick to turn tail and run at the first sign of trouble.

There was more discussion as to the best man to be captain of the *Victoria*. All five of the original captains were now dead or, in the case of Serrano, lost to us, while just two of the original masters remained: Polcevera, master of the *Trinidad*, and Cano, the master of the *Concepción*. Cano actively campaigned for the captaincy, but the men elected *Alguacil major* Espinosa over him by a wide margin. Cano took over as master of the *Victoria*. Polcevera remained Master of the *Trinidad*. Michael de Rodas became mate of the *Victoria*, which would help me endure Cano.

This was now a game of survival. It would be nice to return with the ships' holds full of spices, but just to be able to tell Europe of the enormity of the Pacific Ocean, and the strait at the southern end of South America would be a great accomplishment.

I was pleased with my new ship. The *Victoria* was the best sailor of the two remaining ships. She had been the newest and soundest of the five original ships. She cost thirty thousand *Maravedis* more than the *Trinidad*, even though the *Trinidad* was close to half again as large as the *Victoria*. If I had to stake my life on three masts and a keel getting me back to Spain, it would be on the *Victoria*. I now had a good ship and good men, including my countrymen Michael and Philip. In the shuffling of the crews, San Andrés followed me to the *Victoria*. He confided in me that he'd seen Carvalho in action and wanted no part of any ship he commanded. I was also glad to see the Italian Pigafetta move to the *Victoria*. He didn't say so, but I suspected his opinion of Carvalho was the same as mine. His linguistic talents and coolness under pressure were sure to be useful. Unfortunately, this was all offset by having Cano as master of the *Victoria*.

"So you are to be our pilot, ah, Albo?" said Cano the first time we stood together on the poop deck of the *Victoria*. His voice sounded like an old gate opening.

"Magellan gave it a lot of thought before he promoted me to pilot. Would you prefer to have a different pilot?"

"I'd rather have one authorized by the *Casa de Contratación*."

I laughed. "You can make that request."

Cano stared at me, not knowing what to make of my laughter. "You'll have to do, I suppose."

"Master Cano, I've sailed the seas as long as you."

"Perhaps, but in the Mediterranean, and the eastern Mediterranean at that. That sea is a mere puddle compared to the Atlantic Ocean and the Bay of Biscay where I learned my trade," spat out Cano.

"Huh. Most of your days at sea have also been in the Mediterranean. And I've never sold my master's or my king's ship without permission."

"You know I had no choice. The bankers were demanding payment and the king's monies never came. I was absolved of any misdoing."

"And I've never mutinied against my Captain," I persisted.

Cano glared at me. "He was leading us to ruin."

"But he found the strait to the South Seas."

Cano turned. As he walked away he muttered, "But Magellan is dead."

Evening, July 28, Year of our Lord 1521
Brunei

Mate Michael and I stood on the deck of the *Victoria*. Our longboat plied the broad river to and from Brunei City all day, as it had for the past three weeks, trading for food.

Ample sacks of rice were now in the hold. Trading had been businesslike and the men felt safe in the city. Small groups would go ashore to see the city and trade with the locals.

Brunei was a large and bustling city with over twenty thousand dwellings. All the cities of the surrounding area paid tribute to Brunei's elderly Moslem Rajah Bolkiah. The houses were of wood set on pilings above the water. It was the largest city I'd seen since Spain. The palace was on solid land with fifty cannon lining its thick brick walls. It rivaled any castle in Europe.

I was frustrated. Initially, Carvalho took us south after abandoning the *Concepción*'s burned hulk, but islands and shoals blocked our way. Then Carvalho led us on a circuitous route seemingly without reason that got us nowhere. I could not understand why the other officers had any faith in him. Finally, Carvalho stumbled on Brunei, which at least had the food we needed.

"Mother of God," I said while mopping sweat from my brow. "I'm ready to move on. We finally have all the supplies we need. It's nearly three months since Cebu and Carvalho hasn't gotten us any closer to the Spice Islands. The men are getting too comfortable here. Did you hear our fellow Greek, Mateo de Corfu, deserted from the *Trinidad* the other day?"

"Why would Mateo want to stay in this hellhole with no hope of returning someday to his home in the Aegean?" asked Michael.

"This may be a hellhole, but it's the best hellhole we've seen since Rio. I'm told Mateo even became a Moslem."

"I never knew him to be a religious man," said Michael.

"I doubt he is now. It's the way we Greeks have survived: by being Christian one day and Moslem the next. Such flexibility helps at times." I thought of my time with Piri Reis.

Michael laughed. "I think everyone is worried about what happens next." Then he turned serious, "I can't understand why no one is willing to pilot us to the Moluccas."

"Every day of delay makes it less likely we will ever see

the Mediterranean. Each day our ships deteriorate a little more," said Michael.

"I know. The *Victoria* needs to be careened soon." We'd recently had to put a second man on the pumps.

San Andrés called over to me, "We have visitors, Pilot. Look downstream."

Six high-sided junks were making their way up the river with the incoming tide. I was surprised when they dropped their anchors just downstream of us, partially blocking our escape route to the sea. The sea meant safety to me. Most of the ship and boat traffic anchored closer to Brunei City, but I had seen few junks of this size and their draft might require staying near us. Their large fore and sterncastles were constructed of bamboo. They rivaled the size of our *naos* and many men crowded their decks. I doubled the watch for the night and admonished them to keep a close eye on the new visitors.

I awoke the next morning to pounding on my door. It was San Andrés summoning me to the deck. Captain Espinosa, Cano, and Michael were already there. Michael pointed towards Brunei City. Over a hundred *praus*, multi-hulled sailboats, accompanied by many smaller boats had set out from the Brunei harbor with the ebbing tide. They were coming towards us.

Carvalho bellowed across the water, "It's an attack. Up anchor. We'll fight our way past the junks."

The first anchor came up in record time. There wasn't time to raise the second; I ordered it slipped.

Michael had the men assembled and waiting on the main deck. Espinosa ordered the preparations for battle. Cannons were loaded. A score each of cocked crossbows and arquebuses with their fuses lit stood at the ready. Filled water buckets were ready to put out fires.

The junks had been quiet, but now their crews scurried about. The *Trinidad* and *Victoria*, freed of their anchors, sailed with the tide towards the junks and, beyond them, freedom. We headed for one junk while the *Trinidad* sailed between two others. As we came alongside our moored target, Espinosa ordered a broadside with the five culverins on the starboard side. The thunderous discharge of the guns drowned out the cries of the junk's crew. Our target shuddered with the impact of the round shot; bamboo splinters flew through the air. Powder and shot fed the cannon, and another volley went into the junk, holing it at the water line. One of its masts teetered and fell across the deck. Its deck was a shambles of rigging, yards, and broken bamboo. Michael had the boarding party assembled.

"Do you want to grapple the junk?" asked Michael.

Captain Espinosa shouted through the din, "No."

"Why are we letting the junk go, Captain?" asked Cano.

"*To ensure our survival.* We can defeat the junks, but that is for naught if it allows the *praus* to overwhelm us. Why risk danger to the *Victoria* or our crew when we can simply be gone from here?"

The tide had already carried us beyond the junk. Instead of helping their sister ships, the three junks not engaged by us cut their anchors and made towards the northern shore with the clear intention of beaching themselves.

The smell of burnt gunpowder filled the air and gun smoke drifted in clouds over the water. Through the haze, I saw the *Trinidad* had one junk in its grasp. Its other adversary was floundering. Repeated cannon volleys from the *Trinidad* shattered the grappled junk and musket balls and crossbow bolts swept its deck. Bodies lay where they fell and blood mingled with salt water on the deck. Its crew surrendered or jumped overboard as the Spanish boarded. The *Trinidad* then followed us to the safety of the large bay to the east.

It was apparent to me that we'd surprised the junks and they hadn't planned a joint attack with the *praus*. The *praus* never joined the battle, although they could have. Was this danger just another figment of Carvalho's imagination? Those captured on the junk included a prince and three attractive women, who we presumed to be princesses. We held the prince for ransom. Carvalho announced we would take the three princesses to King Carlos. Their presence supported the idea that the junks were not part of a battle fleet. What warship would have them aboard? My already low confidence in Carvalho's judgment fell another notch.

Brunei ended badly. Carvalho lost a man in the assault on the junk. Three crewmembers, including Carvalho's Brazilian son, were ashore when the battle in Brunei began. We returned the next day for them and our anchors. A *prau* came out with the rajah's emissary. He said the rajah was very angry, the *praus* had meant us no harm, and had been en route to attack a nearby pagan village. He then tossed three severed native heads aboard as proof of the rajah's story. Carvalho then invited the emissary to his cabin to talk in private. That was the last time we saw the captured prince. When our three crewmen, including Carvalho's son, weren't returned by noon as Carvalho claimed the rajah had promised, he ordered us to sail.

Eight weeks later, Michael and I were overseeing the final details of the belated overhaul of the *Victoria* on an islet several days sail northeast of Brunei. Anchored nearby was the *Trinidad*. For the past six weeks, we had replaced worm-eaten wood of our hull and recaulked the planks using the last of the Canary Island pitch. Unfortunately, the tides did not have enough variation to repair the planks near the keel.

Master Cano was in a tent ashore. Captain Espinosa was on the *Trinidad* about something. It seemed that with Carvalho in command something always needed attention.

"Pilot, Mate, Captain Espinosa asks for you to come to the *Trinidad*." I looked up to see Ginés curly head looking over a stack of worm-eaten wood.

"Why? Is something wrong?"

"By Christ's Blood, yes. It turns out Captain General Carvalho has been treating the three women captured in Brunei as his private harem."

"I thought we were taking those virgins to King Carlos,"

said Michael.

"Virgins? I can't vouch for what they were when we took them aboard in Brunei, but I'm positive they aren't virgins now," smirked Ginés. "They were enthusiastically screwing Carvalho when I looked into his tent."

"So why does Captain Espinosa want us?" I asked.

"It gets worse. Captain Espinosa had Carvalho's cabin searched. You know that prince who was captured along with the three wenches?"

"The one who escaped the night we returned to Brunei. Carvalho came close to giving the night watch lashes for it."

"Well, maybe he didn't escape. Captain Espinosa found a stash of gold in Carvalho's cabin. It has the rajah of Brunei's mark on it."

"So?" asked Michael.

"It was a bribe the Sultan paid. The prince didn't escape after all. Carvalho let him go," Ginés's voice rose in excitement.

I thought for a moment. "So he took a bribe to release the prince, but wasn't willing to pay a maravedi for the release of our two men and his son from the rajah. We should leave him here."

"You aren't the only one thinking he's not fit to be Captain General. There's going to be an election."

Carvalho remained mute in an angry meeting. He offered no defense. We declared that he forfeit his ill-gotten gains. In the end, what saved him from marooning was he was the sole original remaining pilot. We voted that Espinosa replaced Carvalho as captain general and captain of the *Trinidad*. Carvalho remained the *Trinidad's* pilot, while Cano replaced Espinosa as captain of the *Victoria* and Michael replaced Cano as master.

Even under Espinosa, we were still unable to find pilots to take us to the Moluccas. Our supply of trade goods continued to dwindle as we purchased food. Eventually, all that was left in our holds were those items earmarked for the purchase of spices. To survive, we resorted to preying on the junks and *barangays* that crisscrossed these waters. No Asian vessel was a match for our cannon. We took what we wanted. Seized goods filled our holds. We kept the more distinguished personages for ransom. Life at sea here was no different than the Mediterranean where the Ottoman and the Christian vessels saw one another as proper pickings. For all, including myself, the thrill of the chase, the capture, and examination of the spoils was exhilarating.

TWENTY-THREE – TIDORE

November eighth, 1520 was my best day since our landfall in Asia. We were finally approaching the volcanic island of Tidore, one of the Spice Islands, after over two years at sea. A month earlier, we found a native pilot who claimed to have been in Francisco Serrão's house in Ternate and to know the Rajah of Tidore. He urged us to go to Tidore instead of Ternate. He claimed the Tidore rajah hated the Portuguese.

Many times, I'd wondered if we'd ever see these mythological islands. I'd known in Seville that we were sailing into the unknown. I'd expected storms and, while I hadn't expected the starvation and scurvy of the Pacific Ocean ordeal, such things happen. The mutiny, Magellan's religious empire building, and the loss of most the officers in the massacre at Cebu, I hadn't imagined. I hoped this rajah, the Rajah of Tidore, was as honest and cooperative as our pilot claimed. It was important to get the cloves purchased, the ships loaded, and to sail for Spain.

I'd spent many hours studying Magellan's Portuguese *roteiros* for the Indian Ocean and East Indies after his death. From them I knew we had six to eight weeks before the monsoons blew in from the south. Once these arrived, we would be unable to make headway against them and be forced to wait months before the winds would be right for a return across the Indian Ocean, around Africa, and back to Spain. There was the possibility of returning eastward across the Pacific Ocean to Spanish Mexico, but I wanted to avoid it. The westward voyage across the Pacific had been bad enough even though we had good winds the entire way.

Tidore was an island six or seven miles in diameter. A large volcanic cone rose over a mile at the island's southern end. The island was lush with vegetation, which reached high up the volcano. From Serrão's letters to Magellan that I'd read, I knew that the clove trees grew only on the mountains of Tidore, its neighbor Ternate to the northwest, and a few other neighboring islands.

The sun was but three hours from setting when we entered Tidore's harbor on the eastern side of the island. We fired a salute from our cannons and dropped anchor. A large *prau* soon approached us. I joined Captain General Espinosa, Pigafetta, and Carvalho on the deck of the *Trinidad*. A steady drum beat marked time as two banks of oars in unison propelled the *prau*. This native ship was just as majestic as any Mediterranean galley as it circled our *naos* twice and glided to a graceful stop a ship's length away from the *Trinidad*. A man, all dressed in white, sat under a canopy at the *prau's* stern.

"I think he expects us to go to his ship, Captain General," observed Pigafetta. Pigafetta had become the expedition's interpreter. He had a natural knack with languages and sensitivity to the nuances of speech and customs of the native people.

"Well, let's go. This is what we've sailed halfway around the world for," said Espinosa. "Come along." He gestured to Pigafetta and me. "Work some charm like you did on the Rajah Colambu."

A skiff took us to the *prau*. I think I portrayed a calm exterior, but inside my stomach churned. Beginnings are very important. Our future was in the hands of this rajah. Two warriors helped us aboard and escorted us to its stern. There, under the silk canopy, sat the rajah on a raised platform. A young man behind him held a scepter; four others stood close by with gold jars. Nine men who appeared to be chiefs sat beside him.

The rajah sat erect wearing a white shirt made of linen. Gold thread embroidered its neck and sleeves. White cloth covered him from his waist to his feet, which were bare and brown. His head appeared shaven with a silk headdress topped with a crown of flowers. His arms were tanned and powerful. Unlike the obese Humabon, there was little fat on him. The lines of his face betrayed his age as being in his forties.

Espinosa, Pigafetta, and I bowed and sat before the rajah. He said nothing at first, but his welcoming eyes focused first on Espinosa for several minutes and then Pigafetta and me. He motioned with his right hand and a man stepped forward who translated the rajah's speech into Portuguese.

"I have dreamt for some time of your ships coming from far away. I have dreamt of people and ships that are like the Portuguese, but not the Portuguese. I have dreamt of the people on these ships being honorable and true friends, unlike the Portuguese. I am the Rajah Almanzor of Tidore and am pleased you are here."

The tension within me evaporated with these words.

"And we have dreamt of being here for many months," said Pigafetta. "We bring greetings from the great Carlos, King of Spain and Emperor of the Christian World. We come in peace, seeking an alliance with your great kingdom. We carry many goods and seek to trade to our mutual benefit."

The conversation continued for some time. I was elated at our reception. We invited the rajah aboard the *Trinidad* for refreshments and the presentation of gifts from King Carlos.

He climbed aboard the *Trinidad*. Each officer in turn approached, bowed, and kissed his hand. Pigafetta led him up the ladder to the quarterdeck. Erect and with every move, every muscle exuding his royalty, Almanzor sat in the red velvet chair that awaited him. His son, Arief, the man holding the scepter, stood behind him. His chiefs sat by his side.

The officers of the fleet, Espinosa, Cano, Carvalho, and I bowed again and sat on pillows on the deck before him. Espinosa made a signal. Out came a yellow Turkish velvet robe, which he presented to Almanzor from King Carlos.

"I thank my royal brother for his fine gift. I, and my people, desire to be true friends of your Spanish King Carlos. We seek a true alliance as brothers to one another, unlike the people of Ternate, who are servants to the Portuguese King," replied Almanzor.

"And our King also seeks to be your brother. Our King is ruler of Spain, which is many times the size of Portugal in land and people. Our King is also Emperor of the Holy Roman Empire, which makes him first among all kings of the Christian world," answered Pigafetta.

Almanzor broke out into a broad smile and threw up his arms on each side as if in a welcoming embrace.

"I welcome you here as if you were King Carlos himself. You and your crew should consider yourself my children and like my children you will ever be welcome in my house."

Espinosa presented gifts to Almanzor and his chiefs. The rajah received the red velvet chair, four cubits of scarlet cloth, crimson satin, fine linen, other cloth and clothing, two caps, six crystal glasses, twelve knives, three large mirrors, seven pairs of scissors and six combs. Arief and the chiefs received similar gifts.

When they were finished, Almanzor said, "Enough, you are too generous. I don't have anything to give King Carlos except my life. I value your gifts, but what I would most treasure is King Carlos's banner and a treaty with King Carlos."

Espinosa spoke, "Our King Carlos also desires a treaty, great rajah, a treaty that would forever memorialize the enduring friendship of our two peoples."

"A treaty would please my people greatly. But what would also bind our people together would be if you left a detachment of your men here when you return to Spain," said Almanzor.

Espinosa replied, "The long voyage has taken its toll on the crew of our ships. We are delighted to leave some men, but they will be few in number. They will be good men, though."

A frown flitted across the rajah's face and he became somber.

Why was he so eager for Spanish troops? Did he fear the Portuguese that much?

Espinosa asked, "A man named Francisco Serrão, a friend of our late Captain General Magellan, lives in the Moluccas. Do you know of him, and where he might be found?"

Almanzor appeared to think for a moment and then replied, "There have been some Portuguese at Ternate. I think one of them was named Serrão. I heard he died some months ago. If I can find out more about him, I will tell you. For now, I suggest you anchor your ships closer to my city. I will tell all that you are under my protection, but you should be on guard. In particular, if any should come to your ships under the cover of darkness, you should kill them. They will mean you harm," said Almanzor.

This didn't sound like an idle warning. Who did he expect to come in the dead of night? Portuguese? Or his rival in Ternate?

Alarm flashed over Espinosa's face. "We appreciate your advice. We are interested in purchasing the fruit of your island, your cloves. What stock do you have for sale?"

"I have some, but not enough dried to fill your ships. I do have a good friend, ruler of the large island to the east, the rajah of Bacchian. He has two junks filled with cloves that he wishes to sell. I will send word to him and go there personally to arrange their shipment here," said Almanzor before he returned to his *prau*.

The next day, a Sunday, we worshiped and rested. Many went ashore to Tidore City. Keen to see what we had sailed so far for, Pigafetta and I, with Arief as our guide, hiked a mountainside to see the fabled clove trees.

We followed Arief up a path along the lower slopes of the old volcano. The air was thick and the cloying sweet smell of tropical flowers enveloped us. After an hour, we came upon a grove of clove trees. The conical trees reached some thirty feet into the sky. Arief asked us to remove our hats before we entered the grove. He explained one must respect the trees when they are in bloom and so we doffed our hats and spoke in whispers. The trees' sturdy brown trunks were around eighteen inches in diameter. Close to the ground, the large trunks split into two or three smaller trunks. The emerging leaves were a bright pink, while the older leaves were laurel-shaped with a dark green color on top and pale green underneath.

Slender, brown-skinned workers were atop ladders throughout the grove. They deftly picked the clove buds from the tips of each branch. The workers ignored the green buds and harvested the pink ones, in which the flower was forming. Arief explained that, if left unpicked, the buds would break into a crimson red flower. The flower would produce a small, pendulous fruit. From the bags around one tree, I estimated it yielded a hundredweight of buds.

We returned following porters carrying the sacks down to a village at the base of the mountain. There natives sat cross-legged while they removed the flower buds from their stems. They did this by placing the buds against the palm and twisting the stems. Arief showed us buds drying on woven mats in the sun. After several days, they turned a reddish brown, which meant they were ready. There were two crops each year. Arief said Tidore produced around sixteen hundred hundredweight of dried cloves a year in poor years and much more when the rain was good. There was maybe one bumper crop every four years.

Three Days Later

I looked up to see Pigafetta and Captain Espinosa returning in a skiff from Tidore City. They had gone early in the morning to meet with Almanzor to negotiate the terms and logistics of the purchase of cloves. Pigafetta reported all had gone well. Almanzor would have a large hut built tomorrow near his palace for our *feitoria*, or trading post. We would be doing business in two days at the latest.

I was having my noonday meal together with the other officers on the *Trinidad's* quarterdeck when a steady drumbeat echoed across the water. The sound was both majestic and ominous. The beat grew louder when two large *praus* rounded the headland to the north. Two decks of rowers propelled each of the *praus*, which made a course straight for our ships. The native galleys were a rich red color, with mythical creatures painted on their bows.

The *praus* coasted to a stop a hundred feet from us.

A foreign accented voice called across in Portuguese, "I have the great honor to present Prince Checchili de Roix of Ternate, honored son of the late Rajah Boleyse."

Espinosa replied, "Greeting from King Carlos of Spain, we are his representatives to Tidore and Ternate of the Molucca Islands. We have come in peace and friendship to seek alliances and trade."

"Prince Checchili wishes to visit aboard your ship to pay his respects. Also aboard are the widow and children of the late Señor Francisco Serrão, a man who may be known to some of you." The speaker was a native standing in the rear of one *prau*. Next to him in a chair sat a man. It was too far to be sure, but he appeared young, with bright red cloths draped about his muscular body.

Espinosa said to Pigafetta out of the side of his mouth, "Go quickly to the Rajah Almanzor. Ask him if we should receive the Ternate Prince."

"We must have a council of the officers, Prince. I have summoned some officers who are ashore. Please wait until they have returned," replied Espinosa.

The Prince waited, although he soon began to pace, and glanced repeatedly towards shore. He spat out an order when Pigafetta returned by himself in the skiff half an hour later. His rowers backed his *prau* away from the *Trinidad.*

Pigafetta reported that the rajah's reply was that we, "should do as we wish."

I was uneasy inviting the prince to our ship. Almanzor might feign indifference, but it could be a test. The other officers felt the same as I. There was no reason to test Almanzor's goodwill. Espinosa, Pigafetta, and I went in a skiff to the prince's *prau* to pay our respects.

The haughty Prince Checchili watched as his men helped us aboard his ship. The translator by his side was a slim male Asian. A native woman, presumably Serrão's wife, stood with wide eyes in the background with a small child clinging to each leg.

Pigafetta delivered greetings from King Carlos and expressed our desire for peace between the peoples of Spain and Ternate. As an expression of our good intentions, we presented gifts of gold cloth, Sicilian silk, knives, mirrors, and scissors.

The prince glanced at these as if they were nothing, and asked us to come to Ternate. Pigafetta replied that we had arranged to take on a load of cloves at Tidore, which would take some time to finish. The prince stared at first Pigafetta and then at Espinosa and finally at me. He gave a command to his servants, who wrapped up the gifts in some cotton. He announced that he must return to Ternate. Dismissed, we boarded our skiff. While doing so, the Portuguese-speaking Asian translator whispered to me. He said he was Manual, a Christian and servant of Pedro Afonso de Lorosa. Lorosa was a Portuguese who came to run the *feitoria* on Ternate after Serrão's death. Manual asked to return with us to the *Trinidad*, to which Espinosa agreed.

Once on our ship, Manual was very talkative. He explained that Tidore and Ternate were traditional bitter enemies with much blood spilt over the years. Nonetheless, the people of both islands disliked the Portuguese. The Rajah Almanzor had hated the Portuguese since Serrão masterminded Tidore's defeat by Ternate ten years earlier. Those in Ternate did not hate the Portuguese as much, but the Portuguese had outworn their welcome.

He then explained the manner of Serrão's poisoning at

the hands of Almanzor at a dinner.

Our friendly rajah had murdered Magellan's friend! When we had asked him about Serrão upon our arrival, he had only vaguely recalled a Portuguese named Serrão, which was a clear deception. Nonetheless, the rajah had done all he had promised to this time, and he hated the Portuguese. By all accounts, Serrão had directed Ternate's defeat of Tidore. Had I been in Almanzor's place, I might have done the same. In the end, I considered Almanzor a better partner than the Ternate prince with his closer relations with the Portuguese.

My fellow officers agreed. Manual returned to Ternate the following day on a small island trading boat.

I went to Tidore City the next morning to check on the hut under construction for our *feitoria.* A score of men were placing the final thatches on the roof when I arrived. When I returned to the *Victoria,* men were unloading the trade goods from the hold. Piles of cloth, German knives, scissors, and other goods took shape on the deck. The longboats and shallop made trips all day to Tidore City. At day's end, five men stayed to guard our merchandise.

Trading began the next day. Everyone was eager to sail for home and Spain. Hence, our merchandise was fairly, if not cheaply, priced. The standard exchange was three feet of good red cloth or twenty-five feet of ordinary cloth for four hundredweight of cloves. The same amount of cloves would also buy fifteen axes, twenty-five pieces of linen, or a hundred and fifty knives.

While we bought cloves in Tidore City, boats arrived at the ships with poultry, pigs, and goats as well as produce for sale. We soon replenished the ships' food stores, although little salt was available to preserve food. Once our goods were in the trading post, we refilled the ships' water casks with fresh water from a spring near the harbor.

Five Days after our Arrival at Tidore

Unexpectedly Almanzor's *prau* pulled alongside the *Trinidad*, and with strong arms, he climbed the rope ladder to the main deck. *Had we somehow offended him?* He requested firmly, but without anger, that we release our prisoners. I had thought the taking of the three girls in Brunei a mistake, but there was no use in arguing with Carvalho about it at the time. All the other prisoners taken since then in our time as pirates were also a mistake. It had been silly to take them with no clear idea how to ransom them, and they were a problem to guard and feed. I felt sure some of them were worth money, but to whom? It was not like in the Mediterranean where everyone knew who would pay a tidy sum for an Ottoman pasha or a Castilian duke. I was relieved when Espinosa turned over our human burden to Almanzor.

Next, he asked us to remove the pigs we had from our ships since they were unclean in his Moslem eyes. I then realized that his informants had been aboard our ships. Well, we had nothing to hide. I hoped Almanzor could say the same.

The rajah lingered on the *Trinidad's* main deck. I wondered why. Within minutes, a boat appeared from the north, following the same route as the Ternate prince a week earlier. Almanzor knew this boat was coming.

Manual was at the ship's bow. Beside him was a tall man with a bushy beard identifying him as European. He announced himself as Pedro Afonso de Lorosa, the Portuguese trader from Ternate that Manual had told us of earlier. Lorosa greeted us like long lost cousins...until he saw the Rajah Almanzor. Then he froze. He hesitated before climbing aboard.

The rajah gave him a bear hug and with a laugh told him, "Pedro, you may be Portuguese and from my rival Ternate, but I know you're an honest man. You should speak the truth to my friends here." And, with that, Almanzor departed.

Lorosa watched in silence as the rajah's *prau* went back to his palace.

"I am tired of these islands," Lorosa said in a soft shaky voice to no one in particular. "The line between life and death here is finer than I would like. Both the Moluccan rajahs and the Portuguese commanders will just as soon kill a man as swat a fly. I sometimes wonder if I'll ever see home again."

"We feel the same way at times too, Señor Lorosa. We lost two dozen of our finest men in a massacre in Cebu north of here. One can never be too careful," observed Espinosa. "Come sup with us and tell us your story. How long have you been in Asia?"

"Too many years, Captain, too many. Sixteen long ones. The last ten have here in Ambon and the Moluccas at the far eastern limit of Portuguese influence. To whom have I the pleasure of speaking?"

"Forgive me. Let me introduce our officers. I am Gonzalo Gómez de Espinosa and Captain General of our little fleet. Señor Juan Bautista de Polcevera, a native of Genoa, is captain and master of the *Trinidad* here. Señor Juan Sebastián Cano is the captain of the *Victoria* anchored to our south. Our pilots are João Lopes Carvalho of Portugal and Francisco Albo of Rhodes. Señor Michael, also of Rhodes, is master of the *Victoria*. Our translator is António Pigafetta of Lombardy. So you can see both ends and the middle of the Mediterranean are represented."

"I am pleased to meet you all. So Magellan is dead as the rumors said?"

"He died in battle near Cebu north of here. That was six months ago."

"I would have liked to have seen him again. He and I sailed in 1505 for India with Almeida's fleet. He was a good man. I remember his bravery when we fought against the Zamorin of Calicut and his Egyptian allies. Even when wounded he was a lion in battle. Later, when I was with Serrão in Malacca, Magellan saved us both from death or slavery when we were attacked without warning."

"None among us ever doubted his resolve or bravery. So you knew Serrão too?"

"Yes, I was with Abreau's three Portuguese ships that were the first to venture east of Malacca to the nutmeg island of Ambon ten years ago. I stayed behind at the *feitoria* in Ambon when Abreau's fleet returned to Malacca. A storm wrecked Serrão's ship on its return voyage, but he turned that misfortune into becoming vizier of Ternate, and one of the most powerful men of this region. Serrão, like Magellan, was a man of great determination, but his luck eventually ran out too."

A dinner was set out on the quarterdeck. There Lorosa continued his story.

"I had wondered if I would ever see you. Word came from Malacca a year ago that your five ships had disappeared from Spain for these islands. King Manuel sent two fleets to stop you. One went to the Cape of Good Hope and one to near Brazil, but both found only empty seas. Then he commanded the Captain General of India, Sequeira, to send six ships here to intercept you. Sequira couldn't spare that many ships because of a Turkish threat, but he did order a large galleon here. That was some time ago."

"It took us much longer to sail here than we expected."

"Word reached here some months ago that you were to the north in Brunei. What took you so long? It is but a few weeks sail from Brunei."

Espinosa glanced at Carvalho. "We could not find a pilot to guide us here."

"Well, you had best not stay here long. The Portuguese commander in Java, António de Brito, will eventually learn that you are here. Brito is a hard, violent man. You'll want to be gone before he arrives. For the moment you are safe, but only because of the ineptness of my Portuguese countrymen."

"How is that?"

"I had spent a year negotiating for a large shipment of

cloves. A week ago, a Portuguese caravel and two junks arrived at Ternate for the cloves. I sent seven men with the two junks over to Bacchian Island to load a shipment I had arranged with the rajah there. While at Bacchian, the Portuguese screwed a couple of the local rajah's wives. That was a bad mistake. The rajah had them executed most painfully and confiscated our junks."

"Those must be the junks the Rajah Almanzor spoke of. He said the Rajah Bacchian had two junks filled with cloves for sale," I said.

"I'm sure it's my cloves. Oh, well. Brito's men paid for them, not me. Anyway, when word of the executions in Bacchian reached Ternate, the caravel couldn't leave fast enough."

"How long ago did it leave?" asked Carvalho. Panic filled his dark eyes.

"No need to worry. It left last Wednesday, two days before your ships arrived. If you had arrived a few days sooner, word of your arrival would be in route to Brito right now. As it stands now it will take weeks, or even months, before Brito learns you are here."

"Well, Señor Lorosa we don't intend to stay here long. Our *feitoria* is already doing a brisk business in Tidore City. It should only be a matter of a week or two before we have a full load to sail with," replied Captain Espinosa.

"And we understand the monsoons will soon shift and prevent us from sailing south and east if we delay too long," I added.

"Your information is correct. How do you intend to return to Spain? Are you going back the way you came?"

"No. Going back east over the Pacific Ocean seems more perilous and less certain than the traditional route. The Pacific Ocean is vast, much larger than we imagined. We lost many men to scurvy on our westward voyage. If the winds had slowed us but one or two weeks more, I think we all would have died of sickness or starvation. No, the westward, Portuguese route around Africa sounds better to us."

"I'm ready to go home. It may look like a tropical paradise here, but it isn't. The fever cut down many of my comrades. The rajahs can be generous, but you are also at their mercy. The Portuguese commanders aren't any better. Instead of supporting Serrão here in the Moluccas with more men and money, they were jealous and asked him to return to Malacca. Most of the commanders just want to make their own fortunes any way they can, and if that means turning on their countrymen, so be it. Of course, they are just following the example of our good King Manuel, who likes his gold better than his subjects."

The afternoon became the evening. Our talk with Lorosa continued. Lorosa agreed to a salary and to sign on as an officer of the fleet. The plan was he would pilot us south to Ambon for some nutmeg and then westward to the Cape of Good Hope. Pigafetta, Lorosa, and I talked until three in the morning. Lorosa returned to Ternate the next day to prepare for his family's departure.

We slaughtered the pigs that were offensive to Almanzor and hid their carcasses behind sails on the quarterdeck of the *Victoria*.

The store of merchandise in Tidore City diminished each day while the pile of clove sacks grew. It became clear there was not enough to fill our ships' holds. As promised, Almanzor went to the Rajah of Bacchian to bargain for the cloves that filled the confiscated Portuguese junks. Meanwhile, the rajahs of the surrounding islands came, one by one, to visit. Each enjoyed demonstrations of the Spanish arms: the cannon, matchlocks, and crossbows. We signed peace treaties with most of them.

Boats filled with cloves came from Ternate each day wanting to trade, but we were true to our agreement with Almanzor. We traded for food with the Ternate boats, but refused even the most lucrative offers of cloves. I felt sure Almanzor's spies would tell him of this and his confidence in our word should grow because of our faithfulness.

Some days later, a *prau* nosed up to the *Trinidad*. I summoned Espinosa as Arief and several warriors climbed aboard, followed by Almanzor.

"Good news, Captain General," boomed Almanzor. "Tomorrow it will be time to start loading your ships. Today the junks arrive from Bacchian and stacks of cloves are reaching the rafters of your *feitoria* ashore."

Espinosa's face broke into one of his rare smiles. "That is great news. Again, we thank you for your assistance."

"You have large ships. It will take a month to fill them full."

"But that will be too late. The monsoons may have come by then. We must leave sooner," I said.

"Rajah, we must expedite the loading. We appreciate your hospitality, but we must return to our King Carlos with word of your friendship. Only then can a larger fleet return to Tidore," said Espinosa.

"Well, perhaps we should concentrate on first loading one ship. The second ship can leave later."

"It is best that they sail together."

"Leave some of your soldiers behind with their cannon."

We had already decided to do this. Espinosa paused and then announced, "We'll leave some cannons, arquebuses, four barrels of powder, and five men in the *feitoria*."

"Thank you, Captain General. Return soon. Return with a great fleet. The Portuguese will fear such a fleet. Meanwhile, we will double the number of laborers. We will load your ships in fifteen days. That will be a record. Now please come tonight to my palace. It is our custom to have a great feast before the first cloves are loaded."

My stomach grew tense. Espinosa and I cast knowing glances at one another. What little of Carvalho's face not hidden by his beard turned white. Was Almanzor planning a repeat of the Cebu massacre? We knew Almanzor was capable of killing since Magellan's cousin Serrão had evidently died by poison at his hands.

"Let me inform the other officers, Rajah," replied Espinosa smoothly, not giving a hint of his concern.

We retreated to the poop deck where Cano, Michael, and Pigafetta joined us.

"I think we should go," said Espinosa. "I consider myself a good judge of men, and I believe him true to his word."

"That's my opinion also," said Pigafetta.

"I think we would be crazy to go. Having barely survived the massacre at Cebu, I'm not eager to leave my bones here in Tidore. Why in the name of God would we take this chance?" argued Carvalho.

"But the Rajah Almanzor is our friend," replied Pigafetta.

"Wasn't the Rajah Humabon also our friend and a Christian to boot? That didn't stop him from butchering our shipmates. We've known this Moor rajah for scarcely two weeks. I haven't any reason to believe he is less homicidal than the Rajah Humabon," said Carvalho.

"And what of the Rajah Almanzor's murder of Serrão? Every time I see the spring where we fill our water casks, I think of Serrão's men being killed there after he was poisoned. You may go if you want, but I'll oversee the loading of the ships," argued Cano in his raspy voice.

"Don't you think you are being overly cautious? This man hates Ternate and the Portuguese. He has no reason to alienate us and every reason to cement his friendship with us," countered Pigafetta.

"Agreed. But I still think going to his feast is an unnecessary risk…it's a chance I'm not willing to take," said Carvalho.

"Let's celebrate with the rajah," I suggested, "but tell him it is our tradition to have the meal aboard the departing ships. Let's invite him to a feast here on the *Trinidad* tomorrow night."

"An excellent idea, we won't offend the rajah, while ensuring our heads stay attached to our necks. Señors, let's do as our canny Greek suggests," said Espinosa.

The loading of cloves continued for another three weeks after the feast. Soon the holds of the *Trinidad* and *Victoria* were close to full. Lorosa arrived with his wife and children. In a few days, the ships could depart.

Espinosa, Lorosa, and I were watching the loading of the last cloves when a familiar drumbeat echoed over the water. A reddish *prau* rounded the headland to the north and made for the *Trinidad*.

Lorosa squinted at the ship and announced, "It is a royal *prau* of Ternate. I don't think it's here to offer us best wishes for our return voyage."

The *prau* slid to a stop. Prince Checchili de Roix stood in its stern under a silken canopy. He cried out, "Is Señor Pedro Afonso de Lorosa aboard?"

Lorosa hesitated before he stepped forward. "I am here with my friends, Prince Checchili. What do you wish?"

"I wish you to return to Ternate with me, Señor Lorosa. You have a good trading business there."

"No longer, I will be sailing with my friends."

"But I need your business acumen beside me in Ternate."

Turning to us, Lorosa said, "He doesn't want my head to advise him. He wants my head to give to Brito." He turned back to the prince. "I have no more business on Ternate, Prince. Please give my regards to your brothers."

For a moment a look of frustration crossed the prince's face, but he regained his composure. He addressed Espinosa, "May I come aboard your ship, Captain?"

Many warriors lined the *prau's* side. Espinosa shook his head in refusal. "We are busy getting ready for our voyage, your Excellency, and aren't prepared to properly entertain a guest of your stature. Please forgive us, but a visit at this time is out of the question."

The prince then shouted in a loud voice, "Señor Lorosa, you, and all with you, do not have my permission to leave. You all leave at your own peril." He barked out an order. His *prau* turned, gathered speed, and headed north back to Ternate.

What did he mean by his threat? Had he already warned Brito of our arrival? I was anxious to be away before the murderous Portuguese arrived.

TWENTY-FOUR – WE LEAVE TIDORE

December 18, Year of our Lord 1521

"Weight the anchors, mate," I ordered. San Andrés and three other *grumetes* strained against the capstan of the first anchor while four Moluccans worked the second anchor to the customary chantey. The men were enthusiastic. They were going home. There was no one waiting for me in Spain, or even Greece. Still I longed for real wine from grapes, olives, and the aroma of wheat bread fresh out of the oven. And cheese. I coveted the nutty flavor of cheese. Nonetheless, I had no illusions about the long voyage ahead, despite the festive atmosphere of the ships' departure.

Three large *praus* lay near the *Trinidad* and *Victoria* along with many smaller ones. The largest *prau* with three banks of oars manned by a hundred and twenty men flew the colors of the Rajah of Bacchian. The aged Rajah of Bacchian had stayed over from his wedding three days earlier to a daughter of Almanzor.

The other two *praus* were the flagships of Almanzor and Prince Checchili de Roix.

After securing the anchors, I ordered yards and sails hoisted. Twenty *marineros* and *grumetes* grunted as they got the topsails in place, followed by the main and foresails. I looked on with pride as a fresh breeze filled out new cotton sails, which were every bit as good as the ones the ship bore when it put out from Spain two years earlier. Emblazoned on the main and foresails was the cross of Saint James. Inscribed under it was *'Ésta es la enseña de nuestra Buenaventura,'* 'This is the figure of our good fortune.' The flag of King Carlos topped the mainmast; pennants topped the fore and mizzenmasts. *I'd never seen a smarter looking ship.* I even felt almost as well dressed as Pigafetta in a new doublet made by Lorosa's wife.

"Take her out of the harbor, mate," said Cano.

"The *Trinidad* is slow getting its anchor up," observed Michael.

Michael, one would think, would be happy at finally sailing for Spain. Instead, his face wore its typical mask of perpetual worry.

I looked towards our sister ship. There was no obvious problem. "We'll tack about until the *Trinidad* joins us."

An hour passed and the *Trinidad* still had not left her anchorage. *What in the name of the Blessed Virgin was taking so long?* I ordered the *Victoria* back. As we neared the *Trinidad*, I saw that not only was she still anchored, but she also had an ominous list to port.

Once within hailing distance, I called across, "Pilot Carvalho, what is the problem?"

"We have a serious leak. One anchor fouled fast. We doubled up the men on the capstan and finally broke it free. But the ship's hull was torqued so much in the process that now water is pouring into our hold."

Doubled up the men? You fool. That old hull can't take that kind of torture. You should have simply cut the anchor line.

"Where is it leaking?"

"We don't know. We can hear water rushing in, but the hold is so full of cloves we can't see where the leak is."

"Do you have the pumps manned?"

"Of course. I have *grumetes* working hard at the pumps. I think they're keeping up with the water coming in, but we've been unable to correct the list."

Cano ordered the *Victoria* anchored and sent over help to relieve the tired men on the *Trinidad's* pumps.

Two Days Later

All the officers of the Fleet assembled for council. Two days of work on the *Trinidad* left it as leaky as ever. Almanzor had pearl divers search the outside of the *Trinidad's* hull for the leak, but they were unable to find it.

Captain General Espinosa started the council, "It's clear we're going to have to unload the *Trinidad* and perhaps even beach her to find and repair this leak. We'll will be sailing no time soon."

"But the monsoon winds will soon be shifting. We must sail or we'll be delayed for nearly a year," said Carvalho.

"That means the *Victoria* should sail now. At least then one ship will make it to Spain and tell King Carlos of our accomplishments," said Espinosa.

"I hate leaving you here, but I think you are right," I agreed. "The *Victoria* should sail. What are your plans for the *Trinidad*? Will you wait a year? I'm sure that will make the Rajah Almanzor happy."

"It would be too risky to stay. Every day I fear Brito will arrive with a flotilla and overwhelm us. Once the *Trinidad's* hull is sound we'll sail east across the Pacific Ocean to Spanish Mexico," replied Espinosa.

"I'm still concerned about doing that. No one has attempted it before," said Carvalho.

"And no one had ever sailed westward over the Pacific Ocean before we did it. No one even knew there was an ocean there," said Espinosa.

"Perhaps we should not tempt fate another time. Perhaps we should wait until after the monsoons," replied Carvalho.

"Then even if the Portuguese don't get us, the *Trinidad's* wood will be rotten and joints begging for caulk by that time. I think we should at least try the eastward path. If we fail, we can always return and try the westward route next year," argued Espinosa.

"Well, we can attempt it, if you insist," relented Carvalho.

"Are you agreed, the *Victoria* sails tomorrow?" I asked

Cano.

"The sooner the better," he replied.

"I think our ship, like the *Trinidad*, is overloaded. We should take off some of the cloves," suggested Master Michael.

"I think that's a good idea. Remove fifty or sixty hundredweight. We don't want to suffer the *Trinidad's* fate," replied Cano.

"I'll have it done before midnight," Michael replied.

Soon the men were unloading the cloves to be stored on Tidore. The cloves left behind would diminish King Carlos's profit, but Magellan had signed the contract with the King, not us. Perhaps the sole thing Cano and I agreed upon was our desire that we do return. And, it was the King's cloves being hoisted out of the hold, not the crews' cloves. Michael and I each had two sacks of cloves stored below, while the *marineros* and *grumetes* had one each.

Word of the *Victoria's* departure without the *Trinidad* passed like lightning among the crews. In the morning, Ginés visited with a bag filled with hundreds of letters.

He gave the sack to me. His eyes turned misty when he gave a letter to me, "This is for my wife Fidelia."

"I will be sure it is delivered."

"I will pray to the Virgin Mary that your voyage is swift," said Ginés. He looked at San Andrés as he helped ready the *Victoria's* sails and sighed. "Good luck, Pilot."

"We'll need some of that. I'll see you in Seville," I said with a smile. I liked the curly headed Ginés. He was as good a *marinero* as I'd ever seen, but I doubted I'd see him again in Seville, or any other place here on Earth.

When we sailed, Ginés followed the *Victoria* in the *Trinidad's* shallop for several miles before turning back. I watched with sad eyes as the shallop's sail grew smaller against Tidore's outline as he returned to his stricken ship. I said a short prayer for my friends on the *Trinidad*. It could not hurt.

Then I turned back to the work at hand. I was satisfied. I'd done everything possible to prepare the *Victoria* and its crew for the long voyage ahead. The *Victoria*'s hold was full of twenty-six tons of precious, pungent cloves including my two bags and two more for Andrew's widow. She was crewed by forty-seven Europeans plus thirteen Moluccans to fill out the ranks. Two pilots provided by Almanzor would guide us to Timor. After that, we'd sail west into waters for which no *roteiro* existed until we reached the Cape of Good Hope. Once at the Cape, I had Magellan's Portuguese *roteiros* to guide me the length of the Atlantic Ocean to Spain.

Sweet spring water filled the *Victoria's* water tanks. Four small *praus* loaded with firewood met us at Mare Island south of Tidore. Water and fuel should be ample. Food, though, could be a problem. There was far less than I liked. There was ample fresh food, but little preserved food other than rice compared to when the *Victoria* left Spain. Maybe we could buy more food along the way. And, what about the scurvy? Would that scourge reappear to savage us on the return voyage?

The sun was setting on our first day. Philip gnawed on a drumstick, his cap at its usual jaunty angle. We were eating our way through the fowl caged on the deck and our fresh vegetables while we could. Before long, it would be back to our more typical stew and rice.

"So now that we're at sea, what exactly is the plan to get back to Spain? I know we're going the western route, but I'm hurt you wouldn't tell me the details while we were in Tidore," said Philip.

I smiled. "If it had been left to me no one would have even known whether we were sailing west or east."

"Why's that?" Philip tossed the remains of his chicken leg overboard, and wiped his fingers on his pants.

"If Prince Checchili didn't send notice of our departure to Brito, then I'm sure someone else did. There was no need to advertise our plans to the Portuguese."

"I wouldn't have told a soul, Albo."

I laughed. "Not intentionally I am sure, but you probably would have told some wench in Tidore."

Philip shrugged his shoulders. "By Zeus's beard, how do we get back to Spain?"

"We're going to sail west across the Indian Ocean, around the Cape of Good Hope and then north to Sanlúcar."

"So what is different? That is the usual Portuguese route."

"No it isn't. Their normal route would be to sail first to Malacca, to the south and west of here. From there the Portuguese sail west to Cochin in India where their ships convoy up and sail to the east coast of Africa and then to the Cape of Good Hope. Finally they sail up the west coast of Africa to Lisbon, with a stop at the Cape Verde Islands."

"So how will we sail differently?" asked Philip as he scratched idly at the scar by his eye.

"We're going to sail south, southeast to Timor, skirting the Portuguese base at Ambon along the way."

"I heard the Portuguese trader Lorosa speak of Ambon. I thought we were going to stop there."

"Ambon is the nutmeg island. Lorosa was going to guide us to a hidden port to take on a load of nutmeg and mace undetected by the Portuguese. However, Lorosa stayed with the *Trinidad*. We do have his man Manual with us, but Cano and I don't see any reason to risk capture by the Portuguese there. Our hold is full with cloves anyway. We'll avoid Ambon and make for the island of Timor. That island is east of the Portuguese base in Java."

"Why Timor?"

"The Rajah Almanzor told us it's a good sized island where we should be able to buy food. We'll need more food, because after leaving Timor we're going to sail south until we clear the East Indies. Then we'll turn west across the Indian Ocean to the Cape of Good Hope. We'll be well south of the standard Portuguese route to the Cape of Good Hope."

"Do you have a *roteiro* for that route?" asked Philip.

His question cut to the heart of my concerns. "No, few, if any, ships have traversed the Indian Ocean at the latitude we'll sail. That part of the Indian Ocean is nearly as unknown as the Pacific Ocean was before we crossed it. We may discover new lands."

"I don't want to discover new lands. I just want to get home with my sack of cloves."

"I hope we find places where we can buy fresh food, but nothing is guaranteed. Otherwise, you're right. We'll be short of food by the time we reach the Cape of Good Hope. At least, the distance will be less than that of the Pacific Ocean. Once at the Cape we'll take the usual Portuguese route home only we won't stop at the Cape Verde."

"I wish I hadn't asked, Pilot. It sounds as risky as sailing the Pacific."

Philip was right, but we had no choice.

"It will be risky, but we've survived many dangerous things to get this far. My biggest concern is the wind pattern of the Indian Ocean. The Portuguese *roteiros* say little about the winds in the southern part of the ocean we will be sailing. We'll need good winds to get across the ocean quickly and safely."

Storms had been conspicuously rare during our time on the far side of the world. That ended on the sail to Timor. One evening in the approaching dusk, an immense thunderhead rose into the heavens. Rain obscured the horizon. Lightning crisscrossed the sky as if gods were dueling. I felt the thunder's low rumble in my spine.

I turned to Cano. "I think we should be dropping the sails."

"Not yet. Let's wait until we're closer to shore," replied Cano in his gravelly voice.

I steered the *Victoria* towards the shelter of a small island. Despite the approaching storm, the air was quiet, with barely a light breeze propelling the ship.

"Philip, take some men and get ready to drop the

anchors. I'll want two of them down."

"I'll be ready Pilot."

"Mate. Be ready to take down the sails at a moment's notice."

The mate started shouting orders to his men.

I waited for Cano's order, while the gray trouble slowly advanced towards us.

"Now. Captain?" I asked.

Cano looked over the side at the water below. "Not yet."

A sudden gust of wind rocked the ship, then another and another. The sudden ferocity of the storm's onset surprised me.

"Now," ordered Cano.

"Strike the sails, Mate," I shouted over the wind.

The men dropped the main and foresail yards, leaving the sails in a heap on the deck. They cut the bowsprit loose.

Along with Master Michael and San Andrés, I brought down the lateen sail.

"By the Virgin Mary, get the top sails down, Mate," I urged. The sea had been placid minutes before. Now white-tipped waves crashed across the main deck. I braced myself as the ship shuddered. Rain pelted the deck. I clutched the binnacle as a huge wave hit. It threw Cano against the railing.

The wind worked against the high sterncastle and pivoted the ship about until its bow headed into the storm. The men worked frantically to get the topsails down.

The wind whistled through the rigging. A crack came from overhead. The foretopmast gave way at its splice to the foremast. The foretopmast, yard, and foretopsail blew back into the mainmast.

I shouted, "Let the anchors go. Watch out overhead."

Philip worked furiously to release the anchors. A loud snap. I looked up to see sails, ropes, and wood coming towards me. I threw myself onto the deck. A yard slammed into the binnacle near my head. I looked around. Snarled ropes, ripped canvas, and splintered yards covered the deck. A long length of foretopmast leaned against the starboard rail where Cano had been standing. Cano? Mother of God, where was Cano?

I stood up and glanced forward. The anchors seemed to be holding. Like a monkey in a mango tree, I climbed across the fallen rigging to where I'd last seen Cano all the while searching for him through the tangled thicket of ropes and canvas. He was nowhere.

"Michael. We've lost Cano. By the merciful Mary, where is he?"

Michael scrambled through the rope jungle to me.

I looked over the side. Cano was in the water hanging onto a rope trailing from the foretopmast. The fallen topmast had one end caught on the railing while its other end dragged in the water. A wave hit, and Cano lost his grip on the rope and his head disappeared underwater. When he resurfaced twenty feet further away, his eyes met mine.

"Save me."

"Throw some lines off the stern," I ordered Michael.

I took off my doublet and jumped over the side. The warm salt water burned my eyes as the initial plunge took me well below the surface. I swam upward, took a breath of air, and looked around. Cano was to my right. A few strong strokes brought me beside him.

"Are you hurt?"

"No…I don't think so."

To my left was one of the lines that Michael had thrown out.

"We need to get to that line, Cano."

"I can't swim."

By the Virgin Mary, why wouldn't a mariner learn to swim?

"Grab hold of me."

Cano clutched me. I took a deep breath, and started out for Michael's line. One stroke, two strokes, and soon the line was in my grasp, but I lost it when a wave lifted us away from the ship and another crashed over us.

When we surfaced, the *Victoria* was disappearing from view.

"My God. We're dead," gasped Cano.

Cano adjusted his grasp, pinning one of my arms, and driving us both under. With my free arm, I slugged Cano with all my strength. He went limp. I put my left arm around Cano, and treaded water. I kicked to raise my head higher and looked again for the *Victoria*. It must still be close by, but in the driving rain, I couldn't see it and I didn't even know its direction. All I could do was keep our heads above water. We were dead unless I found some flotsam to hang onto, or if God smiled on us and blew us into shore.

My sight became blurry from the salt water. It seemed like we'd been in the water for an hour without seeing a barrel or spar. I'd swallowed seawater two or three times after misjudging waves. My legs were cramping and my arms were leaden.

Maybe it's my time. No, not now. I can go on a little longer. I thought of letting Cano go. I'd survive longer if I did and shore shouldn't be far away. If I knew where it was, I could make it, but the water around me all looked the same.

A small log materialized before me.

Something to grab onto, to support me. Salvation had arrived. I grasped it. I relaxed a little to give my tired muscles a rest. I then realized it wasn't a log. I clutched an oar. San Andrés's dark face loomed over me. A giant hand reached out. It grasped Cano and pulled him into the longboat while I held tight to the oar. Then it was my turn. I lay in the bottom of the boat staring up at San Andrés's dark eyes.

I croaked, "Thanks."

Philip held the tiller in the stern with one hand while pulling down his cap in the wind and rain. "Welcome aboard, Pilot," he said with a crooked smile.

I lay a minute, shivering; the seawater I'd drunk rose to the back of my throat. I pulled myself to the boat's gunwale and vomited until only dry heaves were left in me. I clung to the railing until my stomach settled, then turned to Philip, blinked and tried to rub the salt out of my eyes. *No. I'm seeing right. The Victoria was a floating hulk at the storm's mercy.*

Philip saw my surprise and said, "I have the anchors down. I think they'll hold unless the storm rolls double sixes. Our ship is in need of some work."

Two weeks later, I was supervising the final refitting of the *Victoria*. We'd lost both top masts, so a work party went ashore to find suitable replacements. The men felled two trees, pulled them to the shore, shaped them into new topmasts, and floated them to our ship. Then came the tricky job of splicing them into the lower masts.

Cano sidled up to me. I suddenly realized how much older he now looked than when I'd first met him in Seville. Lines crisscrossed across his face that weren't there before, and gray hairs now peppered his dark beard and hair.

"I haven't thanked you for saving me," he said with a throaty voice.

"No, you haven't."

Cano stood in silence.

I arched my eyebrow. "Well."

Cano grunted. Then he smiled. "Thanks, Pilot, for saving my life."

"You're welcome."

"I'm actually sort of surprised you did it."

I let out a belly laugh, "And so am I, so am I."

"Why did you do it?"

"I would do the same for any man on this ship."

Cano laughed. "Oh…I had hoped I was someone special." With that, he walked away.

That was all the thanks I ever got.

Somewhere in the Indian Ocean — Over three months later

I pointed at the chart sprawled across the table in Cano's cabin. "We are close to the longitude of the Cape of Good Hope by my dead reckoning."

"Should we turn north? Are we clear of the cape?" asked Cano.

"I don't think so. I've been careful in my plotting, but it's been months since our last known position. The many tacks have made it difficult to estimate our longitude."

After leaving Timor, the winds were favorable. Timor had been disappointing. It was a large island but the villages were small and poor. The natives bargained hard for the little food they had to sell. Tensions were high when we sailed for the Cape of Good Hope. Two men deserted rather than face scurvy again. Philip filled a small bag with soil to ward off the disease and religiously touched it each day.

Two days from Timor, the wind abandoned us and our ship lay motionless in the dark blue water. Would this be a repeat of the doldrums off Africa? Thanks to the Blessed Virgin Mary, this was not to be the case, and soon strong winds arose from the southeast. We made good time on a southwesterly course meant to take us far from Portuguese eyes. I began to think the voyage would be swift and uneventful. A change of the wind to the west dashed those hopes.

We tacked for weeks against these headwinds. At least we had favorable winds for the entire transit of the Pacific. The Indian Ocean was smaller, but more difficult to transit because we had to fight our way across it.

Our fresh food was gone, the men exhausted, and the water stale when an island appeared upwind. I swore to myself. It was if the gods were conspiring against us. It was impossible to tack to the island. Cano, Michael, and I talked. We decided to drop the sails and drift in hopes the wind would change. We badly needed landfall to replenish our food and water. The next day the wind had shifted enough that we were able to close the island, but cliffs barred our landing on it. We had to sail on. No other land appeared. Now, days later, we were somewhere near the Cape of Good Hope. The temperature wasn't as bad as that in Patagonia, but we'd left the warmth of the tropics far behind.

"We have to do something," said Michael. "The men are fading. The tacks would be bad enough if the weather was warm and the men well fed. But…"

I sensed desperation in Michael's voice. *Has Michael given up?*

"I know. We need some woolen clothes for the men," I said.

"Just fine, Pilot. Tell me if you see a fine flock of sheep and I'll have the cabin boys weave their fleece into some nice coats," grunted Cano.

"The Moluccans are doing worst of all. I don't think they've ever seen temperatures this low before," said Michael.

"Get what work out of them that you can," ordered Cano. "Maybe have the Moluccans man the pumps instead of working the sails. That will keep them a little warmer."

I regretted that we'd been unable to careen the *Victoria* properly near Brunei. There must be some leaks near the keel, and they were getting worse. Men had to work the pumps around the clock to keep us afloat.

"I think we should continue west for another couple of weeks before we head north," I ventured.

"I think by then we'll have no choice. Rice and foul water won't keep these men going much longer than that," said Michael.

"I know. I see signs of scurvy too," I replied.

"Land, land," shouted San Andrés from the topmast. Fifty scarecrows pulled themselves to the side to see Africa. Hopes high, I climbed the rigging to sit beside San Andrés, weaved my hand through the ropes for support, and waited, as the *Victoria* grew closer. The shore did not look right. *By Satan's blood, we are too far east.* The shore ran from the southwest to the northeast. That meant we were on the east side of the Cape of Good Hope. A river mouth was visible. That would be the Rio del Infante. *By the Devil's Horns, that meant we were some five hundred miles east of the cape.*

I looked up. It was cloudy, too cloudy to shoot the sun. If I could fix the latitude, then I'd be sure this was the Rio del

Infante. No matter. We had to be east of the cape. A ribbon of white marked where waves broke against the shore. That dashed any thoughts of sending a boat in for water and food. The crew would be sorely disappointed.

I returned to the deck. The men crowded around me.

"Are we past the Cape?" asked Hernández, a Castilian *marinero*. Hernández kept his beard shaved short. He had taken a saber in the face while fighting the Moors in North Africa. A scar ran from his right eye to his jaw like the furrow of a plow through wheat stubble. His right hand was missing two fingers from the same battle.

"No. We must sail a little farther."

"Farther? My stomach won't take it. We must land now."

"We can't. Look at those breakers. We can't hazard the longboat there."

"We must have food. I know the signs of scurvy. Lorenzo is already near death with it. It is only a matter of time until we all die," argued a second *marinero*.

"I say we should make for Mozambique," said Hernández.

"And what would you do there?" asked Cano.

"I would live. I would eat. By the Blessed Virgin, if we continue as you've led us, we'll all die." Several men beside Hernández nodded in agreement.

"The Portuguese are more likely to give you a rope necklace than a meal. At best, I think we'd be staring at roaches crawling up the walls of a Portuguese prison cell for a long time," I said.

"A fast death might be better than wasting away here," a ragged *marinero* scowled.

"We made it across the Pacific. The Atlantic will be child's play by comparison."

"Maybe we need a new captain and pilot," said Hernández. His three good fingers and palm wrapped around the hilt of his knife.

"Draw that and you'll be dancing from the end of the yardarm," shouted Cano.

"I'm with Cano." I fingered my dagger. "I say on to Spain, where fame awaits us, and your King Carlos will give us our just rewards."

Hernández looked at Cano and me. Michael, Pigafetta, San Andrés, and Philip stood close behind us.

"Damn Greeks. Strange company you keep, Captain Cano. I demand a vote."

Cano looked at me. I nodded. "That would be fair. A vote then," said Cano.

I didn't want a vote, but Cano and my command of the ship was only possible with the crew's acknowledgement of our leadership. I felt strongly that heading north to the Portuguese would be a fatal mistake, so my palms were moist as the votes were cast.

TWENTY-FIVE – THE SOUTHERN ATLANTIC

The vote was three to one to sail on. It took us eleven days to make the cape. My joy at rounding the Cape of Good Hope was short-lived. A bad squall hit and dislodged the foremast. We had to lie to a day for repairs.

Two weeks after the nascent mutiny, the *Victoria* entered Saldanha Bay fifty miles north of the Cape of Good Hope on the western coast of Africa. We consigned the first victim of scurvy to the deep south of the cape. The second, a French *grumete*, succumbed along the way to Saldanha Bay. The supernumeraries' forecastle cabin was an infirmary holding half a dozen Europeans and an equal number of Moluccans. Even the dark giant San Andrés showed signs of the scurvy, although he still worked as hard as any man did at the sails and pumps. To hold up our baggy pants, we cinched our rope belts tight about our stomachs. We had to find food.

I looked forward to the sweet, fresh water of the river flowing into the bay. I was tired of four-month-old water that smelled of mildew. Fresh water to drink and boil our rice in was not enough. We needed more food and the *roteiros* said there was little at this bay. I'd even finished the last of my marmelada. I'd husbanded my little stash as long as I could but it was gone.

When we rounded the spit that protected the bay from the ocean, we saw a ship anchored dead ahead flying the Portuguese flag. *Blessed Virgin, have we sailed this far only for the Portuguese to capture us? Why are they here?* I looked upward. Just this morning, Cano ran up a new Spanish flag to replace the tattered one we had flown since Tidore. It was too late to lower it. Well, maybe we could brazen our way through.

As we drew closer, I saw the top masts of the Portuguese ship were broken away. Weary faces looked our way from the damaged ship.

Cano spoke first, "God save you, captain, and your good company."

A tired-looking man came to the railing of the Portuguese ship's poop deck and said, "And God save you, captain, and your good company."

"What is your name and where are you bound?" asked Cano.

"I am Captain Pedro Cuaresma, of the Santa Maria. We are bound for India, or at least we were until a storm disabled us." He gestured towards his top masts. "And who are you?"

"I am Captain Juan Sebastián el Cano of the *Victoria*. We are bound for Spain."

"Well, forgive me, but I have much work to attend to. It's urgent that we sail before the winds change." With that, the Spanish captain turned his back on us.

"He's a rude man, but it suits us just fine," I said. "Let's anchor near the river's mouth."

"I say we stay two days here. Let the men touch the earth; maybe it will ward away any further scurvy. Master Michael, have work parties refill our water tanks and cut firewood," said Cano.

I hoped letting the men ashore would help with the scurvy, but my intuition told me it would take better food. Another *marinero* died before we left.

The Cape was six weeks behind us. I wiggled a tooth that was loose. I'd felt myself immune to the scurvy. Now I knew I wasn't. Still I was better off than the other men were. We'd lost eleven of the original crew and ten of the Moluccans to scurvy, starvation, and exposure. Every other day we tossed another scrawny corpse overboard. San Andrés had joined the weakest men in the forecastle sick cabin. I'd become inured to pitching my dead shipmates into the brine, but the sight of the giant San Andrés half delirious in bed reminded me of Master Gunner Andrew's decline in the Pacific. It troubled me deeply.

Thank the Blessed Virgin the winds had been favorable, but the constant pumping was wearing out the men. Even Cano, Michael, Pigafetta, and I manned the pumps. We'd made a frustrating landfall on the African coast. Philip and a crew took the longboat ashore, but he'd been unable to find any fresh food.

I went to Cano after the last death and said, "This can't go on. We won't reach the Canaries at this rate."

Cano stared back with sunken eyes, "You're thinking we need to risk stopping at the Cape Verde?"

I gave a little laugh, "You've read my mind."

"I think we have no choice," replied Cano. "Let's call a council."

There were no dissenters when we met. There was no other choice. We'd have to risk the Portuguese Cape Verde. The authorities there might throw us in irons, but the alternative was to starve to death at sea. Maybe our fears were unwarranted. After all, the Portuguese ship at the Cape had ignored us. Maybe King Carlos and the Portuguese King had reached a truce. Whatever was the truth, we needed food and maybe slaves to work the pumps.

TWENTY-SIX – CAPE VERDE ISLANDS

Four caravels lined the main quay when I poked the *Victoria's* nose into Riberia Grande's harbor at the southern tip of São Tiago island in the Cape Verde. A large building near the dock had European architecture. Portuguese were walking about the small town. These were the first Europeans other than Lorosa and my shipmates that I'd seen since three years ago in Tenerife. *Will they welcome us, or will this be an ignoble end to our long journey?*

Pigafetta was his usual font of knowledge about the islands. São Tiago was one of the largest of the volcanic Cape Verde Islands off the western horn of Africa. Another seven large and many smaller islands made up the archipelago. Riberia Grande was the administrative and economic hub of the isles. First settled less than a century earlier, initially raising sugar cane was their primary business. The discovery of New Spain changed that. The plantations there needed workers for their cane fields. The natives there were initially enslaved, but as their numbers dwindled from European diseases, blacks from Africa filled the void. The Cape Verde were a natural way station for the slaving ships on their route to New Spain from Africa.

We elected Martin Méndez, the clerk of the *Victoria* and the most senior Castilian aboard the *Victoria*, to go ashore. With some trepidation, I watched Méndez's longboat tie up at the quay. Reaching Spain, fame, and wealth hinged on Méndez's success in convincing the harbormaster of a tale of woe: that we were separated by a hurricane from a convoy returning from New Spain and needed help.

I waited with Cano, Michael, and Pigafetta for the boat's return. Our stomachs were empty. Our hope was almost exhausted. Would Martin be successful? Would we be sucking oranges and roasting pork tonight, or would we be lying on the dank floor of some fetid jail?

Finally, our longboat returned with Méndez at the helm. I took it as a good sign that the Portuguese working on the docks looked as lazy as before. We quietly rejoiced when Méndez said the harbormaster was sympathetic to our plight. Before long we'd unloaded two longboats full of food. We gorged ourselves on oranges, bananas, olives, and dates while we slow roasted a dozen fowl. I so wanted to eat some of the wheat bread from the harbor bakery, but I knew I'd lose one or more of my loose teeth if I attempted to do so. I squeezed an orange into San Andrés's mouth before I fed him some mashed bananas.

More food arrived over the next few days. Philip took some of the stronger men to refill our water casks. He was eager for a dice game, but I told Michael to go everywhere with him, and to keep Philip out of any gambling dens. All went well, except we exhausted our gold and we still didn't have enough food for the remainder of the voyage to Spain. The Portuguese traders refused to honor a draft on the Haro Bank. The Portuguese King had banned the bank from Portuguese territories because of its sponsorship of our expedition.

It puzzled me that Mendéz reported the Portuguese ashore said it was Thursday. My own log made it Wednesday, as did Pigafetta's journal. How could we both have missed a day? This perplexed me until later an astrologer in Spain explained to me that our sailing around the world had caused us to lose a day. I still don't entirely understand why, but it most assuredly happened.

Five days later Cano, Michael, and I met in Cano's cabin.

"The men are looking much better already," I said. My teeth were firmer in my mouth. The light in San Andrés's dark eyes had returned and he was able to sit up in bed for the first time in a week.

"It's amazing how quickly the men recover from the scurvy once they get to land and fresh food," seconded Michael.

"Even so, I'd like to get more food and buy some slaves to man the pumps," grunted Cano as he studied the chart that I had prepared for him. "We still have a long ways to sail."

"I think we can get by with what we've purchased," I said.

"Why not get more?" said Cano.

"How will we pay for it? All the gold is gone," said Michael.

"Cloves," grunted Cano. "I'll send Méndez with three hundredweight of cloves. That should pay for a couple more boatloads of food and half a dozen slaves."

"Won't that push our luck? Cloves? Where the hell would a ship from New Spain get cloves?"

"Méndez can be persuasive. Let him try," said Cano.

"I don't think we should risk it," said Michael.

"As captain, I think we should; we can put it to a vote of the crew."

"You'd give them the choice of sailing now or getting more food and slaves to man the pumps? I know how they'll vote. Go ahead. But just one more trip and let's raise anchor and be ready to be off when the longboat returns," I said.

Once the longboat had cast off, I moved the *Victoria* outside of the harbor and waited. The longboat returned low in the water at noon with more food.

"Time to be off. I think we've stretched our luck far enough," I said while the men unloaded rice and salt cod.

"One more, just one more trip. Let's see if Méndez can buy some slaves."

"We've enough food to make it home. Let's get out of here."

"I say one more trip."

The longboat did not return by sunset.

The next morning I moved the *Victoria* closer in. I was apprehensive, having worried all night about the longboat. It carried thirteen men, over a third of the crew, including Philip.

There was no sign of our men, although a large skiff set off from the pier and headed our way.

I headed the *Victoria* into the wind, spilling some air from the sails. Our ship lost way as the skiff grew near. An official sat, back erect, in the stern. Once it was within hailing distance, the rowers raised their oars. The stern-faced official stood and shouted in a baritone voice, "In the name of King Manuel of Portugal I command you to surrender."

"Surrender? Why?" replied Cano.

The official's eyebrows rose. "Why, because you and your crew have committed illegal acts by Portuguese law."

"We've done nothing illegal."

"You've trespassed on Portuguese territory and traded without paying the proper tariffs."

"We've done nothing of the sort."

"Your men in our custody say otherwise. You must surrender immediately." The official folded his arms, as if we had no other choice.

Who ratted us out to the Portuguese authorities? Not my countryman Philip. It must have been one of the Portuguese crewmen, but which one? May God strike him down. He might have consigned us all to death.

"And what would become of the *Victoria* and its crew?"

"Your ship is by rights a Portuguese prize. It's now the king's property."

"And the crew?" rasped Cano.

"Your men will be taken to Lisbon and tried before the proper authorities."

"You've no right to do this!" shouted an irate Cano.

"You must return our men and our longboat," Michael and I said at the same time.

The official seemed taken aback by the vehemence of our

response. He sat down.

"I will tell the governor your response. Do you have anything else to say?"

"Honor the property of King Carlos and return the longboat along with its men," replied Cano.

I watched as the skiff made its way back to the dock. Thirty minutes after it reached the dock, we saw men running about. They were readying the four caravels for sea.

"Any one wish to surrender?" asked Cano.

"Hell no," I replied. "Let's take our chances with the sea."

I hated to abandon Philip, but it was not like leaving Captain Serrano in Cebu. Here, the Portuguese would easily overwhelm us if we attempted a rescue. Besides, Philip might have the best of it. Portuguese prison food was bound to be better than ours aboard the *Victoria*.

"The course is west," I ordered the *marinero* on the tiller. The *Victoria* gathered speed as its sails caught the wind and headed out of the harbor.

TWENTY-SEVEN – THE EARTH ENCIRCLED

We took the *Victoria* west until it was out of sight of Portuguese eyes and then turned south, away from Spain. I expected the pursuing Portuguese ships would search to the north, the most direct route to Spain. I also knew that, even given our head start, the barnacle clad and under-manned *Victoria* would not be able to out sail the Portuguese ships. We had to elude the Portuguese through guile. The *Victoria* continued south for two days and a night. After nightfall of the second day, we turned west for a day, both to elude the Portuguese and to skirt the more westward of the Cape Verde. Only then did I order the tillerman to head the *Victoria* to north and home.

We had barely enough men to sail the *Victoria*. Two men worked the pumps, a man was at the tiller, and Cano, Michael, or I was at the binnacle to con the ship. The few remaining fit men labored to manage the sails. Twenty-two sick and weak men remained of the sixty we had left the Moluccas with.

From Magellan's *roteiros*, I knew we couldn't sail northeast directly to Spain. If we did, we'd be sailing straight into the trade winds that three years ago took us from Sanlúcar to the Canaries. Instead, we had to sail north until we found the western trade winds north of the Portuguese Azores.

The Azores Islands appeared in the distance off our port bow on August fourth. We were so close to being home, but the scurvy had returned. It was tempting to put in at the Azores, which would be a common landfall for a Spanish ship from the West Indies, but word of us may already have reached there from the Cape Verde Islands. We couldn't chance it. We would never be able to repeat our escape at the Cape Verde.

We sailed on. The scurvy claimed its last victim, a French *marinero*, two days after sighting the Azores. He appeared to be recovering after the Cape Verde, but when the fresh food was gone, he fell into a long, slow decline ending in his death. A week passed and then another. Where were the west trade winds?

Then the wind switched to from the west and we turned our bow towards Spain and Sanlúcar and home.

I remember the *Victoria's* pilot's cabin, my home for a year of my life. It was the second best cabin on the *Victoria*, but I don't miss its rough-hewn plank walls and bug-ridden bed. I regularly had the mattress beaten and aired, but I still woke up with welts inflicted by my nighttime companions.

It was there I inked the final entries in my personal logbook, the basis of these memoirs, two days before we reached Spain. I kept this log locked with my Mediterranean *roteiros* in an oak chest under my bed. Then I turned to the logbook Magellan had given me and wrote:

"September, 1522.

On the 4th day of the said month, in the morning, we saw land, and it was Cape St. Vincent, and it was to the northeast of us, so we changed our course to the S.E., to get away from that Cape."

This was the last entry in this log. Any novice pilot could find his way from Cape St. Vincent to Sanlúcar.

Just shy of three years had passed since the five proud ships of the Armada of the Moluccas had stood out from Sanlúcar with pennants flying. Sanlúcar's harbor pilot Pedro Sordo's warning had proved prophetic. Only one ship of five returned and intrigues of the Armada's officers were almost our undoing. However, my idle boast to Pedro had also come true. I had made it. I had survived. Even more, I had piloted the first ship to circumnavigate the globe, a feat that eclipsed those of da Gama and Columbus.

A knock stirred me from my thoughts.

"Enter."

António Pigafetta's smiling face peered around the door. In his hands were two glasses and a bottle of wine. "Will you join me in a toast, Pilot? A toast to our return."

I laughed. "Of course. Where did you get the bottle?"

"The Cape Verde."

"Sit down and pour."

Pigafetta pulled a three-legged stool over to my table. I watched as the red elixir plunged into the glasses, took one, savored the wine's aroma, and met Pigafetta's glass with a clink across the table.

"To God, to Magellan, and to our encirclement of the world," said Pigafetta.

"And to our stout ship and our crew," I said.

I let the wine caress my tongue and swallowed.

Pigafetta spoke, "Making a log entry?"

"Yes. I want my log ready to give to the *Casa de Contratación*. You know how particular they can be."

"I can imagine, although thankfully my dealings with them were few. What do you intend to do once we're back?"

"I hope the *Casa* will commission me as a pilot."

"Do you think they will do that?"

"They should. Who else do they have who has piloted a ship halfway around the world?"

Pigafetta grimaced. "They should. But 'should' doesn't seem to enter in the *Casa's* thinking at times."

"Well, if they won't hire me, I am sure there are others that will. Anyway, I have thirty-two months of back pay as I calculate it; eleven of that as mate and twenty-one as pilot. They owe me nearly seventy-five thousand *Maravedis*. I also have my two hundredweight of cloves. I shouldn't have to work for a while." I'd received, like the rest of the crew, a four-month advance of pay before leaving.

"Do you think they will give you pilot pay?"

I scowled. "Why not? I have my commission signed by Magellan."

"I hope you are right."

"And what are you going to do?"

"I've made copies of my journal, which I will give King Carlos and maybe King Francis. After that I think I'll return to home in Vicenza and make my journal into a book."

I eyed Pigafetta's faded, patched, and darned doublet. "You look more like a beggar than someone who keeps the company of kings."

Pigafetta laughed. "And you too. We look like wretches you might see begging in the Patio de los Naranjos in Seville."

"Yes, but you come from a different world than me, António. A world of kings and popes. You'll soon have a new linen doublet and fine multi-colored hose. My world is of the water and the mast."

"You are made for that world, Pilot."

TWENTY-EIGHT – SANLÚCAR

September 6th, Year of our Lord 1522

"The *Victoria* is a floating specter," said Pedro Sordo with a grimace. Pedro, who piloted us over the Guadalquivir River's bar three years earlier and warned me of the dangers facing me, had met us in his launch to guide us into Sanlúcar.

I laughed, "At least she floats."

The *Victoria* listed to port as she struggled to keep her precious cargo afloat. Gaunt men worked the sweeps. The merciful flooding tide gave us an assist towards Sanlúcar. Other cadaverous sailors worked the pumps to evict water from the hold. The *Victoria's* sails were tattered. Raw wood showed through where tar once blackened the hull.

"So you piloted the *Victoria* home."

"Halfway around the world from the Moluccas."

"What of the other pilots?"

"I left Carvalho in the Moluccas. Pilot Major Gómez's ship vanished in the Strait. The others are dead."

"There have been rumors from the Portuguese that Magellan was dead."

"The rumors are true. He was killed by heathens."

"What of the other men and ships?" asked Pedro.

"Many souls met their maker from scurvy and native treachery. We left nearly sixty on the *Trinidad* in the Moluccas. The *Santiago* wrecked before we found the Strait to the South Seas. The *San Antonio* disappeared over two years ago in that Strait. We had to abandon the *Concepción* for lack of crew."

"I guided the *San Antonio* over the bar last year."

"So Pilot Major Gomez defected?"

"He bragged of finding the Strait to the South Sea. He also claimed Magellan murdered our Spanish captains. The Bishop Fonseca was incensed at the marooning of his son. He began planning a rescue expedition, but it was aborted."

"Oh…Actually the fools mutinied. Thank you for your advice to be wary of intrigues." My first thought was that Pilot Major Gomez's return could be trouble for us, but the more I thought about it, the less I was concerned. While Gomez and Cano were on opposite sides in the mutiny, they were united in their dislike for Magellan. Fortunately, neither man knew my role in the mutiny. Also, I'd always kept a professional relationship with Gomez, and I believed he respected me.

"Be wary. Some people will prefer the Pilot Major's version of events. He is still a pilot for *Casa de Contratación*. It is fashionable here to disparage Magellan."

"I speak the truth. Has anything changed here?"

"Ottoman power is growing. There is a new Sultan, Suleiman, who is young and ambitious. His armies advance in Central Europe. Belgrade has fallen to him. Word just arrived that he is besieging your Rhodes with a hundred thousand men and hundreds of ships."

"It is lost then."

"The Knights of Rhodes vow not."

"Will Spain, Pope Leo, or Venice go to their aid?"

"I'm sure there will be talk, but will they act? I don't know. Pope Leo is dead. King Carlos's advisor is now Pope Adrian VI. A Dutch Pope!"

"The Cardinal Adrian struck me as an honest man."

"Perhaps, but what can one man do? It gets worse. A renegade Greek allied with Suleiman named Barbarossa commands a great fleet from Algiers. He is a scourge. Nowhere is safe from him. Last year he captured some of our ships returning from New Spain within sight of Cadiz."

"Enough. Tonight I want strong, red wine, olives, and

garlic. And cheese. I haven't had any cheese for over two years."

"You need some proper clothes too," said Pedro eyeing my filthy rags. "And a bath in fresh water."

After securing the *Victoria*, we disembarked. Michael kissed the earth. I stood in silence, the ground swaying in my mind, relishing the feel of solid ground beneath my feet for the first time since the Cape of Good Hope. Pigafetta started to walk the cobbled streets to the Church of Nuestra Señora Barrameda. As if by unspoken order, the other men and I followed him, barefoot in single file. There we prayed.

EPILOGUE

King Carlos requested Cano's presence at Valladolid upon our return. The king asked that he bring along two others along with all their papers. Cano, somewhat to my surprise, chose the barber-surgeon Bustamente and me. Pigafetta, or perhaps Michael, should have gone in Bustamente's stead, but the surgeon was the most senior Castilian remaining in our small crew. I met the great king. The young man impressed me with his astute questions. Afterward his men interviewed me at great length and I gave them my logbook, which made clear the Spice Islands were in the Portuguese sphere. What happened to the logbook, I know not. Since its revelations were counter to the crown's desires, it might have found a place on some dark and forgotten shelf.

So, I spoke the truth, but only of what they needed to know. My role in quelling the mutiny remained a secret. They paid for my travel and I received a fine set of new clothes. Most important, I received all back pay and the monies for my cloves. I kept my secret roteiros well hidden. The Casa rejected my application to become a pilot for Spain. And so, I sought employment elsewhere, but that is another story.

THE SURVIVORS

The men who survived to reach Sanlúcar on the *Victoria* on September 6, 1522 were:

Captain Juan Sebastian Cano, Basque, originally Master of the *Concepción*

Pilot Francisco Albo, Rhodes, originally Mate of the *Trinidad*

Master Michael de Rodas, Rhodes, originally Mate of the *Victoria*

Mate Juan de Acurio, Basque, originally Mate of the *Concepción*

Barber Hernando de Bustemente, Castile, originally of the *Concepción*

Marinero Francisco Rodrigues, Portugal, originally of the *Concepción*

Marinero Juan Rodrigues, Castile, originally of the *Concepción*

Marinero António Hernandez Colmenero, Castile, originally of the *Trinidad*

Marinero Diego Gallega, Castile, originally of the *Victoria*

Marinero Níccolo de Napoles, Naples, originally of the *Victoria*

Marinero Michael Sanchez, Rhodes, originally of the *Victoria*

Grumete Juan de San Andrés, Canary Islands, originally of the *Trinidad*

Grumete Juan de Arratia, Castile, originally of the *Victoria*

Man-at-arms Martin de Judicibus, Genoa, originally of the *Victoria*

Supernumerary António Pigafetta, Italy, originally of the *Trinidad*

Supernumerary Juan the Martin, Italy, originally of the *Victoria*

Cabin Boy, Diego Garcia, originally of the *San Antonio*

Cabin Boy, Juan de Zubileta, originally of the *Victoria*

Three Unnamed Moluccans

The crew of the longboat captured at the Cape Verde Islands - The thirteen, including Philip de Rodas and Manual, Lorosa's loyal man, fared comparatively well, and were all repatriated to Spain over the following year.

The crew of the *Trinidad* – Carvalho died in Tidore of a fever before the *Trinidad* attempted an eastern passage of the Pacific Ocean. Storms and starvation drove it back to the Moluccas, where the crew threw themselves at the mercy of the Portuguese Brito. Brito gave them no mercy. He imprisoned Espinosa, Ginés, Polcevera, and the remainder of the crew. Brito summarily beheaded Lorosa. Only four—Espinosa, Ginés, and two others—ever returned alive to Spain. The leaky *Trinidad* sank in the Moluccas.

Kenneth D. Schultz

PERSONS

Those who sailed on the Armada:

The Spanish clique:

Cano – Juan Sebastián el Cano – A Basque who is Master of the *Concepción*.

Cartagena – Juan Cartagena – *Conjunta persona* with Magellan per a letter signed by King Carlos, which is believed authored by Bishop Fonseca. Exactly what *Conjunta persona* meant is unclear, although he was clearly second in command of the Armada. He was also Inspector General of the Armada and the Captain of the *San Antonio*. Commonly believed to be the bastard child of Bishop Fonseca.

Coca – Antonio Coca – Castilian Chief Accountant for the fleet initially aboard the *San Antonio* and believed related to Bishop Fonseca.

Mendoza – Luis Mendoza – Spanish Captain of the *Victoria*. Treasurer of the Armada.

Quesada – Gaspar Quesada – Spanish Captain of the *Concepción*.

Magellan's clique:

Magellan – Fernando Magellan – Captain General of the Armada of the Moluccas. A minor Portuguese nobleman aged around forty when the armada sails.

Carvalho – João Lopes Carvalho – Portuguese Pilot of the *Concepción*.

Duarte – Duarte Barbosa – Magellan's brother-in-law. His father was originally from Portugal, but had loyally served the Spanish crown for years. Like Magellan, Duarte

256

was an experienced sailor and a veteran of the Portuguese spice trade to India.

Mesquita – Álvaro de Mesquita – Portuguese and a cousin of Magellan.

Ravelo – Cristóbal Ravelo – Portuguese. Commonly believed to be Magellan's bastard son.

Enrique – Asiatic slave of Magellan bought in Malacca.

Others of the armada:

Antón – Antón de Noya – Castilian *grumete* on the *Trinidad*.

Espinosa – Gonzalo Gómez de Espinosa – Castilian *Alguacil major*, master-at-arms for the Armada and the *Trinidad*.

Ginés – Ginés de Mafra – Castilian *marinero* on the *Trinidad*.

Pilot Major Estéban Gómez – Most senior pilot of the armada. His plan for an expedition to the Spice Islands similar to Magellan's was rejected by King Carlos.

Michael – Michael de Rodas – Mariner from Rhodes, mate of the *Victoria*, and friend of Albo.

Father Pedro de Valderrama – Chaplain of the *Trinidad*. From Andalusia.

Polcevera – Giovanni de Polcevera – From Genoa. Master of the *Trinidad*.

Pigafetta – António Pigafetta – A Lombard from present day Italy and a supernumerary on the *Trinidad*.

Philip – Philip de Rodas – From Rhodes. A *marinero* of the *Victoria* and a friend of Albo.

Salamón – Antón Salamón – Sicilian master of the *Victoria*.

San Andrés – Juan de San Andrés – Canary Island *grumete* on the *Trinidad*.

Serrano – Juan Rodríguez Serrano – Castilian Captain and Pilot of the *Santiago*.

Others:

Almanzor – Rajah Almanzor – Rajah of Tidore, one of the two main Spice Islands where the clove tree grows indigenously.

Da Gama – Dom Vasco da Gama – Portuguese who pioneered the sea route to India around the south tip of Africa.

King Carlos I – King of Spain. With title Charles V, he is also newly elected Holy Roman Emperor.

Fonseca – Bishop Juan Rodríguez de Fonseca – Castilian head of the *Casa de Contratación*. Was Isabella's confessor.

Piri Reis – An Ottoman cartographer and captain.

Serrão – Francisco Serrão – Portuguese Grand Vizier of Ternate and a childhood friend of Magellan.

See my website at www.kennethdschultz.com if you want to know what became of some of the people in Albo's memoirs, including Almanzor, Michael, and Cano.

SPANISH NAMES AND TERMS

Alguacil major – The *alguacil major* was responsible for keeping the peace on the armada's ships and to carry out any judgements or orders of the Captain General. To assist in this he had several men-at-arms on the various ships.

Ampolleta – An half-hour glass which a *grumete* would faithfully turn to keep time.

Arquebus – An early form of musket. When the trigger was pulled, an already burning fuse touched a flash pan filled with gunpowder. This burning powder would then light the main powder charge in the barrel via a touchhole. The need for a constantly burning fuse and gunpowder in the open were a problem under wet and rainy conditions.

Barangay – An Asiatic galley propelled by rowers and a sail.

Binnacle – A waist-high stand at the front of the poop deck with a compass and place for the half hour glasses, charts, and logs.

Bonnet – An additional sail that was laced onto an already existing sail to increase its area, and hence its propelling power. Used if there is a strong to moderate wind.

Casa de Contratación – A powerful Spanish government agency in Seville. It totally controlled all exploration and Spanish colonies. In the name of the king, it controlled and taxed all trade with the colonies, conducted all exploration, and approved all pilots. Queen Isabella of Columbus fame established it in 1503.

Casi casi – An Asian blood oath.

Culverin – An early cannon, around twelve foot long and a four to five inch bore. They fired solid shot at long range or to damage ships at shorter distances. Bags of smaller balls would be fired at shorter ranges against personnel.

Cuirass – Armor that protects the front of the torso.

Feitoria – A fortified trading station.

Farol – A light that was lit on the stern of each vessel at night.

Grumetes – An unexperienced or minimally trained seaman

Jardines – Toilets suspended from the poop deck. The name comes from the gardens where toilets traditionally were.

Maravedis – Spanish unit of currency. Albo's pay as first mate was 2,000 *Maravedis* per month. A *grumete* received 800 per month, while a Pilot received 30,000 *Maravedis* per year or 2,500 per month as a base pay.

Marinero – An experienced seaman.

Nao – A sailing ship, typically with two large masts, and a lateen sail on the stern. These ships were the sailing workhorses of their time.

Roteiro – Sailing instructions from one place to another. This is much more than a map or chart as in the days of sailing ships information about winds and currents through the seasons was critical.

Shallop – Each ship had several small boats. Most trailed longboats along behind. The *Trinidad* had a larger single-masted boat, called a shallop. All ships also carried dingies.

Supernumeraries – Extra men beyond the sailors and men directly involved with the operation of the fleet. Many were relatives or otherwise connected with the officers of the fleet. Some, like Duarte, had experience in the Portuguese spice trade to India. These men, along with *Alguacil major* Espinosa's men, formed the core of a military force. They also constituted a pool of men to choose from to replace any of the officers of the armada should the need arise.

BOOKS BY THE AUTHOR

Science fiction

Truth-Teller Rebellion
Truth-Teller Revenge
Mindfield (coming soon)

Thrillers

Download (as K.D. Schultz)

Historical Fiction

Magellan's Navigator

Visit me at:
Website: kennethdschultz.com
Facebook: www.facebook.com/KennethDSchultz

The Author

Ken lives in the quaint fishing village of Poulsbo, Washington, with his wife Teresa, his Vizsla Ruby, and Pomeranian emergency backup dog Otto.

Made in the USA
Middletown, DE
04 December 2018